Blackest of Lies

BILL AITKEN

Cover design by Rachel Harrison rachelkateharrison@gmail.com

ISBN: 1511498137
ISBN-13: 978-1511498135

DEDICATION

This book is dedicated to the memory of Lord Kitchener of Khartoum and the officers and men of *HMS Hampshire* who lost their lives on the evening of 5 June 1916.

CONTENTS

ACKNOWLEDGMENTS

This book has been rattling around in my head for more years than I care to remember. I have bored for Britain on the subject and to all those who suffered as a result, I apologise from the bottom of my heart.

My wife and I visited Broome House a few years back and were warmly received by Ms O'Shaughnessy, who showed us around and let us view Kitchener's bedroom. It was an eerie feeling to say the least. My thanks go to Broome for all the help they gave, then and afterwards. They do weekly tours, by the way – well worth a visit.

My greatest thanks, however, is reserved for my friend since childhood in darkest Glasgow – David Neilson – who heroically waded through tons of verbal manure to distil the tiny fraction worth keeping. It reminded me constantly of Marie Curie and her Pitchblende. Without his help, suggestions and guidance, this book would never have been in a state to launch on a defenceless public.

PROLOGUE

Saturday 20 May 1916 0255 hours, Barham, Kent

The parched road wandered up the hill and vanished behind a line of ancient trees. But the quiet beauty of the rolling Kent landscape was lost on Gallagher – he was just too angry as he stumped along, head down. It was bad enough that he had missed his way several times that night, despite a brilliant moon, but – worst of all – this lout Riordan had been foisted on him by Brigade with no explanations and no reasons. "He goes along, Sean." Gallagher was a loner and preferred it that way. Riordan was a distraction he could well do without – tonight of all nights.

He glanced across at him: a huge brute, dressed like Gallagher as a farm labourer. Riordan's idea of 'blending in' usually ended in explosive violence. There was no disguising what he was – a thug – the sort of would-be hard man whose only real value was extorting money from drunks for "The Cause" and doling out the odd punishment beating. Gallagher felt demeaned by the order to bring him along and he wondered, not for the first time, whether Brigade had a private agenda in mind. Perhaps Riordan was along as a minder to see that things were done by the book. He mulled that one over for a minute or two – nasty undercurrents were moving around back home like bad cess. No doubt he'd come in for a knock or two if he didn't watch his tail. He snorted in the darkness and shook the thought out of his head – Riordan would keep.

Beyond the summit, the road trickled down the gentle reverse slope for a hundred yards or so and then snapped to the right, enclosing two sides of the flat, green-covered graveyard of a church. Straight ahead, some farm buildings clung to the edge of the narrow valley.

A clump of stunted bushes nearby lent much-needed support to an ancient stile. Gallagher stopped for a moment under the dark pool of shadow it cast over the grass verge and looked slowly around, sniffing the air. It was warm and still, carrying even the sound of a dog barking somewhere over on the other side of the valley. Satisfied that no-one was watching the church, they trotted across the road, their boots sparking a flinty rhythm, and passed through the little gate in the low, drystone wall. A narrow path led them through the gravestones.

Just ahead, they could see the more imposing thatch of the main entrance and its shorter route to the porch, out of sight on the other side of the building. Their own path called at a small side door and, from there, it continued around the building to join with the broader thoroughfare. Gallagher tried the handle, only to find it locked.

Riordan chuckled. "What now, Sean?"

Gallagher stood quite still. "Shut up," he said. 'I've told you twice already to mind your tongue, son. You're here on sufferance. Don't you forget it or they'll find you floatin' back to Dublin." He paused and looked up at the taller man. "Are we clear on that?"

The moonlight cast deep shadows below the younger man's eyes, but there was little mistaking the expression. Gallagher felt rather than saw the nod.

They walked in silence around the corner and stopped at a curt flight of narrow steps to the right leading down to a door two or three feet below ground level. Gallagher looked cautiously around and then turned to Riordan. "Now, for your information, it was a toss-up whether we could get in by the other door. This one here leads into the vestry. If the first one's shut, this one's usually open."

"How d'you know?"

Gallagher sighed in exasperation. "Because we have a man in the house, you clown. It's arranged. What did you think – we'd kick Special Branch in the arse without a plan and half a dozen backups?" He paused and considered his next words. "Has all of this penetrated that thick skull of yours? This is meant to be payback, in spades, for Easter Monday but – get it into your head – the Specials have got this place sewn up tighter than a bloody drum. No surprises – that's the only way we're going to get out of this alive. Christ, that's why we were down in his gardens this afternoon, checking out the lie of the land. If all this stuff turns to worms, we'll be needin' another way out. I never leave things to chance and that, son, includes you. So just shut up and do what I say."

The door opened with only a token creak and they slipped into the claustrophobic room beyond. The smell of old stone, wood and polish enveloped them, pulling Gallagher back to his childhood in Donegal and the old priest in Buncrana castigating him yet again for missing confession.

"Ah, you're a bad sort, Sean," he would say, "and you'll come to a bad end." He would limp away, shaking his head and leaving the ten year old boy standing barefoot by the side of Lough Swilly, fishing rod in hand, trying to catch something – anything – to put food into the mouths of his mother and sisters after their miserable crops had failed yet again.

Riordan closed the door while Gallagher, turning to his left, walked through the archway leading into the main body of the church. He struck a match and moved round to the far wall. In the dim light, he could see the inside face of the locked side door they had tried earlier and, to its right, a large marble monument.

"Right. You see that big marble thing? Well, there's a two foot gap between the back of it and the wall. That's where we're going."

They moved to the rear of the polished stone and Gallagher braced his back against the church wall, pushing his feet against the monument. "Give me a hand for Christ sake," he said to the other man. With a high-pitched screech, the huge block inched forward on rails, uncovering a short set of steps, just visible in the guttering light of the match. "This is the start of the tunnel. It goes all the way to the Hall."

"Christ Almighty!" said Riordan in a reverent whisper. "Who made it, anyway?"

Gallagher shook the match to death and struck another. "He did – or else he fixed it up. He's mad for them. Our lad at the Hall says that he's even built one from his flint cottage to the stables so that he doesn't get himself wet walking over to the horses. The whole estate's riddled with them. Some of them were there even before he bought the place. Probably smugglers' tunnels or something like that but this one here was built for the lord of the manor to get to church on rainy days. It didn't have this lump on top of it at first. It's supposed to have been a just a wee trapdoor in plain view but the Specials made the vicar have it covered over by this thing so that bad people, like you and me, wouldn't be able to use it. If you ask me, anyone can see it stands out like a dog's balls. It wasn't made to go here."

The match flickered out, burning his fingers. Cursing, he turned to Riordan and handed him the box and a dark lantern. "Here. Light this and follow me down."

The tunnel, as he had expected, was dank and dripping but it had sufficient proportions to allow a normal sized man to walk along without touching the brick-lined walls. Gallagher waited for Riordan to arrive behind him, took charge of the lantern and led the way into the gloom ahead. The weak flame reflected off greasy walls and highlighted the inverted forest of delicate stalactites, suspended from the corbelled roof. The floor was slimed in a thin treacherous film of algae and chalky mud fed by the water dripping in the darkness ahead.

The tunnel snaked its way in sympathy with the contours of the land between the church and Broome Hall so, by the time they reached its abrupt end, they were filthy and wet through, courtesy of several falls in the slippery mud. Some steep steps, a little broader than the corresponding ones back in the church, led up to what could only be the underside of a large flagstone. Gallagher swore quietly to himself. He had been hoping for a trapdoor or something easy like that. This would be heavy and bloody noisy. He covered the lantern.

"Here, you. Make yourself useful. Get up in front of me and put your shoulder to this stone."

Riordan had positioned himself to lever the stone up when he felt Gallagher's breath at his right ear.

"But make a sound with it and, so help me, I'll gut you where you stand and leave you here to rot in the mud."

He smiled to himself as he felt the younger man tremble in the oppressive darkness. Gallagher's complete indifference to his own life, never mind anyone else's, was notorious. It was a useful reputation to have in stressful times.

"Gimme a break, Sean, I won't."

To their surprise, the stone slid upwards without a sound, stopping just beyond the vertical. It turned out to be hinged at one end and fitted into a wooden frame, sunken out of sight below the level of the flagged floor.

Gallagher nudged the other man. "Leave your boots on the top step. When we leave, I don't want these bastards knowing how we got in. We might want to use the tunnel again. And that means watching what we brush up against in the house, as well. We'll be pretty manky after having landed on our arses half a dozen times in that muck."

Cautiously, he climbed up and looked around to get his bearings. The moon glared through large windows, throwing brilliant highlights on polished copperware and carving deep shadows beyond stocky furniture. Below, still kneeling on the steps, Riordan heard the snap of Gallagher's fingers, to say that it was safe to join him.

They had come up at the rear of the kitchen, between the large chopping table in the middle of the floor and the enormous enamel sink ranged against the back wall. Gallagher drew his gun, a large-calibre Mauser, fitted its silencer and turned to Riordan. "Ready?" Seeing him nod, he padded around the table towards the large oak door and stood with his hand on the handle, waiting for the other man to join him.

"OK, now, we go through here and then along the main hall for a bit, turn right and up the main staircase. That brings us to a corridor. About halfway along it, there'll be a short flight of steps goin' up to the left. That takes us to the door of his bedroom. There's a lot of buildin' works being done to the house right now, so you make damn sure you don't trip over any buckets or such like. But there should be no risk of bumpin' into anyone else in the place. He won't stand for any Specials in the house so that means you only need to watch where you put your big feet."

Seeing that Gallagher was about to go through the door, Riordan plucked at his sleeve. "Wait a minute, wait a minute! I thought you said he was livin' in the flint cottage and using his tunnel to the stables and all that."

Gallagher checked his frustration with Riordan. "That's right, he usually does. But he's just come down from London and seein' that the bedroom's been finished he's decided to stay the night in the house itself. It's goin' to be his first and *his last."*

Inch by inch, Gallagher opened the door and entered the short corridor leading to the main hall which was long with a high ceiling supported by heavy beams. On the left were the large windows and the main door that gave the building its characteristic look from the main sweep. On the right, no less than two enormous stone fireplaces dominated the wall. Gallagher snorted at the extravagance of the man, remembering the miserable cottage of his own childhood with its ever-smoking peat fire. The smell of it was in his nostrils still.

He pulled at Riordan's jacket and they glided along the hall to a door leading to the staircase corridor. They began to climb the first flight of broad, carpeted steps. On top of each upright of the massive, carved wooden balustrade, unicorns and other mythical animals reared rampant behind wooden shields. Glancing around to check that they were still alone, Gallagher peered at the carvings in the blue moonlight, discovering an erect penis behind each shield.

"Jesus, would you look at that, now."

"What is it, Sean?"

"Never you mind. You're too young anyhow. Keep moving." He pushed Riordan ahead of him up the steps to the first landing were they both stopped. This part of the building was in thick, deep blackness.

Gallagher whispered into Riordan's ear. "Right, so. At the top of this flight, we go into the last corridor. Straight ahead and we get to his bedroom steps in about ten yards. We do this with no fanfare - no talkin' and no tippin' over in the dark. You just follow me. Don't get involved and don't say anything. You're just here as a witness."

"Right you are, Sean."

Gallagher plucked at him once again and they moved, as one, up the stairs and into the corridor. Here, the going was a little better. A nightlight was burning at the far end. It cast a dim, sepulchral yellow glow along the walls and sketched faint highlights on the painted columns flanking the bedroom stairs ahead.

Five seconds saw them at the bedroom door, a few feet above the level of the corridor. With care, Gallagher tried the handle and, finding it unlocked, opened the door. It turned on its well-oiled hinges, raising only the gentlest whisper from the deep carpet. As they entered, moonlight drenched them through large bay windows overlooking the rear lawn. The room boasted several slender pillars, similar to the ones at the bottom of the stairs, giving it a rather odd, cluttered look. Gallagher turned to his right, around the open door, where he had been told he'd find the bed. Its head was touching the wall through which they had entered.

They walked round to the foot and looked back at the man, deep in his slumbers. He had kicked the covers down to his waist in the warmth of this, his last, early summer.

Gallagher raised the gun and pointed it at his target. Once upon a time, he might have woken his victim – he still knew one or two like that – to amuse himself with the simple pleasures of telling his target why he was about to die. He despised Riordan for his crowding desire to see this one beg for his life but he was now too much a master of his art to squander time on pointless theatrics. He pulled the trigger and the gun gave a metallic thud, startling in the confines of the bedroom. His victim arched in a spasm and gasped several times as three more bullets followed. Gallagher retrieved the casings from their smouldering burn holes in the carpet and pulled Riordan towards the door.

"It's done. Back down to the kitchen and through the tunnel again." Riordan remained frozen in fascination, staring at the body. "Move right now or, so help me, I'll put the next four in your ear."

Riordan turned with a start and followed him to the door. Gallagher took one glance back to make sure that nothing had been left behind and then removed the key from the bedroom side, locking the door behind him. That would give them a little more time in the morning while the staff dithered about forcing it or not.

Behind them in the bedroom, motes of dust and feathers from the pillows glinted in the moonlight as they settled on the face and body of Horatio, Lord Kitchener of Khartoum, Secretary of State for War.

CHAPTER 1

Saturday 20 May 1916 0730 hours – 1700 hours

Hubert stepped out of the hallway into a side street in Holborn and closed the outer door of his block of flats behind him. He pocketed the keys and turned to cross to the other side, leaping back – out of sheer reflex – as the black Rolls-Royce Silver Ghost screeched to a halt at the kerb, missing him by an inch or so. A moustachioed man in his late middle-age, narrow-chested despite a bulky greatcoat, popped his head out. "Get in, Hubert!" he ordered. "Don't waste time asking stupid questions – get in beside the driver!"

Hubert jumped in and slammed the door behind him, turning to look at the other man. The car sped off, causing two brassy Clydesdales to jingle their Covent Garden waggon to an abrupt halt at the corner of the street. Hubert grinned at the violent oaths echoing after them as they screeched round into Judd Street and then on to the Euston Road. He raised his eyebrows at the Head of MI5,

Major Vernon Kell. "What's going on, sir?"

"We have the mother of all disasters on our hands, Hubert," said Kell, with a slight stutter, as the car rounded another corner on two wheels.

A corner of Hubert's mouth curved up in a sardonic smile. The very thought of having the 'mother of all disasters' at the same time as the 'war to end all wars' seemed seriously bad luck, to say the least. "How's that?"

"Last night, or sometime this morning, Lord Kitchener was assassinated at his home down at Broome."

Hubert's jaw slackened. "What?"

"Quite." Kell pointed to the other occupant of the back seat. "This is Colonel Fitzgerald, Lord Kitchener's Personal Staff Officer. Sir, this is Lieutenant Christophe Hubert, late of Princess Patricia's Canadian Light Infantry. He's only been with us for a few weeks but I've stolen him from my second-in-command, Holt-Wilson, to assist us on this."

Hubert and Fitzgerald somehow found each other's hand in the violence of the driving.

"Hubert will liaise between myself, you and Special Branch."

Fitzgerald nodded without humour or cordiality and Kell turned back to Hubert. "We're off right now – good God, Mason, have a care with your driving! – we're off to collect Assistant Commissioner Thompson from Downing Street." He paused for emphasis. "Special Branch was responsible for Lord Kitchener's protection squad."

Hubert sat silent for a moment until he saw Kell waiting for some sort of reply. "I'm sorry … I'm sorry but this has completely floored me. Kitchener assassinated!" He nodded to Fitzgerald. "My sympathies, Colonel." Hubert glanced back at Kell. "I fancy the Commissioner's interview won't be a happy one."

Kell grunted. "I very much doubt it. But we'll need his help, and the Colonel's here, to work out how we're going to handle this. It goes without saying that this will never be secret for long – but we have to squeeze every second we can out of the gap before it *does* leak out. And that means getting down to Broome and putting a lid on it, PDQ."

Hubert's mind was still frozen but two years of fighting in Belgium, seeing men blown apart within feet of him, had trained him to shake off that sort of mental paralysis and *think*. "First thoughts, then – perhaps we could announce that Kitchener has developed influenza? There's a lot of it about, according to the papers. Keep him at home for a couple of weeks?"

Fitzgerald leaned forward holding on to a door strap. "I have already made it perfectly clear to Major Kell that Lord Kitchener would *never* let himself be absent for that length of time. He was always very reluctant to delegate things. It wouldn't be long before some document would need his personal attention and it would be brought down to Broome. The game would then be up."

To Hubert, Fitzgerald's voice sounded thick – plummy, but thick – as though his tongue was somehow too big for his mouth. "How long, then?"

Fitzgerald, thrown against the side of the car by another frightening manoeuvre, thought for a moment. "Three days!"

Kell swivelled slightly to look at him, appalled. "You cannot be serious, surely!"

"Three days," said Fitzgerald. "Three days."

****

Gallagher stuck out a rigid arm to stop Riordan walking in front of one of those big black Rolls' that was roaring along the road not far from Kings Cross. Sure, the Specials would be expecting them to take the train from Euston up the west coast to Liverpool and catch the ferry there back to Ireland. But he had a better idea – up the east coast to Edinburgh from Kings Cross and then west to catch the Larne ferry. Exasperated, he glowered at Riordan and pulled him by the sleeve across the road. "Didn't your Mammie ever tell you about traffic, you moron? The last thing I want is some copper identifying your mortal remains on the Euston-bloody-Road. Get your wits about you. If you have any."

Within minutes, they were striding on to the main concourse of Kings Cross railway station. Gallagher thrust a hand at Riordan. "Right – here's some money to get your own ticket. Make yourself scarce for half an hour or so and then buy it. I don't want to see you until we board the train. It won't take them long to work out there was two of us in that bedroom."

Riordan nodded without comprehension.

Gallagher sighed in frustration. "Christ. So … they'll be looking for a *couple* of Micks, if they've got any sense. You follow?"

"Right, Sean. I'll just go off and get meself a cup of tea or something and see you later."

"That sounds grand. I'll get my own ticket right now and meet you on the Edinburgh platform five minutes before the off."

Riordan wandered away in search of his tea while Gallagher, glancing around under his eyebrows, wandered over to a set of postal trollies loaded with bags. He walked past them until he found one marked 'Exeter'. It would be taken over to Paddington, maybe, and out on a mail train from there. Doing a final check around to make sure there was no one watching, he took both guns – his and Riordan's – wiped them clean and pushed their dismantled sections deep into several different mail sacks. Someone in Land's End, or some other bloody horrible place, was going to get a hell of a shock.

Like a man without a care in the world, he strolled back to the concourse and went to buy his own ticket.

****

Kell tapped the driver on the shoulder. "There he is, Mason!" The car swung over and crunched to a halt just outside the entrance to Downing Street. A man wearing a rather old-fashioned soft hat, formal coat and wing collar made to get into the car but paused for a moment, hand upraised and eyes screwed shut.

He groaned and stood, crouched, for a moment. "Damn it!" he said and got into the car, sitting in the middle between Kell and Fitzgerald. Kell introduced him to the other two men. "Gentlemen, this is Commissioner Thompson of Special Branch."

"Special Branch!" said Fitzgerald, making no attempt to offer his hand.

The car roared off again, throwing Thompson into the back seat. "Dear God!" He held up his hand again. "Wait a minute …" He held up his hand again and sneezed violently. "Sorry! Bloody cold … can't shift it." He wiped a rather large mottled nose with a garish handkerchief and sniffed loud enough to be heard above the roar of the car.

"Wonderful!" said Fitzgerald, *sotto voce*.

The car continued to snake among the other vehicles on

the road at terrific speeds, stopping only once on account of a traffic policeman. Thompson leaned out of the window and yelled obscenities at him. After that, the way was clear and they picked up speed through the eastern suburbs of London.

Thompson looked over at Kell. "You'll want to know what happened at my meeting with Asquith, I suppose, Kell."

"I thought I'd wait until you were ready, Commissioner."

"It was bloody awful, as you might imagine."

"Do we have any leads?" asked Hubert.

Kell interjected. "Sorry, this is one of my officers – Lieutenant Christophe Hubert."

Thompson nodded grimly, "Pleasure. As to the question of leads, we just might. But it's still conjecture, really."

"Why am I not surprised?" Fitzgerald's lisped disdain was very clear.

Thompson looked carefully at him. "Are you trying to tell me something, Colonel?"

"You need me to be more explicit? Very well, it was your department that was charged with protecting Lord Kitchener, *the* most important person in the Empire at this moment in time. Now he is dead – shot in his sleep, unable even to defend himself."

Seeing Thompson about to explode, Hubert broke into the conversation. "What did you mean by 'conjecture'?"

Thompson turned slowly to face him, keeping his eyes fixed on Fitzgerald until the last moment. "Kitchener was shot four times at close range. We're still working on the bullets but they're probably from a Mauser. My waters tell me we're looking at the work of the IRB."

Hubert sat in silence for a moment, letting the appalling idea percolate through. His first reaction was one of simple disbelief. They very idea that *anyone* in Britain would want to kill the driving force behind the war was lunacy. He pulled his collar up against the chill of the morning air blasting through the open side window of the car. "The Irish! For God's sake ... let me be clear – are we talking about the Irish Republican Brotherhood?" he asked, stunned by the thought.

Thomson nodded grimly.

"But … *why*?"

Fitzgerald cleared his throat. "Well, if it is the IRB, the Harp issue might be at the back of it. Lord Kitchener received a request from the Irish regiments at the Front for permission to wear the symbol of the harp on their tunics. He never really had much time for the concept of Welsh and Irish regiments. I've no idea if this was behind his refusal but refuse he did."

Thompson slid towards Kell as the car rounded a corner at speed. "This upset our Hibernian brothers and the IRB used the matter as the excuse they needed to issue a death warrant. Of course, you never know, his assassination at this precise time – perhaps it's simple tit for tat."

"You mean retaliation for the Easter Uprising?" Hubert mused.

"Exactly. Personally, I think it's more about antagonism to the prospect of British troops back in Ireland after the War – killing Kitchener might make the Government think again, that sort of thing. At any rate, we set ourselves to watching one or two promising Murphies but we were caught with our trousers around our ankles." Thompson sat in grim silence for a moment and then glanced back at Hubert. “The thing is that the Mauser is the preferred weapon of a very nasty piece of work called Sean Gallagher."

"Gallagher!" said Kell. He looked at Hubert. "Gallagher is one of the IRB's most effective killers. Commissioner Thompson and I have chased him up and down the country – and always he manages to stay one step ahead of us. Speed the day we can put a rope round his neck."

Thompson picked up the story again. "He’s a strange mixture of parts – quite well educated within the limits of his class. But something went wrong inside him a long time ago: he’s the most ruthless man I've ever heard of. A devil with the ladies, too. If he's involved, we'll have one hell of a time of it.” Thompson shook his head in thought. “Then again, to be fair to the IRB, God bless 'em, we know that Gallagher is a very much loner and the evidence we have so far points to *two* men. That may rule him out and it’s not as though Kitchener didn’t have enough enemies elsewhere to keep us busy. Some of those are very powerful indeed. We’re spoiled for choice, really, when it comes to potential suspects.”

“Do you think it might have anything to do with Casement and his lot?” prompted Hubert.

“Well, that’s certainly *one* possibility. Casement is a traitor and we’ll surely hang him if he sets foot again on British soil but we don’t even have to look that far. There are members of our own Government who were, shall we say, less than enamoured with Lord Kitchener. They’re not beyond the odd, seriously dirty trick. I can’t say any more than that at the moment but that’s the reason we had men down at Broome to protect him.”

Kell slipped his gloves off and toyed absent-mindedly

with them for a moment. "And now we're in the eye of the storm."

Thompson nodded. "The PM wants us to keep this under wraps until we can work up something that will stop it turning into a world-class disaster – God knows what, though. You can imagine his reaction when I told him. This is the worst thing that could have happened to us."

"Worst time, too," said Fitzgerald, moodily.

"Indeed – the Branch is stretched wafer thin right now rounding up strays from the Uprising so most of my people are not even on the mainland." He cleared his throat and spoke more authoritatively. "The bottom line is that damage limitation is the order of the day. We can take any action – any – to soften the blow on the country and the war effort. 'All resources, all solutions, without restriction' are ours to command – the PM's very words. And that, as far as it goes, is the current state of this bag of nails we have on our hands."

"And now we're going down to the scene of the crime, as it were. What's the plan?" asked Hubert.

"Well, clearly, I have to conduct an investigation into what went wrong and you can all testify that everything is above board."

Hubert watched the thunderstorm approach. A few bumps on the road delayed Kell's retort but, when it came, it was icy cold. "I'm only going to say this once, Commissioner – we are *both* responsible for the internal security of this country. If you think I'm going to restrict myself to 'testifying', as you quaintly express it, you're deluding yourself. There will be no decisions taken without my complete agreement and if you cannot accept this right from the outset, we can turn this car around, go back to the PM and sort the matter out."

Hubert watched the exchange with interest. He had learned early on that there was no love lost between MI5 and Special Branch. Military Intelligence did all the spadework to build a case against an enemy agent but it had no ultimate power of arrest. They were required by law to hand their prey over to Special Branch for the legal process to take its course. MI5 had to stay in the shadows while Special Branch got all the glory – it was an old story but it still made Hubert smile to see it in action.

Thompson said nothing but his face told volumes. Taking the awkward silence as agreement, Kell continued, "But one thing's absolutely certain: no-one must ever even *think* that this might have been the work of the IRB – *ever* – or we're just building another problem for the country to solve after the war. How we're going to do that is the rub. We need time. Time to work out some sort of plan – a cover story of a heart attack or something like that brought on by overwork. He was in his late sixties, after all. Anything that could reasonably take him out of public view without delay."

Fitzgerald blinked several times and plucked at some imaginary threads on his uniform. "You're talking about Lord Kitchener as though he were a stone in your shoe, Kell," he barked across Thompson, irritated by other's dispassionate manner. "He was a great soldier and a great *man*, too. None of us were fit to bull his boots. Don't you dare forget that. We have lost our best leader at a desperate time because of the incompetence of those who were meant to protect him." He looked, with some significance, at Thompson.

Kell remained unruffled. "I meant nothing of the sort, Colonel, nor can you lay any blame at my door, since it was Special Branch – not MI5 – that was in charge of his safety. It looks as though the IRB have succeeded in bringing down Lord Kitchener but I have to make sure that they don't bring down the county with him. Public morale is a critical measuring stick for my department. We're losing thousands of our youngest and fittest men at the Front almost on a daily basis. The Russians are just deserting in droves because of corruption at the highest levels inside their General Staff. And, of course, the French are as hopeless as usual. Against that sort of backdrop, losing Kitchener could be the final straw for the country."

Hubert looked sharply at Kell. He had seen some very brave Frenchmen on the field of battle and, as for his own ancestry …

But Kell was in full swing. "You see a very different war from the one Thompson and I have to fight. Not everyone supports the war and even those who do are getting monstrous weary of it. The War Office might be in touch with what's happening at the Front but you have little idea of what it's doing to the British people."

"Now just a …"

Kell held up a hand. "No, please hear me out. Every single day, Thompson and I have to hunt down all sorts of traitors and spies and malcontents. I dread to think how Britain will react to the news that Lord Kitchener has been gunned down in cold blood by citizens of our own country." Kell sat back in his seat. "You can be sure of one thing, though – if civilian morale drops any further, we can just pack up and surrender to the Kaiser. Kitchener's death is devastating – as you rightly say, he was a great man but we have higher priorities now."

Fitzgerald sniffed in disdain and looked out of the window at the passing countryside.

Kell had it right, though, Hubert thought. This certainly was one hell of a disaster. The war, pretty much, was over if they couldn't put a patch over this. There was no-one with Kitchener's grasp of the current military situation to slip in and save the day – no-one of his stature, even. What made it worse was the fact that it was also very unusual, to say the least, to have a serving military officer holding a government portfolio. It was highly unlikely that someone else from the General Staff could pick up the torch without fumbling it. He remembered, still with a tinge of disbelief, that Kitchener couldn't even speak in the House because he was *unelected* – Minister of State for War and he was debarred from opening his mouth in Westminster. That had to be done by his Under-Secretary – a ludicrous state of affairs – but, right from the start, the King and the Prime Minister wanted Kitchener and no-one else. Now he was dead. The thought that Germany might actually win simply because this would sink British morale too low to be resurrected …

Thompson trumpeted into his handkerchief, bringing Hubert sharply back to reality. "Nor do I need you, Kell, to labour the point that my men slipped up. I will deal with that later, as I have already made clear. But, look here, we're in danger of drifting from the point, which is to decide what, in God's name, to do next." He jerked his chin at Hubert, still facing them in the front passenger seat. "Lieutenant, you are new to this – a fresh eye, perhaps. What's your initial reaction?"

From the corner of his eye, Hubert could see Kell glare at Thompson's impertinence. He smiled to himself but, yet, with a touch of irritation. Clearly, as a *very* junior officer, he would have nothing of value to contribute in Kell's eyes. But then, Kell had not fought in this conflict whereas Hubert knew how the men, particularly the younger ones, worshipped Kitchener. His posters and photographs were everywhere, sternly pointing out the 'road to duty'. It was inevitable that he would be proclaimed almost a demi-god by those serving under him – which made the Irish connection all the more incredible.

He cleared his throat. "As Major Kell said, we cannot let English troops know that Kitchener was killed by the IRB – if that is, indeed, the case."

Thompson nodded agreement: nothing had been proven yet. Hubert pressed further. "I'm of French Swiss-Canadian parentage so, to a certain extent, I think I can view Anglo-Irish relations from something of a distance but, even so, I have absolutely no doubt that we'd have internecine war in the trenches if this came out – the English against the Irish. Kitchener was like a God to the British Army."

"We know he was popular but surely that's overstating the case a tad."

Hubert cast his mind back to the carnage he had left behind at Ypres. "Well, think about this. When the mud had set on the Ypres Salient after one of the larger pushes, the Red Cross were trying to identify some of our boys who had died on the field. They came across a young lad – no more than a schoolboy, really – but there he was, lying face down in the mud of an empty trench. His only company was a couple of mutilated horses that had been blown in by the blast of a shell. In one hand he had his empty Enfield and, in the other, a crumpled, blood-stained photograph of Lord Kitchener, torn from a magazine." He paused and smiled sardonically at the others. "Not much more than a child, I agree, and probably very impressionable, but men grow up quickly over there, Commissioner. It's either that or not growing up ever. Clearly, this lad had worshipped Kitchener – and he wouldn't have been the only one – so, one sniff of this business and all hell will break loose. We'll lose the War within the week."

"Point taken. But a *week* – that quickly?" asked Thompson.

Hubert paused as the driver honked the horn like some demented goose. "I do. And it's for that very reason that I can't really take this idea of the Irish being involved. Surely it can't be in their own interests to allow the Hun to win the War? I mean, Ireland would fall with Britain. What makes you think they're behind this – apart from the type of gun?"

"As I said – Gallagher. We had reports that he was seen in London recently. As usual, he buggered off and disappeared God knows where. Now, perhaps, we know." Thompson shook his head emphatically. "But you're wrong if you feel that an English defeat wouldn't serve the Irish cause. There's strong evidence the IRB have been in close talks with the Hun over who gets what after Britannia sinks below the waves. At any rate, Gallagher is just too important to be here without a suitable target in mind. The IRB don't waste his talents – although it *is* rumoured there's some rough and tumble going on at their Dublin Brigade HQ. One or two of his colleagues-in-arms seem to be less than happy about the way he ploughs a lonely furrow – but that's beside the point."

"And what, exactly is to the point, Commissioner?" asked Fitzgerald.

Thompson shifted arthritically in his seat as the firmly sprung car hit a rut in the road. "What *is* to the point, Colonel, is the fact that the Mauser is his preferred weapon. It's a little bulky, but you can be assured that when you pull the trigger, anything in front of the business end is going to feel terminally unwell. And the clincher, I suppose, is that we simply have nothing on the Hun espionage front to suggest enemy involvement – they're all playing nice with their sketchbooks and cameras." He chuckled and wiped his nose. "Well, the ones we didn't sweep up on Day One of the War, that is."

"I'll bet that pleased the Kaiser," said Hubert.

"It did that. Apparently, he raved for the best part of two hours when he heard the news. Steinhauer must have had his ears reamed out." Seeing Hubert's eyebrows raised in question, he added, "Steinhauer's Major Kell's opposite number."

Kell uncrossed his legs in irritation. "All very interesting but, as you say, we're drifting from the point. Colonel Fitzgerald has set us a limit of three days before things start to unravel. What are we to do?"

****

Riordan collapsed like a sack of potatoes into the seat beside Gallagher, who had been dozing in the corner of the carriage. Wartime wreaked havoc with train timetables and the compartments were packed to bursting, despite the early hour. Using a combination of natural cunning and brute force, Riordan had been able to secure the seats. He beamed at the standing passengers in a vain attempt to show them just how inoffensive he was. Gallagher stirred himself, allowing Riordan to lean sideways, whispering like a Guy Fawkes conspirator out of the corner of his mouth.

"So why didn't you phone Brigade, Sean?"

It had been arranged that a successful conclusion of the job was to be signalled by calling a particular Dublin telephone twice for three rings each. Seemed innocuous enough but Gallagher's sixth sense had kittens when MacNeill suggested it. And Gallagher was a man who always listened very carefully to his instincts – they had kept him alive for most of his thirty-five years and he had too many enemies in the IRB to allow them the luxury of knowing that the job was done. He wasn't about to risk personal or political betrayal. Right from the start, he had decided that that he – and no-one else – would choose the time and the place to break the news to the likes of MacNeill.

The train clattered across a series of points in one of the few bursts of speed it had attempted since leaving London. The journey to Stranraer was going to take forever at this rate. He glanced around to see who might be listening and then looked Riordan warily in the eye.

"Will you shut up talkin' about it till we get back home?" he said in an undertone.

"Well, Sean, I just don't want to get into any trouble with Brigade. Y'see? If they tell you to do somethin', you just don't go around doin' it your own way. Not if you want to hang on to your knees you don't, anyway." He paused. "When *are* you goin' to let them know?"

Once again, Gallagher had the impression that Riordan was not as Bog Irish as he let on. Was he really there as back-up or was he insurance for the boys at Brigade? He went over the events of the previous week. Was there anything that could be used against him back home? Nothing sprang to mind. His instincts had led him true but it was definitely time to clam up on friend Riordan.

Gallagher leaned over to whisper in Riordan's ear, "I'll tell them in me own good ..." Gallagher suddenly saw the greasy glint of a pistol butt – a Mauser – catching the yellow, flickering light of the carriage underneath his companion's well-worn jacket. *The bastard had watched him hide the guns at the station!* This was none too good – he was unarmed while Riordan was not and if that gun was to make its way 'somehow' into the hands of the Brits, wiped clean or not, he was as good as hanged. Inside, he knew that he had to get that back gun from Riordan and there was probably only one way to do it.

"Like I say, I'll tell them in me own good time."

****

Hubert wondered what they would find down at Broome – the body of Kitchener himself, perhaps? The thought of seeing him, lying there in his nightgown, was repellent and he had already made up his mind to refuse to view the body. Some things, he thought, should be left to memory.

The villages of Bishopsbourne and Kingston slid past as their car bounced along at speed. Eventually, a large gate appeared on the right, barred by a huge farmer's waggon. Two serious-looking men were standing hidden behind the flanking pillars. They scrutinised the passes of the driver and, while one pushed the gates inward, the other grabbed the bridles of the Shires and pulled the cart out of the way just far enough to allow the cars to pass through. Hubert heard one of the horses stamp heavily as it helped reposition the barrier as soon as the Rolls had moved off. They continued down the winding road that led to the bottom of the shallow valley and the Hall beyond.

Moments later he found himself in the main drawing room of Broome House, being welcomed by a couple of large crackling fires. Although the day had been warm, the valley was in shadow and still had the chill of lingering spring. He looked around, wondering why Kitchener had never fitted electricity, or even gas.

Thompson, on the other hand, set things in motion without delay. All daytime staff who had been in attendance at the time of the shooting had been detained in the house and were waiting in the main kitchen area. Hubert could see the Commissioner was a man on a mission – it had been *his* people who had failed to preserve Kitchener's life and he'd want to find out quickly what went wrong. Looking over at Fitzgerald and remembering his reaction at being introduced to Thompson, it was clear the former wanted blood but was biding his time.

Thompson turned to Kell, who was warming himself in front of the fire, looking at an unfinished coat of arms. It had been drawn in charcoal and chalk on the centrepiece of one of the large granite mantelpieces. “I'm off to question MacLaughlin. He was supposed to be in charge of Kitchener's security detail. It might be best if you were to begin with the domestic staff. See what you can find out. None of the house staff were in the building last night because of the work going on so the head gardener sounds like a good bet to start with. At any rate, we'd better push on. This is going to take most of the day – and probably well into the evening."

Kell turned from the fire and caught sight of Hubert, standing at ease near one of the windows. “Hubert? Are you quite well?”

Fitzgerald turned to look at Hubert and noticed the tell-tale pallor and shallow chest movement caused by exposure to chlorine gas. “Belgium, Hubert?” he asked, gently.

“Yes, sir. I was invalided out from the return match at Ypres last year.” He had no intention of going into details. Whoever said that time was a healer clearly hadn’t served in the trenches up to his eyeballs in filth. The noise, the crying, the gas were still too raw to be a subject of casual conversation for a country drawing room. Oddly enough, he sensed that Fitzgerald had no desire to discuss it either – something he had noticed in officers, particularly senior ones, who had never experienced trench warfare at close quarters – a strange sort of shame at being miles away from a type of conflict they just didn’t understand.

He suppressed a cough that threatened to send him into another racking fit. ‘Dry land drowning’, it was called, where damaged lungs wept fluids that ended in violent coughing spasms. He hated the weakness it brought and the knowledge that his life was inevitably shortened. Exactly how long he had was anyone's guess, but one thing was for sure – *he* wouldn't be seeing any telegrams from the King.

"I wonder if I might just go and splash my face a little?"

Kell gestured at a double set of doors. "Yes, of course."

****

Fitzgerald rang for the butler to call for Dudeney the gardener. A few minutes later, Kell opened the door in response to a soft knock, and ushered in an old man who looked to be in his seventies. The visitor insinuated himself into the room, slicking down his thin white hair and ducking his head to Fitzgerald.

"Ah, Dudeney, come over here. I must ask you a few questions concerning the dreadful events of today," said Fitzgerald in a tone he reserved for servants and junior officers.

Kell raised a laconic eyebrow. "If you please, Colonel, allow *me* to conduct this investigation."

For a moment, there was a strained silence in the room, underlined by a sibilant wheezing from Kell – like Hubert, the journey in the damp air had done him no good. Fitzgerald nodded abruptly and sat down, allowing Kell to turn his attention back to Dudeney.

"Sit yourself down, Mr Dudeney – over here. My name is Kell, Major Kell. Colonel Fitzgerald, you already know, of course. Now, I'm sorry to say that I'm going to ask you to think back over everything that took place here, this morning."

Dudeney turned his rheumy eyes to the fire. "We still

can't believe it, sir, if you know what I mean. His Lordship being killed like that – murdered in his own home." The old man looked tearfully up at the standing Kell. "And I think it might've been all my fault," he said.

****

Hubert jerked back to the present. For a brief moment, he stared without comprehension at the sink he was leaning on and then stood up, sweating, as he realised he was *not* gasping his last in the glutinous mud of the Ypres Salient. Flashbacks were likely to remain part of his life for a while – 'just the mind struggling to come to terms with memory,' they had said – but this was the first time since the beginning of the year and it was a shock he could happily have done without. It was as good as a doctor's note telling him he still had a long way to go. Swaying a little, he unpinned his uniform shirt collar, loosened the tie and washed the sweat off his face.

He growled at his pale reflection in the mirror. "Big girl."

He stumbled back into the corridor, adjusting his uniform, and smiled at the sight of the woman waiting for him, holding half a dozen buff folders tightly to her chest. It was Kathleen Sissmore, a pretty 18-year old clerk who had just joined MI5 and was, unaccountably, called Jane by everyone. "You didn't sound too good in there, Chris. Do you want me to get a doctor?"

Hubert laughed in spite of himself – her painfully upper-class English accent always brought out the colonial in him – and she really was very sweet to worry. It seemed that *all* the secretaries and most of the Registry girls were somehow related to officers of the Army or Navy. That was how MI5 worked – word of mouth, a whisper in the ear and suddenly a post would be filled. In his more sardonic moments, he sneeringly called it 'enlightened nepotism' but it did seem to work. He, for one, could hardly complain. If it hadn't been for his father using his influence to lobby the High Commission back home in Canada, he'd have been invalided out of uniform at the end of last year. Instead, here he was – working for MI5 in London as some sort of high-level dogsbody. That's what he liked to tell himself. In fact, he was a key member of Section G(a) – the department charged with the investigation of espionage and suspected persons.

"No, I'm fine, Jane. Don't cluck around me." He beamed at her to remove any offence. "Anyway, what are you doing down here? You should be back in the Registry with all the other Harpies."

She stuck her tongue out at him. "Major Kell wanted administrative support with him and sent me down ahead of you. I had someone hammering on my mother's door at seven this morning." Her mouth trembled despite a valiant effort not to cry. "It's just so … *awful*."

"It's all of that. The question is 'what are we going to do about it'." He coughed, almost retching.

"You've come back to work too soon, Chris. Yes, I know," she said archly, holding up her hand to forestall his reply, "you'd have been sent back home to manage your father's hotels and what-not. You would have hated it and gone round the bend in no time." She smiled, sadness in her eyes. "But that would have been better than gasping your last in England, one breath at a time."

"Hated it? It's *hate* that keeps me going, Jane – I just hate them," he sighed, leaning back against the cloakroom door.

"*Hate* them – who?"

"Who? The Hun. Who else?" He brooded for a moment, and then grinned at her. "It's difficult for you English roses to understand," he said, acknowledging her stage-curtsey. "But people like my lot are sort of Gallic mongrels. I'm part French-Swiss and part French-Canadian. Both sides of me hate what they're doing in France and Belgium. That's why I dropped out of business school in Ottawa the minute the balloon went up." He chuckled at the brief memory. "My old man was mad as a snake. God, was he mad!"

"Whereas now you're twenty-four years old and your lungs are so badly damaged you can't walk up a flight of steps without collapsing. You've done enough, Chris."

"Well, I clung to life at Pops. Now I'm clinging to my uniform. Anyway – look at Kell. He's Director of all he surveys and he's asthmatic as a vicar's wife."

"Pops?"

"Sorry – Poperinghe – the casualty clearing station outside Ypres. That's where most of us ended up. I had an engaging couple of weeks there before being shipped back."

"Chris," she said.

"I'm fine. Honestly." Changing the subject, he jerked a thumb towards the drawing room and lowered his voice. "What do you know about this Thompson chap? Know him well?"

"Not particularly. But you wouldn't believe some of the stuff he's done." She leaned forward in confidence. "He was actually the Prime Minister of Tonga at one point! Can you believe it?"

"You're kidding me – right?"

"No, I swear …"

Interesting." He thought for a moment about how impartial Thompson's 'investigation' could possibly be and pushed himself off the door, saying, "Well, anyway, I'd better get back in there with Kell and Fitzgerald."

****

Hubert walked back in to see an old man twisting his cap in an agony of despair.

Kell turned at the sound of the door closing. "Ah, Hubert, hope you're feeling a little better? Mr Dudeney here is the Head Gardener. He thinks he may have played a part in the tragedy."

Hubert smiled at the thought of the inoffensive old man causing the death of his employer but Kell, more experienced perhaps, was reserving judgement in the absence of facts.

"So, why do you say that, Mr Dudeney?" Hubert asked.

"Well, I couldn't find them, could I?

"Whom?"

"The two men." Dudeney looked back at Kell with watery eyes and said, "His Lordship calls me over to the rose beds yesterday. Just before lunch it must have been. 'Dudeney', says he, 'have we taken on any new men?' Well, I says 'No, my lord. In fact, we've had to let men go, for the War an' all.'"

"And what did he say to that?"

"He says, 'I've just seen two workmen I don't recognise.' So I says, 'If you'll point them out to me next time, your lordship, I'll tell you who they are.' And then he goes back to his roses. Proper beauties they are. His Lordship worked on them every minute he could. I remember the state of those beds before he bought the place ..."

Kell dragged him back to the moment. "Yes, I'm sure, Mr Dudeney but if we can get back to the question of these two mysterious men. Did Lord Kitchener describe them?"

"His lordship said that one of them was a little taller than me, so that would make him about five foot seven. He said he had thick black, curly hair. The other one was tall, perhaps about six foot, with brownish hair and a pock-marked face."

"What about clothes and so forth?"

"Never said nothing about that – just working men."

"Well, never mind. Did you or His Lordship see them again?"

Dudeney dragged his gaze away from Kell and stared into the fire once more. "That's just it, sir, I kept a weather eye open for them, so to speak, but one thing drives out another, you know how it is, and I just lost track o' time. I was looking after the clearing of the flowerbeds along the top wall. We needed some bedding plants and young Jim was all busy with the raking, so I goes off to the potting shed to get them."

Hubert was beginning to warm to the old man. His maternal grandfather had been the one to emigrate to Canada from Switzerland in the middle of the previous century. A proud, independent sort, he had wrested most of his 500 acre farm from virgin forest with his own hands. All that remained of him now were a few, stiff-looking cabinet portraits and the farm itself but, somehow, that was enough to tell you all you needed to know about him. Dudeney here had that sort of 'feel' but, clearly, events were beginning to prove a little too much for him. He walked over to a yew side table near the armchairs and poured a generous measure of brandy from one of the decanters. "Here you go, Mr Dudeney, have a drink of this. It'll do you the power of good."

Dudeney glanced at Fitzgerald and, receiving a peremptory nod, accepted the drink. After a few sips, he was ready to continue.

"Go on. What then, sir?" asked Hubert.

"Well, we never did see anything more of them and I never thought about it for the rest of the day." He took another sip of his drink as the memory tightened his stomach. "Then, this morning, as I'm getting the tools together to do the borders around the back of the Hall, I hears all this commotion and banging on His Lordship's bedroom just above where I was workin'. One of the tweenies sticks her head out to me from downstairs to say that they can't wake him up. So, I gets my ladder and climbs up to his window. And that's when I saw him." Dudeney looked at Hubert with a glint of fire in his eyes. "They shouldn't have done that. Not like that. Not in his sleep when he couldn't defend hisself. It were wicked."

Hubert suppressed a shiver at the thought of someone like Gallagher creeping in while he was asleep. 'Wicked' was the word for it, all right.

"What did you do then?" asked Hubert.

"For a while, I couldn't do anything, sir. I just stood up there, shaking. I don't know for how long. The door was locked and there was no key, so I went back out through the window to find Mr MacLaughlin. He and his men broke through the door from the corridor side to check that His Lordship was dead and then he called his boss up in London."

"And that's all you can tell us?"

"That's right, sir. We was all herded into the kitchen by Mr MacLaughlin and told not to stir an inch from the place."

Kell and Hubert glanced at each other. It was fairly obvious that little more would be gleaned from the gardener. "Well, that will be all for the moment, Mr Dudeney," said Kell. "We'll call you again if we need you."

The old gardener stood up, stiff with lumbago, and shuffled off towards the door, placing the empty brandy glass on the table as he passed it. Then he turned and looked at Kell across the room. "Who is going to run the War for us now, sir? That's what I wants to know. Does this mean the Hun's going to win? I mean, who do we have who can hold a candle to the likes of him?"

But it was Fitzgerald who turned around in his seat. "Who, indeed, Dudeney? Who, indeed?"

****

Thompson had been searching for MacLaughlin for the best part of twenty minutes before he thought of going to the kitchen. He opened the door and looked in to see a crowd of frightened faces. MacLaughlin and his men were taking statements from the house staff. Thompson caught his eye and cocked a beckoning finger. MacLaughlin went visibly white and followed Thompson out into the corridor.

"Where can we speak, MacLaughlin?"

"The housekeeper's parlour is just along here, sir, if you'll follow me."

Once in the room, Thompson sat down in a flowery armchair and looked up at the other man. He did not invite him to sit down.

"Right, MacLaughlin, let's have it. What the hell happened?"

MacLaughlin swallowed quickly to wet his dry throat and said, "I don't know, sir, and that's the truth of it. Somehow, they gained access during the night. I had four officers patrolling the grounds but somehow they managed it. There's evidence that two men reconnoitred the area yesterday and certainly the carpets in the bedroom show traces of two sets of footprints – no boots. Apart from that, we simply have no clue as to how they got in. Or out again, for that matter."

Thompson let the silence hang in the air for a moment. "Have you any idea of the trouble we are in? You were briefed in the minutest of detail as to the IRB threat. You had everything you needed to ensure the safety of Lord Kitchener, but now he's dead. Worst of all, I'm saddled with that bloody headmaster Kell sermonising over how we failed to look after our charge. If it weren't for the fact that they're all busy chasing Micks from the Uprising just like us, we'd have his entire *department* crawling all over the place."

"Sir, we did everything by the book. There is no way they could have slipped past us and ..."

Thompson held up a hand. "Spare me. The fact of the matter is that he *has* been murdered. Arresting those responsible is incidental to the sheer enormity of the problem the War Office is going to have to face. Catching and hanging the bastards will be as nothing to the mess we have to clear up."

He sneezed into a handkerchief and then looked up at MacLaughlin through red-rimmed eyes. "You're not an ambitious man, MacLaughlin, I hope. As far as the Branch is concerned, your career is pretty much dead in the water. Others will have to decide on what we can salvage from this balls-up but you, for the moment, can carry on with the due process of law and catch the killers. Do you think your demonstrably limited capabilities could cope with that?"

"Yes, sir."

"Then take yourself out of my sight, there's a good chap."

MacLaughlin made for the door. As he was leaving, Thompson said, "Send Fredericks to me."

Alone in the corridor, MacLaughlin grimaced and punched the wall in sheer frustration. Fredericks was his up-and-coming subordinate. 'Up-and-passing', now. He opened the door into the kitchen. There he was, beavering away with the statements. Bastard!

"Fredericks!" he called, "Thompson wants you. In the housekeeper's parlour. Move yourself."

****

An hour later, Thompson re-joined Kell in the main drawing room. He poured himself a drink from the brandy decanter, flopped into a seat and then looked over at Kell. "Well," he said, "I've seen the scene of the crime, as it were. Young Fredericks showed me the form. Smart young lad, that. Nothing to be seen in the bedroom apart from a few footprints and four burn holes in the carpet from the spent cartridges. Two sets of prints, though, on one of the pillars. It could rule out Gallagher, if he's still a loner these days but, on the other hand, we have a bullet and it's definitely a Mauser. Went clean through the skull and embedded itself in the base of the headboard."

Fitzgerald screwed his eyes shut. "Please!"

Thompson snorted to himself and then continued, "From the description, it sounds like our man. If we can snatch Gallagher and he still has the gun, we could be in business. I've set Fredericks to alert road, rail and ports. We might catch him on his way home." He wiped his nose and took a pull at the brandy. "But only if our luck changes."

"Anything from the staff?" asked Hubert.

Thompson held his glass out at arm's length and looked at it with an incredulous frown. "Do you know, I can barely taste this stuff? *Damn* cold! Sorry – the staff – very little, so far. No one remembers seeing anything out of the ordinary. Bloody useless ... wait a minute." He exploded into his handkerchief again. "God, I feel awful. Anyway, I have set everything in motion. We'll round up the usual Celts and see what we can get out of them. That, of course, is the least of our worries."

"I agree," said Kell. "Time we decided upon tactics. As I said before, I think that a sudden heart attack or influenza should be the message and ..."

"Won't work," said Thompson thickly, wiping his nose.

"And why not?"

Thompson scratched his head in bemusement. "I've been thinking about this. If this *is* the work of the IRB, and there is nothing to suggest otherwise, what do you think their next move would be if we tried to cover up the death in any way? They'd have their involvement spread across every newspaper that would print it – especially abroad."

"We are able to deal with the newspapers – any which do not co-operate, we close down. They know that."

"Same problem – *and* you can't close down foreign publications. But the mere fact that we consider the circumstances of Lord Kitchener's death to be so questionable as to render it unfit for public consumption would be enough for the unwashed to start a campaign for disclosure. Repington, for a start, would have a field day."

"You have a point," said Kell, reluctantly.

Hubert looked up. "Is this the Colonel Repington I met when we went down to the Standards Committee a few weeks back? The Military Correspondent of some newspaper or other?"

"The 'Daily Express'. Yes, the very same man – and that makes him a creature of Lord Northcliffe – our 'foremost newspaper magnate', as he likes to be known. Both of them hated Lord Kitchener to the death and they have made no secret of their utter disdain for his handling of the War. They've caused this country no end of trouble, between the two of them."

"But he was a soldier himself. Wait a minute - wasn't there something about his having been forced to resign his commission, years ago?"

"An affair with some official's wife", said Kell, "and that is why he is now justly reduced to the status of newspaper hack. However, Northcliffe's rags have an undeniable influence on the masses, which makes Repington's ravings doubly dangerous."

Thompson weighed in. "Absolutely right. In fact, one of my lads told me he had heard the good Colonel referred to as the 'twenty-third member of the Cabinet'! Ridiculous."

"He was universally detested," snapped Fitzgerald, irritably straightening a fold in his tunic. "A constant thorn in our sides. Indeed, you may remember, Kell, Lord Kitchener actually banned him from the entire Western Front because of his irresponsible scaremongering over the alleged lack of artillery shells."

“Indeed I do. I understand he had only allowed him back a few weeks ago.”

“Well, there are bigger fish to fry right now,” said Hubert, turning to Fitzgerald. “What about this suggestion, sir, that we could arrange to have Lord Kitchener develop flu or something of the kind? Enough to give him reason to remain at home for a week or two. That would give us a little more time. We already control the grounds and the house. We can decide who has access to him."

Fitzgerald gave a snort of exasperation. "Did you listen to anything I said on the way down from London, Lieutenant? Lord Kitchener is – was – a very dynamic leader. He expected a lot of his subordinates – perhaps too much. When he found others lacking, he tended to take on their tasks himself. He was not a delegator in important matters. That, in turn, means that pivotal strategies conceived and directed by him are under way with no one at the helm. He could not be absent from London for more than a few days without his presence being required."

Thompson nodded in agreement. "And when it becomes known that the government – for remember, gentlemen, we do this on the orders of the Prime Minister, himself – has tried to keep the matter of Lord Kitchener's murder a secret, heads will roll. There is no doubt that the present government will fall and that’s something we cannot allow in the current crisis. The King, for one, will not be pleased. He was fond of His Lordship, as was Lady Asquith. He’ll be devastated by the news, however it comes to his ears."

"Well,” said Kell, "we have little choice. At the most, the news can be kept quiet for no more than a few days. After that, the Prime Minister will have to announce it to the House after first informing His Majesty. And then God help us all."

Hubert pulled gently at his lower lip, deep in thought. "We don't even have a few days."

Thompson looked up from his handkerchief. "What do you mean?"

"The IRB High Command will be desperate to jump the gun on us, if you'll pardon the metaphor. As soon as Gallagher, or whoever is responsible for the hit, confirms a successful operation, they'll set their publicity machine in motion, as Commissioner Thompson says. It'll be round the world inside twenty-four hours."

Thompson nodded. "I believe you have the right of it, Hubert. MacNeill will be hopping about like a schoolboy needing a pee when he hears the news." Fitzgerald shuddered at the simile and turned to watch the fire, allowing the other to continue, "And matters will only be made worse by any attempt on our part to suppress things. The bastards have us well and truly stitched up."

Hubert paced about the room, deep in thought, his eye falling on the unfinished charcoal drawing on the front of one the mantelpieces. The hairs on the back of his neck stood up as the idea struck him. Kell, sitting as he was, across the room, could see the change in expression and followed Hubert's eye line to the fireplace.

"What is it, Hubert?"

Hubert held up his hand for silence while he revolved the idea, the ridiculous idea, around his mind for a few seconds.

"Hubert ...?"

"There might be a way out of this. A temporary one, to be sure, but good enough for Government work."

Thompson sat forward eagerly. "If you have anything that can save our balls, man, let's hear it!"

Hubert faced his audience and ticked off the points on the fingers of his left hand. "Our problem is that the IRB *know*, or shortly will know, that they've been successful. It is only a matter of time before they announce the fact to the world. We have a day, two at the outset, before that happens. Lord Kitchener can't be absent from the War Office for long without suspicions being aroused. The problem is that we can't suppress the news even for that length of time. It could be that the IRB are just waiting to see if we attempt a cover up. Any announcement of an 'illness' and they would spread the news of his murder to the four winds. There'd be demands to produce a walking, talking Secretary of State for War – something we would find difficult."

"Get to the point, lad. What can we *do*?"

"We have to arrange matters so that Lord Kitchener resumes work on Monday morning as usual. Wednesday, at the absolute outside."

"Are you mad?" asked Fitzgerald.

Thompson held up his hand to silence him. "Go on," he said.

"With Lord Kitchener still apparently treading the boards, the IRB can hardly accuse us of suppressing the news of his death."

Fitzgerald raised his eyes to the ceiling in scorn. "And how are we to achieve this … this *miracle*?"

Hubert looked at the other two and, suddenly, Thompson saw the light. His eyes widened. "A double, by God! Do you mean that you actually *know* someone who could pose successfully as Kitchener?"

"Impossible," said Kell and Fitzgerald at the same time, almost.

Hubert knew that this *was* the answer – the only *possible* answer, given the circumstances. It was all about *time*. "No, hear me out fully. There's no suggestion that we walk out into the street and find ourselves another Field Marshal. All we have to do is to produce a man who looks sufficiently like him from a distance to fool others. We can arrange things at the War Office to minimise visits from those who might see through the act. The deception only has to last for a week or so while 'His Lordship' becomes progressively more affected by pressure of work. I can't see the IRB trying to claim responsibility when Kitchener appears to be walking around large as life. Remember, it's *our* playing field. *We're* in control."

Fitzgerald snorted. "Hubert, have you any idea how ridiculous this whole thing ..."

"Let's just wait a moment, there, Colonel," said Thompson, "I'm beginning to get the feeling that our lieutenant here wouldn't come up with this sort of idea without something in mind." He leaned over, poured himself another brandy and looked appreciatively at Chris. "Let's hear the rest, Hubert."

CHAPTER 2

Saturday 20 May 1916 1700 hours – Sunday 21 May 1916 1600 hours

Hubert leaned against the massive stonework of the mantelpiece and gazed into the embers of the fire for a few moments. Folding his arms, he turned around, leaning back against one of the granite uprights. "As you know, I was involved in the Second Ypres thing last year. I won't go into the miserable details but the upshot was that I ended up in a casualty clearing station in Poperinghe."

"It's a little town quite close to the battlefield," he said, seeing Thompson silently ask the question.

"Complete with Military Cross, Hubert. Let's not forget that," said Kell in his best Headmaster's voice.

Hubert continued as if he Kell hadn't interrupted. "I spent about a month there in pretty bad shape. Afterwards, I was transferred back to Blighty and deposited on the doorstep of the Royal Victoria hospital at Netley. It took some time, but I recovered much of my health there and it's not stretching the truth to say that it was all due to one man – Henry Farmer – Colonel Henry Farmer of the Royal Army Medical Corps. Best doctor I have ever known." Hubert gazed into the middle distance, immersed in unpleasant memories. "A decent man."

"What about him, Hubert?" asked Thompson.

"Sorry." Hubert brought his faculties back into order and continued. "The thing was that, from time to time, the patients and staff would put on their little revues. You know the sort of thing. A chance to have a laugh, forget about the war. All good clean fun – *and* it gives some of the lads the chance to dress up in ladies' clothes." He ruminated dispassionately about the whole business of amateur dramatics in the Armed Forces. "Never understood that sort of thing. So peculiarly British. Anyway, Henry's turn was to wear the most ridiculous false moustache you've ever seen and do his bit as 'Kitchener'."

Fitzgerald bristled. Whether it was at the moustache story or the fact that someone had been taking Kitchener's name in vain was difficult to tell.

"The point is he was pretty good at it. In fact, he'd actually met Kitchener at Gallipoli and had spoken to him so I'm told he had the voice to a tee. What I'm saying is that I'm sure Colonel Farmer could pose as the real thing for a *short time* if we avoid placing him in positions where he has to make military decisions or voice an opinion or be interviewed by people who know him. He just has to be *seen at a distance.*" He paused. "You'll forgive me, Colonel", he said, glancing at Fitzgerald, "but Lord Kitchener was known as a rather reticent, unapproachable individual. That could well work in our favour. No-one is going to walk up to him and engage him in weighty matters without an appointment and an agenda under his arm. And it could be done in the three days you stipulated. I'm confident of that."

Hubert had shot his bolt and stood in the ensuing silence, waiting for some sort of reaction from the other three. It did not take long.

"I have never heard anything so preposterous in my entire life," said Fitzgerald, spluttering. "The very thought that some *barber surgeon* could stand in the shoes of a man of Lord Kitchener's stature and get away with it is beyond the pale, to say the least."

"Well, actually, he's a microbiologist, specialising in the infection of wounds but he's had to be a bit of an all-rounder due to current circumstances."

Fitzgerald froze him with a stare. "How can you possibly imagine that he would have the presence to carry the thing off, even at a distance? I will have absolutely nothing to do with such an imbecilic idea." Fitzgerald was evidently not impressed.

"And you will tell the PM this, personally, Colonel?" said Thompson quietly. Fitzgerald looked like a stopped clock, allowing Thompson to turn his attention back to Hubert. "I have to admit, I thought you had something there, Hubert, but ..."

"Well, let's just think about it for a moment, sir," said Chris. He looked around at the other three. It was plain from Fitzgerald's face that he, for one, would not think about it for a second, but he persisted. "Colonel Farmer is now working in a discreet little convalescent home in Hampstead – Farnham House – I did some time there, after Netley. I can meet with him tonight or tomorrow morning and talk it over with him. He is about the same build as Lord Kitchener – perhaps a little more weight – but nothing strenuous from the tailoring point of view. Colonel

Fitzgerald could provide us with Lord Kitchener's normal undress uniform and that side of things could be sorted out right away. Taking Monday to alter the others, we're left with all day Tuesday and perhaps Wednesday, if we can spin a good enough yarn at the War Office. We can use that time to give Henry the basic grounding he'd need to survive a day in London. He simply has to be seen entering and leaving the building for the thing to work. In fact, he doesn't have to speak to a soul all day if we can shift his diary around. The main thing is to be *seen.*"

"That will mean bringing his personal staff into the secret, Hubert." said Kell. "How many others have to be told before that secret is common knowledge?"

"Well, that's not necessarily true," Fitzgerald conceded. "His ADC and suchlike can be given tasks out of the building. Out of town, even. It is his secretary who is the key to the matter. She guards the outer office. Nothing gets through to Lord Kitchener without her permission. I have seen generals turned away from her desk empty-handed." He paused, as the thought struck him. "Poor Joan. She'll be devastated."

Thompson looked across at Kell. Could it *possibly* work? After all, doubles had been used throughout history. Why not now? "And you think that a day or two would be enough for this doctor to carry it off, Hubert?" he asked.

"Well, remember, he's not just 'a doctor'. He is a senior military officer – that's enormously in his favour and saves us a lot of time. Personally, I think that he should be seen about town on Wednesday. As I say, no-one in their right mind is going to try to sit Lord Kitchener down and interrogate him about intimate family matters, so I would think that only the briefest details need to be gone into. The same applies to the military situation and his secretary can help him by avoiding situations where Henry would be caged in a room with someone who knows him well. Current names, places and decisions are the critical things and most of that we could deal with in a day. Just get him into the public eye and we are safe for a while. It gives us time to *think*."

"And what exactly are your thoughts, Kell?" said Thompson.

"I agree with Colonel Fitzgerald. It is the most preposterous thing I have heard in my life. However, having said that, I cannot conceive of any alternative. But I would stipulate one thing, Commissioner."

"What's that?"

"This Colonel Farmer must be a willing volunteer."

"Rubbish. He is a serving officer and we have the direct orders of the PM to ..."

"Totally irrelevant. If he has to have any chance of preserving the illusion of Lord Kitchener's continued existence, he must be comfortable in the role. The alternative is immediate disclosure and we will end up in worse trouble than we are in now, if that is possible."

"You're right, of course." said Thompson, nodding. "Hubert, it's all down to you. You know the man. Will he do it?"

"I don't know. All I can do is to ask him."

"Right you are. Well, I think that settles that, Kell." He grabbed frantically at his handkerchief and sneezed loudly. "Apologies. Let's get Hubert packed off to Outer Hampstead, or wherever, while we read the Riot Act to the domestic staff. In fact, it might not be such a bad idea to keep them here until this Colonel Farmer looks the part. The IRB thing applies to them, too. They would find it a bit difficult to run off to the newspapers shouting about His

Lordship's death when he's walking about, apparently, large as life." He looked around. "Well, I'm feeling a lot happier now that we have something to work towards." He levered himself out of the armchair and walked over to the brandy decanter.

"Who's for a drink?"

****

In a shabby, darkened room on the top floor of a run-down Dublin tenement, MacNeill leaned back in a rickety chair. He hated the foul-smelling dump but it was safe. It was the rats that bothered him – that mediaeval aura of death and disease their very name conjured up. It made his skin crawl but, as usual, he had to push personal matters to the back of his mind – he had business to attend to. As Brigade Intelligence Officer, it was his job to mastermind the death of Britain's 'most honoured military hero', the architect of the war. He smiled at how he was about to wipe that damn-your-eyes look off those bloody stupid posters. *Britain needs you.* 'Aye', he thought, 'but Ireland doesn't need *you*, you old bugger.' He took a deep drag of his cigarette and exhaled slowly.

He tilted his head further back into the shadow of one corner of the room and looked listlessly over at the other two men. Academics – he despised them. They could thump tables with the best of them about a free Ireland while they passed the port around but ask them to hold a gun to a man's head and blow his brains out and they'd wet themselves. He sneered at them from the darkness while still acknowledging the sad fact that he needed them. They were his wordsmiths, his voices to the outside world, his political arm.

"Well then, Padhraig, how are you going to release the

news?"

Padhraig Chesney thought carefully before answering. The presence of the Grim Reaper quite so near at hand unsettled him. He cleared his throat nervously before answering, "I don't think we should leap into print as soon as we hear Sean's done the business."

"Why?"

"Well, we can catch them twice if we time it right."

"How?"

He looked around the room for support and, finding none, licked his lips with a pale, flickering tongue. "Once Kitchener is dead, the British Government will have to find some way of announcing the fact. From the trouble we've already made about the Harp business, not to mention Easter Monday, it's going to be fairly obvious that we did it. But the Brits will never be able to admit that to the public so they'll try to concoct all sorts of fairy stories to explain away the real truth."

"And that's when we make our move?"

"That's when we make our move. Not only will we hit the headlines with a blow by blow account of the execution, but we'll also show Asquith up for the liar he is. When we announce Kitchener's death, it'll be the end of Britain as far as the war's concerned and we'll squeeze even more out of it when the country gets to know that *their own Government* lied through their teeth at them. It'll wreck the political landscape and bring the Government down. We'll wipe out morale at home and Government control at the Front."

MacNeill grunted and leaned forward to stub out his cigarette, bringing his face momentarily into the pale light of a low-wattage bulb. He looked up without moving his head. "What about you, Iain? You're our tame newspaper editor."

Iain Devlin's involvement with extremists was an open secret in journalistic circles and, privately, he revelled in the smell of danger that hung around men like MacNeill as long as he didn't come too close to it. This was too close to it. He sat, hunched up, with his elbows on his knees, head down. "I don't agree, Eoin. I think the more time you give to Special Branch to think something up, the more chance there is of losing the advantage. It'll always be harder to announce our involvement after the news becomes public. But if we can be the *first* to spread the news, no-one can deny it was us." He looked up. "What about Casement and his boys? I still have a couple of my lads standing by to get the story about Kitchener and his boyfriends from Dan Bailey. He was supposed to be coming over from Germany with Roger but now that Gallagher's going to kill the ould bastard, what's the point of running the story?"

MacNeill sighed with impatience. "You just don't get it, do you? The point, Iain, is that we don't just want to kill Kitchener. We want to *destroy* him! So, when Dan gets to Dublin, you run the story at the same time as we announce Kitchener's execution. And, in any case, we don't give a tinker's cuss about Casement. If he had his way, there would have been no Easter Rising and he would have had nothin' to do with Bailey's 'revelations' so he's not the man for us. Not any more. Gallagher will kill Kitchener for us and then we'll have some fun."

"Have you heard from Sean yet?"

MacNeill leaned back in the chair and darkness closed over his face once more. "No. It was supposed to be some time this weekend. So unless something has come up, we should hear in the next few hours."

"How will he get in touch, then?"

MacNeill looked sharply at the other man and said quietly, "That's none of your business, Iain. Leave that sort of stuff to people like me and Sean. Don't you go worrying your head about it, so. Y'hear?"

Devlin gabbled something in excuse but MacNeill ignored him. "I like the idea of hitting the Brits twice for the same operation. Maximise the effect. It's good economics." He paused and mulled the matter over for a few minutes, while the others kept their silence in the gloom. "OK, we'll go for the double whammy, as the Yanks would call it."

Chesney grinned quietly at Devlin until MacNeill leaned forward once more, lowering the front legs of his chair on to the floor. The faint light filtering through the torn blinds glittered in his dead eyes. "But Padhraig," he said, "be right."

****

In the end, Hubert drove down the following morning. The events of the previous day and his fragile, early-convalescent health had proved more than he was yet able to bear. Kell, uncharacteristically, insisted Chris got himself a good night's rest before setting off. The situation at Broome was well-enough in hand now and there was nothing to be gained from Hubert collapsing before sorting out this Farmer idea.

Arriving at Farnham House, Hubert had the driver stop the car at the foot of the long gravel sweep. It was early Sunday morning and he had slept most of the journey up from Kent. He got out and walked forward to speak to him. "OK, Tom, make yourself scarce for a couple of hours. Back here at eleven o' clock."

"Right-o, sir."

The car puttered away and Hubert turned towards the house that sat among the trees a little way up the hill. The long path stretched before him, leading under the huge cedar tree in front of the rather fussy colonnaded entrance. He walked slowly up the drive, fighting off gathering memories of the terrors he suffered in these same grounds while his wounds healed. The constant fear of asphyxiation from damaged lungs was a perpetual nightmare. It would never completely go – he knew that. Even now, he would still wake in a sweat some nights, drowning in his mind. *Some wounds never heal.* He smiled at the cliché and strode forward, shaking off the misery of those early days back at Netley.

As he drew level with the cedar, he left the path and walked across the grass towards it. He saw himself, once again, reading below those massive branches. He had picked a tattered book up from the tiny library, just off the hall and had paced carefully outside for a breath of air. Even sitting down on one of these massive roots had demanded more of him than he could give in those early days and he had slid abrasively down the mossy trunk, scoring the leather of his Sam Browne. Reaching behind his back, he absent-mindedly fingered the mark on the shoulder belt – still there, like his wounds, a permanent scar.

He exhaled tentatively, having learned not to take his lungs by surprise. He had all but forgotten those early days of recovery and yet, now that the trenches were a thing of distant but eternally crushing memory, the duplicity of the whole thing, the vested interests, the flagrant profiteering of men like Zaharoff disgusted him all the more. It seared the altruism out of good men at the Front, turning them into husks of weary cynicism and it confused the hell out of new replacements into thinking they'd volunteered for a different war. And then there was the culture of lies and barely-concealed propaganda. Far from being a support for fragile minds, it was perversely depressing – particularly those jingoistic, 'morale-boosting' journals. Inevitably you'd find them, soon after publication, hanging from nails in the trench latrines. He snorted at the memory of one wag in his platoon referring to the toilets as the 'trench library'. Poor Carel – he got his in the push that gave Hubert his Blighty.

He leaned his head back against the rough trunk, feeling the warmth of the living wood in the early morning sun, percolating through layers of deep shadow above him. God! What he would do for a cigarette, right now! *Off-limits. For ever.*

The crunch of the gravel brought him back to the moment and he looked across to see a nurse approaching. As she came closer, her smile grew into one of recognition. "Lieutenant Hubert," she said, "How lovely to see you again!" The smile faltered a little at the edges, "You're well, I hope?"

"Peak of condition, Shaw, and ready to give you a demonstration, by numbers, on command." He stood up and passed an arm affectionately around her shoulders, turning her back towards the building.

She gave him an old-fashioned look, gently disengaging herself. "I see nothing has changed."

"I was hoping *you* had. I'm a slave eternally to your charms. You *know* that."

"And I've always said you should really be on the Music Halls. I'd pay good money to come and see you in your loud check suit and brown Derby. On second thoughts," she said, fending him off again, "stick with the clichés. I don't want you having a relapse on the front door. I'm just about to go off duty, so mind your blood pressure. What are you doing here, anyway?"

"Shaw, I'm devastated. Is this all I mean to you, then – just starch, catheters and bed pans? You're a cold, uncaring fish but if I can't have you, I'll have to satisfy myself with a glimpse of the Great Man. I warn you, he doesn't have your figure, and my general health may suffer as a result. Is he fit to be seen by decent people or is he still drenched in blood from another vile experiment on humanity?"

"You're disgusting," she said, poking him in the ribs and suppressing a giggle. She passed her hand through his arm and led him towards the house. "If you mean Colonel Farmer, he should be finishing rounds soon. I'll take you up to his office and you can wait there, if you behave yourself." They climbed the few steps to the entrance but, as he placed a hand on the glazed doors, she stopped him. "Seriously, Chris, how *have* you been?"

He turned to look at her and rocked his hand, palm down. "W-e-e-l-l, you know. Ups and downs, downs and ups." He grinned. "I get by."

Briefly, each held the other's gaze. Then, the door being narrow, he pushed ahead of her to hold it open. As she walked past, he saw in her eyes the realisation that his life would not be a long one. He caressed her arm as he watched another little piece of her die quietly inside.

****

Riordan was never at his best at that time in the morning. He stumbled half asleep on to the Stranraer-Larne ferry. Gallagher followed close behind in the stream of passengers boarding the vessel. The idea was to keep away from each other until the ship docked in Ireland and then they could make their way together down to Dublin. Both men stayed on deck, hidden behind different bulkheads – as much for shelter as for secrecy. At that hour, they were unlikely to be noticed by other passengers.

As the ferry left port, Gallagher thought about the gun. If he could get it from Riordan without raising his suspicions, so much the better. If not – too bad. It all depended on whether Riordan was what he was supposed to seem. It had always smelled funny when MacNeill made such an issue of taking Riordan along. "He needs the experience, Sean, and he's a good man to have at your back." Gallagher had no need for strangers at his back, and had said so, but there was no going against MacNeill. Gallagher was well-known for working alone, so MacNeill's insistence on taking along someone like Riordan was a bad sign, whichever way you looked at it. A lot of young bloods were just dying to stand in his shoes. Perhaps one of them had been smart enough to persuade MacNeill to let Gallagher kill Kitchener and then betray him to the Brits. It would force a high-profile trial and bring a monumental publicity coup for the Cause. No – the gun had to go – one way or the other. He'd worry about MacNeill later.

****

Henry Farmer had known better days. Weighing in at sixty-seven years old, he should have been retired from Farnham House long ago. It struck Hubert as he waited in Farmer's office that he *had*, in fact, retired three years ago, only to be recalled when many doctors, including his successor, joined up and left for France. It was the big joke at the time that he only came back in order to leave again with another farewell present. But he knew that Farmer found compensations – many of them – for these broken lads needed a man like Dr Henry Farmer. They came to him as shattered fragments of humanity and left him as close to complete as he could make them, despite the Kaiser's best efforts to the contrary. Hubert knew this all too well.

The door bumped open and Farmer stumbled in, wrestling dyspraxically with his white coat and steadily losing the fight. Pills, stethoscope and thermometer spilled out on to the threshold as he tumbled into the room, one arm locked in a sleeve determined not to give him up without a struggle.

Hubert, reclining in a deep Chesterfield, sipping a coffee, gave a chuckle at the sight. "Graceful as ever, Colonel."

"Hubert! My dear chap, you should have let me know you were coming over! What a pleasure!"

Hubert stood up and they shook hands cordially. There was no mistaking Farmer's genuine joy at seeing him once again.

"Sit down, sit down. It's a bit early for a proper drink, I know, but can I get you a coff ... Ah, you've got one already. Of course! You know where everything is."

"Colonel, for God's sake, take it easy. *You* sit down. We need to chat a little."

"And drop the 'Colonel' thing, for goodness sake. In the privacy of this office, we can both admit that I display all the bumbling charm of your elderly country practitioner. I know my place."

"And what about the scary stuff you did at Gallipoli? And, even long before that, in South Africa? You didn't get full Colonel by attending to coughs and sniffles."

"I say, old man, *you're* not ill, are you? This isn't a professional visit, I hope?"

"Well, it is and it isn't. But it's *my* profession we're talking about."

"Lost me, old fellow."

"Never mind that. Let me get you out of that coat before it strangles you. I have a question to ask."

Farmer had turned round with his back to the other man as he allowed himself to be divested of the maniacal garment. "What's that?"

"How do you fancy being promoted to Field Marshal?"

****

The voyage to Dublin brought over the usual mix of business people and servicemen returning home from leave. It was a simple matter to hide among them. The old tub was like a big, smoking bucket that spewed soot and oil everywhere. In bad weather, you were lucky not to get to the other side looking like a bloody sweep. Liverpool had better boats but it was too dangerous – the 'Specials' there were more likely to be on the lookout for them and none of them would think in a million years the two of them would waste time going all the way up to Scotland. Even Riordan had to admit that Gallagher knew his onions – an arrogant bastard, sure enough – but he knew what was what. Still, Riordan had his orders and it would give him no end of joy to see Gallagher birling at the end of a rope. The Brits wouldn't mess around – he'd be lucky if they didn't lynch him in the bloody streets!

Chuckling to himself at the thought, he suddenly realised that he hadn't seen our Sean in a while. Now, even *he* knew there was no way Gallagher would be getting off the boat in mid-channel but he just might find himself a nice little hole to hide in and head back to the mainland.

Riordan had to make sure he got him back to Brigade HQ. This would make his name and maybe end up in him running his own group so he wasn't about to balls it up. He pushed himself off the bulkhead and went to look for his 'associate'.

In the grey light, as the port smeared into view, Riordan drew the gun, walked over to the companionway and went below to the bogs. The toilet door creaked open as he pushed against its spring and the usual acrid smells hit him.

"Sean? Sean, are you in there, son?"

****

The main periscope of U-75, the *Bruder Walther*, caressed the glassy surface of the early morning English Channel, a little north-east of the Pas de Calais. A creamy wake sprang up behind, a tell-tale effect well-known to the commander, Kapitän-Leutnant Kurt Beitzen. He'd keep the scope up just long enough to make his move – one that had been forced upon him by the attentions of the British Royal Navy. He had other, more pressing, matters to attend to and would have preferred to have stayed submerged but he wasn't being given a choice.

His eyes firmly fixed on the target, he issued depth commands to the helmsman, Karl Stolz, cramped into the conning tower with him. "Up a bit, Karl ... now down ... hold it there." The head of the periscope was now only inches above the surface, offering very little to give them away.

Beitzen stood back from the periscope and called down below, "Willi, bring up the bearing kit." He resumed his watch on the target and was soon joined in the tower by Leutnant Willi Grassl, the Navigation Officer. The boat was now gliding along at a depth of 10.5 metres - perfect for this sort of work.

Things were coming together. "Clear first and third tubes!" shouted Beitzen, automatically registering the expected reply of 'First and third tubes clear!' from the torpedo gunner's mate down below.

"Torpedo depth 4.5 metres!"

."'.. 4.5 metres it is!"

"Twenty degrees more to port, Karl."

The minutes dragged by as Beitzen aimed the boat towards the steamer in his sights. A faint column of smoke from escorting destroyers smudged the sky behind. Things could get hot if he missed and had to put in a repeat performance. "Give me 10 degrees more."

"Five men ready to dress the boat!" he called. When the torpedoes were loosed, the change in trim could easily cause the nose of the boat to lunge above the surface, gift-wrapped for the Royal Navy, as it were. The five man team would rush through the open bulkheads from one end of the boat to the other until balance was achieved. Afterwards, they could make things permanent by re-distributing stores.

"Warrant Officer - note the name of the ship – the *SS Farewell.* A quiet chuckle floated up from the crew down below. An omen, surely, but Stolz gripped the wheel tightly. "God in Heaven, how close do you have to be to read the bloody name!" he whispered. Beitzen brought him back to the matter in hand with a bump as he leapt back from the scope.

"Heads up! Lower periscope and dive full speed to 20 metres ... hard a-port ... both engines full speed ahead!"

The words had barely left his mouth when a grinding

wrench announced the loss of the periscope as the *Farewell*, her captain feeling that something was wrong, made an unexpected turn to throw off the aim of any enemy with designs on her. Beitzen called for silence. The submarine seemed pretty much still in one piece but perhaps they had been seen and more was to come. Up above, propellers slowed to a halt.

"OK Karl, bring us up gently. Standby periscope up."

Suddenly, everything happened at once. "Clear first tube ... fire!" Within seconds, a violent concussion told its own story. The *Farewell* was for the bottom.

"Every man forward! Take us down to 40 metres, Karl - fast! Silence in the boat!"

At 38 metres, they rasped onto the sandy floor of the English Channel. All pumps, the engines and compass-dynamo were switched off to reduce noise. Time, now, for the inevitable fireworks as *Farewell's* escorts rushed about dropping countless depth charges. The next half hour was every submariner's nightmare as the hull was pounded by massive, endless concussions. The crew dashed from leak to leak inside but, in its own good time, the torment subsided and the screws of the escorting destroyers could be heard fading away into the distance. Throughout the boat a collective sigh floated up into the conning tower as everyone checked each other's cuts and bruises. They had survived again.

During the attack, Stolz detailed the list of course corrections and actions into the steering book, a duty required of the helmsman. As silence descended upon them, he jerked his attention up from the page. Beitzen noticed the movement.

"What is it, Karl?" he said. Stolz held up his hand for silence and grabbed the earphones. There was no doubt about it - something was ticking on the outside of the hull. For a moment he turned the problem over in his mind until it dawned on him and fear contracted his stomach. He looked up at Beitzen with wide eyes.

"Kapitän ... Kapitän, I think the steamer has settled on top of us!"

****

Gallagher sensed, rather than felt, the vessel kiss against the Larne pier and, moments later, the gangways being run out. He bustled ashore with the rest of the passengers – not so quickly as to arouse suspicion but fast enough to put some distance between himself and the last mortal remains of young Riordan, lying in the toilet with a crushed windpipe. Sweets from a baby. They'd find him soon, of course, but he was unidentifiable – Gallagher had been careful. There would be nothing to trace him back to the IRB. 'Just another senseless murder.' As for the Mauser, it was wiped clean and lying at the bottom of the Irish Sea. He smiled to himself. Whoever was trying to fit him up for the Kitchener operation would be spitting blood when he found out. No witness and, now, no evidence. He turned up his collar against the chill, damp wind and headed off for the railway station.

He was back.

****

Beitzen looked at Stolz as though he was out of his mind. Stolz was a good man and a steady hand in a crisis. If he thought the steamer was on top of them, then it probably was. He called down to the engine room.

"Both engines half speed ahead!"

The boat moved forward in a jerking movement and then came to an abrupt halt.

"Both engines half speed astern!"

Again, it moved a short distance and was brought up short by some unseen obstruction. Beitzen smiled down at Stolz. "Looks like it, Karl," he said, "but let's not put the wind up everyone just yet." He winked to reassure the younger man and called down once more, this time to the control station, "Chief Engineer to the tower!"

Without haste or apparent concern, Chief Petty Officer Roman Bader made his ponderous way up from a lair deep inside the U-boat. Countless years of experience, coupled with a propensity for suspecting the worst in everything had already led him to guess the problem.

****

"This is beyond belief. Surely not, Chris," said Farmer, almost in supplication. "Surely not. The Irish are *with* us at the Front. They're dying alongside our own lads. I have several, even, in this hospital right now with appalling wounds. Their kind couldn't be responsible for killing off a man like Kitchener. I can't believe it!"

"Well, I'm not sure myself but it's the perceived wisdom right now and the assumption we're working on."

"What *will* we do now?"

Hubert saw his opening. "Funnily enough, that's just what I'm here to sort out."

"Anything. How can we help?"

"We want you to impersonate Kitchener."

Farmer stared at him, as though he thought Hubert was mad. "You," he said, choosing his words with care, "have gone completely bonkers!" He stood up and leaned against the fireplace. "That's a technical term we doctors have for total lunatics. How on earth do you expect *me* to convince anyone that I'm the Secretary of State for War, boy?"

"Keep your voice down Henry and have a coffee. As for convincing anyone you can be Kitchener – I've seen you do it."

Farmer looked at him in puzzlement. As the memories trudged their weary way across his face, Hubert stepped in. "That's right, the revues."

Farmer threw his hands in the air and then clasped them behind his head. "Are you seriously telling me that *that's* where you got this reprehensible idea? Good God, man, it was just a lark. I only did it for a few minutes and it was bloody awful. Even the patients said so. When I tried it in the second performance, I was booed *on!* There's no way I could do something monumental like this." He sat down again, breathing heavily.

"Are you quite finished? Fine. Don't get your shirt tails in a flap. I'm going put it all into perspective. Firstly, it's not just me involved in this idea. It goes right to the top. To the top, do you follow me?" Farmer nodded. "Now, I know that you have only ever 'performed', if that's the right word, for a few minutes at a time and we would want a good deal longer than that but it wouldn't be *forever.* The problem is that we expect the IRB, or one of their tame journalists, to start crowing about how they managed to murder an old man in his bed down in Kent and once that particular cat is out of the bag, all hell will break loose, Henry, believe me. We'll have civil war at the Front with our own troops at each other's throats and the War effort at home will just collapse. Within a few weeks, we'll see

Kaiser Bill striding up the Mall. I also know that you are far from perfect ..." He stopped to laugh at Farmer's indignant stare, "... have to be honest, Henry. But the point is that we can ensure no one outside our circle who is really familiar with Kitchener will get anywhere near you. We can do that because we control the game. All we need is for you to play the part for a couple of months ..."

"Two months!"

"Three at the most."

"Three!"

"And during that time you'll be seen by the public – but always from a distance. Who in their right mind is going to walk up to Kitchener out of the blue and start talking to him? You're roughly the right height and build and with the moustache, you'll look just right. The idea is that over the three month period, you'll begin to give all the appearances of being borne down by the workload and the responsibilities of State – you might even 'die' in harness."

"My dear chap, it'd be no lie!"

"So much the better. And your medical knowledge would be invaluable in that respect. At the end of it all, a suitable announcement would be made. No one would be surprised, really. Kitchener isn't – wasn't – a young man and he was used to warmer climates. Two years as Secretary of State for War in a conflict like this would wear *anyone* down. You'll be quietly 'retired' – to a stud farm, or whatever.

"And then what?"

"You can take the moustache off."

"Be serious, you miserable child! Who will direct the War?"

"Do you think Lloyd George could let a chance like this pass him by? He'd be haunting the side-lines, preparing his ad libs."

"But *three months*, Chris!"

"It's in *our* interests to ensure that you are protected from discovery, Henry. If you were found out, we'd be in a far worse position than we are now. Look," he said, "we have your office secretary protecting you, his PSO is in the know, Special Branch is on-side and MI5 is running the show. Couple that with my own modest talents and we *can* pull it off! I know you can do it, Henry. Next time you look at that poster, he'll be talking to you, personally. Your country, this time, needs Henry Farmer."

"Don't you wave the flag at me, you creature of darkness!"

Hubert grinned like a schoolboy. "Just shows how desperate we are. It's the only way, right now, we can think of to buy some time and sort something out."

"No more than three months?"

"Absolutely. We wouldn't want you in longer – you might want the job permanently."

"Chris, I have to be honest -- this thing scares me rigid. If I'm to do it ...." He held up a hand against Hubert's beam of delight. "I say *if* I'm to do this, I'll need you there. I couldn't carry this off without someone around me I know and trust. Even then, it'll probably collapse around my ears."

"I think that's the general idea, anyway, Henry. You know – my idea, so put me in the thick of things to take the blame when it explodes."

Farmer swallowed the last of his coffee, still undecided.

"Look, Henry, just think about it. Come back with me to the War Office and let Kell and Thompson put in their respective oars. No-one is going to force you to do this. In fact, it was Kell's main stipulation. You must be a willing victim – that's the bottom line."

"Very well," he said, quietly, "I'll come and listen to what your Kell has to say. No more than that, mind you. And may God help us all."

****

On the *Walther*, Beitzen had stood the crew down on the pretext of waiting until all danger of sighting by destroyers escorting the convoy had passed. Some were lying around, reading books from the boat's small library, while others busied themselves writing home. Only the constant drip of condensation from the inside of the hull disturbed the silence.

Beitzen looked carefully at Bader, "Think it'll work?"

"What choice do we have, Kapitän?"

"This is true. It's either that or we'd have to figure out some way to get out of the boat and make our way to the surface."

Bader had suggested using both the power of the electric motors and compressed air to lift the hull free of the obstruction but inconsiderate use of air could cause an intolerable leverage on the hull – the immovable object and the irresistible force. The hull could fracture.

"Do it," said Beitzen and then called below, "Look sharp! We're going up and it might be a bumpy ride. Secure loose articles and hold on! Standby to flood tanks on command." He turned to the Chief Engineer, "Very well, Chief, the show's yours. Don't bend my boat. It's the only one I have and it's not paid for."

Slowly, U75 moved against the rigging of the *Farewell,* strangling the boat in its death throws. Once again, the lights dimmed as the motors struggled to make headway. "Blow aft tanks!" called Bader, "Slowly!" The stern lifted, tipping the boat forward. "No dressing!" The last thing he wanted was five bright sparks rushing towards the engine room in an effort to keep the boat level. "Full astern!" U75 moved slowly backwards and upwards but ground to a halt once more. "Flood aft tanks! Blow for'ard tanks! Full ahead!" Again, she moved forwards - a little further, this time – and struck the unseen hand below.

Beitzen glanced at Bader, noting the sweat beginning to gleam on the older man's nose and cheeks. This was all very inconvenient.

"Right," said Bader, "No more pissing about. Flood all tanks and stand by to blow them again on command!" He turned to Beitzen. We're well and truly tied up here, Kapitän. The only thing left is to try and break through whatever it is that's holding us down. If it's just rigging, the upwards force might be enough to snap through it."

"And if it isn't?"

"Well, if it's part of the superstructure that's holding us down, we'll probably crush the tower against it and that'll be that."

Beitzen looked at Bader and Stolz. This was his call and no-one else's. But he had already made the decision when he had agreed to blow his way to the surface. "No choice," he said, hoping the words sounded authoritative enough. "Go for it."

Unknown to them all, the last movement of the boat had freed the stern and the recoil from the forward motion had left only a few radio wires across the *Walther's* bows.

Looking Beitzen in the eye, Bader defiantly bellowed out, “Stand by below! Blow all tanks!”

A deep, grinding roar echoed through the hull of the submarine as she fought against her dead prey. And then, she was free. It was so sudden. An ear-splitting shriek of metal against metal heralded a violent jolt and the boat sped towards the surface.

Stolz looked up at Beitzen, the relief shining through his eyes and the shriek echoing in his ears. “My God, Kapitän, talk about the dead wanting company!”

Beitzen held up a finger. Talk like that was infectious in a small boat. “Now then, Karl. Chief, sort things out. I don’t want us popping up on to the surface like a cork. We don’t know what’s up there. Bring me to periscope depth first.”

Bader made to go below and take charge but Beitzen laid a hand on his shoulder. “Well done, Roman,” he said quietly. Lady Luck had smiled on them. This time.

****

Kell and Thompson headed back up to London in the care of the fearless Mason. Neither had spoken for half an hour, each wrapped in his own thoughts.

“How do you see the Farmer thing, Kell? Is it *really* going to work, do you think?”

“Who can tell? The real question is ‘what choice do we have?’”

“God Almighty!” grunted Thompson, explosively, as the car hit yet another rut. Wartime, clearly, had an effect on road maintenance.

“We either try this or we wait for the IRB

announcement or we announce it ourselves. Not much of a choice really. I just hope to God he's as close to the real thing as Hubert has led us to believe."

"Amen to that. I suppose if we can keep him out of the limelight, it might just work."

Kell paused. "Perhaps."

Thompson glanced quizzingly at him and sneezed loudly. "Is there a problem here you might share with me?"

Kell waited until the other had finished blowing his nose. "Hubert's idea that this might be in revenge for the Government's repression of the Easter Uprising has some merit but we both know that there are groups other than the IRB who have no love for Lord Kitchener. However, since we hope to hide the death from public view, only we and the IRB will know that anything untoward has happened. The others will therefore continue their work blissfully unaware."

"I see what you're getting at. In fact, I meant to tell you that my people are looking into an Indian husband and wife team who are up to no good as regards His Late Lordship. We expect to arrest them in the next week." Thompson coughed lugubriously and turned sharply to Kell. "Did you have anything particular in mind, yourself?"

"Sadly, yes. We both know that Lord Kitchener has many enemies within the Government itself. I could name one very highly placed Minister who is known to be involved in a smear campaign. We have infiltrated a group – the Casement lot – who have been tracking His Lordship's every movement in support of that campaign. Their objective is to create a false case, complete with names, places and dates, with the intention of branding him a homosexual."

"For God's sake!"

"Quite. We have information that Casement is shortly to return to Ireland, courtesy of the German Navy. One of the creatures in his party is a man called Daniel Bailey – a former Sergeant in the Royal Irish Rifles and erstwhile POW of the Germans – they released him to join Casement's faction. We believe he's carrying documents that would lend an aura of veracity to this story and it's his task to release the information to the Irish press when he gets there. My people are working round the clock to find out exactly where he will land so that we can intercept them. The very scandal would spell the end of an impressive career at just exactly the wrong moment – it would have finished the real Kitchener but Heaven knows what it would do to the good doctor."

"I see what you mean. We can hardly call them up and tell them not to bother any more since someone has literally beaten them to the gun, as Hubert puts it."

"Precisely. And so you can see that, while Hubert must give all his attention to keeping this Colonel on the straight and narrow, we have to close down these clandestine operations before they have the chance to give the game completely away. There are just so many groups and individuals bent on Kitchener's destruction that any one of them, at any moment, could expose our subterfuge. We have to re-double our efforts to prevent this – even more so than if he was still alive. That's the irony of it."

"I take your point. And you're perfectly correct – we *have* to make sure we shut the stable door, even though the horse has already bolted, so to speak."

"And then the other thing is this business of information leaks from the War Office."

"Well, yes. My people are heavily into that investigation, too."

"I am aware of that. But the purpose of those leaks has yet to be determined. It is my opinion that political leverage will be made of the information in the near future. And anything which causes the world to look closely at 'Lord Kitchener' is a bad thing." He paused for a moment. "And there is another possibility – one we should seriously examine if the IRB prove to be innocent of this crime."

"Do tell."

"We have, of course, had to inform His Lordship's sister of his demise. She was understandably distraught. The problem is that she is convinced, and convinced loudly, that the Black Hand is behind his murder."

"God save us! Let's not start that hare running!"

****

On the surface, Beitzen and his crew assessed the damage. The main periscope was badly bent and would not retract. That wasn't too much of a problem but it gave the boat a rather sad, deflated look. It would considerably reduce their speed under water.

"Willi?"

"Yes, Kapitän?"

"I haven't mentioned this before but Kiel issued us with a 'Special Mission' moments before we left port. I'm supposed to open sealed orders right about now so I'm going below to find out just what they've landed us with. You have the con."

Beitzen went below to his cabin, opened his safe and extracted the thick manila envelope, marked with 'Secret - Captain's Eyes Only'. He pulled the curtain across and opened his orders. Most of the bulk was taken up with

Admiralty charts – Heligoland and Ireland. *Ireland?* He looked for the expected signal and found a small slip of paper, informing him that he was to make all speed for the island of Heligoland and to collect the Irish Member of Parliament, Sir Roger Casement, and his two companions – Monteith and Bailey – by 0600 hours tomorrow morning. Beitzen was then to transport the said passengers with all speed and to deposit them, under cover of darkness and complete with rubber dinghy, in the Bay of Tralee. He looked at his watch – half past ten – he'd have to move if he was to pick them up. The only issue was the main periscope. Still, he had a standby scope and Kiel would not thank him for taking the safe way out by aborting the mission. He stood up from his bunk and swept the curtain aside.

"Willi?"

"Yes, sir."

"Make course for the Heligoland mole – all speed. Button everything down in the conning tower and let's get under way."

****

Gallagher woke with a start as the train arrived in Dublin. He gathered up his things and waited until the last person in the carriage had left before peeking outside to check for any unwanted attention. There was nothing to tell from the masses of people milling around the station – some arriving home from the Front, others leaving for it and saying goodbyes they thought might be their last. At least, he couldn't see anyone he knew. He stepped down onto the platform and joined the stream of passengers wending towards the barrier. The noise was deafening but, even so, when the familiar voice spoke behind him, he froze and waited for the speaker to take his arm like an old friend.

"Hello, Sean, it's yourself is it?"

"As ever was, Cassidy."

"We've been worrying about you for a day or two, and here you are safe and sound at last."

"Nice to be missed. Who's the gorilla?" Another hand, a large one, had gripped his free arm.

"Don't worry about him, Sean, he's just along for the ride. You've other things to concern yourself with. MacNeill wants a word with you in private. To be honest with you, Sean, I think he has a hair up his arse about something."

Gallagher looked steadily at Cassidy. Another labourer like Riordan, a bit thick and strictly low calibre but good enough for this job. He knew him from the old days, good at mixing Paxo in bathtubs. They'd had some good times together once upon a time but there were no friends in this business – barely even acquaintances. The point was, however, that there was no chance of breaking free, even if he had wanted to, with the King of the Jungle hanging on to him. He stared, through basilisk eyes, at the unknown man.

"Now, then, Sean. Don't you be looking at him like that. MacNeill just wants a talk. No idea what it's about. I was just trying to put the wind up you, so I don't want any problems. OK?"

Gallagher said nothing. During the conversation, they had made their way outside the main concourse of the station onto the street outside where a nondescript car, which had seen better days, was waiting for them.

"Inside, Sean," said Cassidy looking around, "and we'll

take you for a wee hurl around the town. No charge."

CHAPTER 3

Sunday 21 May 1916 1700 hours – Tuesday 23 May 1916 1800 hours

Cassidy led Gallagher up to the bodyguards flanking the open door and whispered a short message. At a curt nod from one of them, Gallagher was pushed into the back room of a pub in a run-down part of Dublin. MacNeill sat at the back of a booth with a half-finished glass of Guinness and the Sunday papers in front of him on a ring-stained wooden table.

"Here he is, Eoin. Picked him up at the station."

"Well done, yourself, Fergus," said MacNeill, "I'll see you later." Cassidy took that as a dismissal and vanished into the darkness, leaving Gallagher standing in the middle of the small room. From somewhere a draught was blowing, swirling the gaslight into twisting shadows in the sticky gloaming. MacNeill picked up his glass and supped a little of the dark liquid, deliberately forgetting to offer

Gallagher a seat. When he finally spoke, it was in a quiet, conversational tone but, for Gallagher, there was no mistaking it - MacNeill *was* mad.

"Where have you been, Sean? We was all that worried about you – no news, no telephone calls. No *nothin'?*" He crashed his fist down on the table, making the liquid slop on to the surface. "There, now, you've made me spill my drink."

Gallagher froze and stared stolidly at the other man. He could sense the two bodyguards moving in the shadows, getting into position in case they were needed.

"Well?" asked MacNeill. "You were given clear instructions as to how to contact us. Either done or blown, you had a signal to follow but I have to get Cassidy pick you up at the bloody station when the RIC are at every street corner looking for us. We can hardly move for them, they're that mad to catch any left-overs from Easter. What are you playin' at, for Christ's sake?"

Gallagher remained silent for a few moments, then said, "The job's done. He's dead." He glimpsed the flicker of excitement flashing in MacNeill's eyes and he knew that he was on firm ground. "I got him fair and square, in the chest and one right between the eyes."

"OK, then, that's the only thing that's keeping you inside your skin, right now. Any problems?" He nodded at the other's shake of the head and then relaxed back into the corner of the booth. He flicked a hand at the empty seat. "Sit down, for God's sake, Sean. Do you want a drink? Feeney, get Sean a Guinness." He turned back to Gallagher, now seated opposite him at the table. "Sean, Sean. Why do you give us so much trouble? Why couldn't you just do as you were told and give the signal? You're goin' to go too far one of these days and land yourself in the shite."

"That's just why I keep clear of the telephones," said Gallagher, contemplating MacNeill. "Just in case anyone wanted to underline the point by arranging a personal tour of Scotland Yard for me."

MacNeill looked shocked and, to tell the truth, played it well. "God, Sean, you're a suspicious bastard, right enough."

"Sure, and that's what keeps me young and clear-complexioned."

MacNeill threw his head back in a loud guffaw. "Good for you, Sean!" The laugh expired on his face as he studied Gallagher for a few moments. "All right, then, let's leave all that on one side for the minute. We've decided that we'll wait for two or three days to see how the Brits try to get out of this one. With any luck, we'll catch them telling fibs to their adorin' public and the fat'll be in the fire, then. Two hits for the price of one – Kitchener *and* the British Government. The bastards have a lot of answering to do for the Dublin Post Office."

"What if they come up with something good - something you can't argue your way out of?"

"We think we've got the angles covered. Anyway, that's the way it's to be."

Gallagher leaned on the filthy table top and rubbed his bleary eyes.

"Tired?" asked MacNeill.

"Tired enough."

"All right, then, be off with you and get some rest. I'll debrief you tomorrow. Lie low for the minute."

Gallagher got up to leave.

"Sean?" MacNeill was looking down at the remains of

his drink. Gallagher, near the door, turned to face him. "I don't see young Riordan."

"Right you are, again, Eoin."

MacNeill looked up to stare into his eyes. "Hope you put him somewhere safe, like."

"I did," said Gallagher, simply, and left.

****

On the following day, Monday, Kell sat back in his chair in his Strand office and gazed at Farmer over steepled fingers. "We're facing a major crisis, Colonel. I know you see the tragic results of it all but I don't think I'm exaggerating when I say that thousands more could be lost, directly and indirectly, as a consequence of the IRB's assassination of Lord Kitchener. The War will be lost without doubt and from the political point of view we'll be back in the Stone Age."

Farmer looked across the room at Hubert and smiled inwardly at his answering wink. It cheered him but could not relieve the feeling in the pit of his stomach. "But, Major Kell, can you really believe that a country doctor could carry off such a preposterous act?"

Kell shifted himself a little and re-arranged one or two items of stationary on his desk, a sure and certain sign that he was concerned.

Farmer leaned forward in his seat. "Please don't misunderstand me. I would do anything for my country. More than that, I would consider it a great honour even to *pretend* to be Kitchener and keep him alive, so to speak, for a little longer but I am terribly afraid I would make a mess of things – a real mess that would just make things worse."

"I feel you underestimate yourself, Colonel and you must also remember that *we* will be controlling the stage, as it were. It is at our discretion alone that you will appear in public or give an interview – anything of that sort. In that respect, you have little to fear. Indeed, we will ask you to do very little in the first week or two until you feel comfortable with the role and we can assess your potential. Honestly, we will ask no more of you than we believe you can deliver. It's not in our interests to ask for more and I'm sure Hubert has stressed all of this already."

Kell paused for a moment – for effect, Hubert suspected. "However, I confess that I *have* thought the matter over since he's been off finding you." He gave a wintry smile. "More than once, in fact. It may be that the Government will still fall when the news is eventually released. Accusations of incompetence, perhaps even collusion, will inevitably be levelled at one prominent figure or other. Public confidence will vanish and the Government will suffer catastrophic upheaval."

He glanced over at Chris and wagged a finger in his general direction. "It's all about *timing*. The great point of Hubert's strategy is that we have a better chance of being able to *choose* the time of disclosure. If we manage matters well, not only might we survive the crisis but the effect might be to turn the country against the enemy with renewed vigour – if you are not found out, that is."

Farmer wiped his forehead with a handkerchief and looked firstly at Hubert and then at Kell. "And Hubert will be able to accompany me? To help me through it? I don't think that I could ..."

"Do not concern yourself with that, Colonel. We will arrange for him to be attached to your staff as a liaison officer. Nothing could be simpler. He will stay with you until we have resolved the situation one way or another."

"Well," said Farmer, "if that's the case, I'll do my best to help you. I just hope it will be good enough."

Kell stood up and walked around to where Farmer was seated. Hubert opened his eyes wide in mock surprise. Kell was not normally demonstrative. "Colonel," said Kell, shaking Farmer's hand, "I cannot begin to tell you how grateful I am. I know I speak for Commissioner Thompson and, indeed, the Prime Minister himself, when I tell you that you are doing a very great thing for your country. It may be, indeed, that this operation will never be publicly known – indeed, it's my intention to ensure it won't – but I hope that the knowledge that you have served your country, as no-one else can, will suffice."

Farmer mumbled something inaudible by way of reply.

Kell became brisk. "And now, there is no time to lose. It is almost eight in the evening and we have to get you measured up for uniforms. We have a tailor standing by in a room to which Hubert will conduct you. As soon as that business is concluded, you must be off to Broome. I left Colonel Fitzgerald down there, yesterday. Tomorrow, you must start the process of becoming Lord Kitchener and, by Tuesday or Wednesday, you will have to be good enough to appear back at the War Office."

Farmer groaned. "Oh, God!"

"Quite. Hubert?"

Hubert took his cue and wheeled a deeply disturbed Farmer out of the room.

****

Farmer was undergoing the ritual indignity of having his inside leg measurement taken. The whole process had dragged over an hour by now, with the tailor chattering incessantly like a little robin.

"Just a little more on the waist than His Lordship, sir, and probably an inch or so shorter in the leg."

"Just take the line of least resistance and grunt intelligently, Henry," said Hubert.

Farmer's complete inability to respond 'intelligently' was written all over his face and Hubert was fidgeting in his seat by this time. Lack of sleep over the past couple of days and trundling around the countryside in cars had conspired to make him bad tempered. Besides, his chest hurt like hell.

"Come on, Solly, shift yourself, will you? The Colonel and I have still to travel down to see Lord Kitchener tonight."

Farmer looked sharply at Hubert, who narrowed his eyes and held his hand up slightly.

"Hold that position just a little longer, sir," said Solly.

"We don't want you to make him a second skin, just alter the uniforms so that you can't see any light through the gaps."

"Doing my best, sir. I'll be as quick as I can but we *do* have standards." He shook his head, primly. "We have our reputation to think of."

Hubert exhaled a stage-sigh and flopped back into the armchair. Another hour later, and Solly was content that he had measured his customer from every possible angle and across all dimensions.

"Now, let me get this straight, sir," he said, taking the pins out of his mouth. "You don't want a brand new uniform made. You have two uniforms of His Lordship's – one daily working and one dress uniform – which you wish me to alter according to the Colonel's measurements."

"Absolutely right, Solly. Can you do it?"

"Certainly, sir. There's more than enough material to cover the alterations."

"As long as it covers the essentials, Solly" said Hubert, chortling.

Solly remained unamused. "Yes, sir, I think we can do that."

"By tomorrow afternoon?"

"Not easy, sir. I told Mr Kell so, too. You can only put so many people to work on a single garment before they start getting in each other's way. But we'll do it."

"Good man, Solly," said Hubert, getting up with an effort, "and Solly ...?"

"Yes, sir?"

"Thanks for not asking *why* – keep doing that, there's a good lad."

"Sir!"

"Yes, I have been told that you are very discrete and that this is not the first time you've been called in by my lot to perform Herculean acts of bespoke work for cloak and dagger stuff. But this is something *really* special." Hubert spluttered an involuntary cough for a moment and continued, "If any word of this were to get out, heads would roll – and I'm not being overly-dramatic when I say that. Understand?"

Solly nodded, rather offended, and started to gather up his working materials.

"I say, old man, are you feeling unwell?" Farmer had been too busy with Solly to notice the pallor in Hubert's face but it was unmistakeable, now.

"Feeling a bit rough, right enough. But we haven't got time to hang about, Henry. We have to get down to Broome, grab a few hours in the sack and then get started on your training."

"Forget it, Chris. You first. I have my bag with me – force of habit." He looked around to see Solly pack up the last of his things and open the door to leave. "Thank you, Solly."

Solly nodded with a smile and went out.

"Right Chris. Strip to the waist and sit on the edge of the couch. Don't argue. You need an examination." He dragged his stethoscope, with an effort, from his medical bag. "I ought to have done it this morning, for you looked bloody awful then, too, but I thought that might have just been the effects of the angelic Shaw. Anyway, you knocked me sideways with this lunatic escapade you've got me into. Sit up and take a deep breath."

Twenty minutes later, Farmer had completed a conscientious and professional examination, given the limitations of the situation. He grimly replaced his equipment in the bag and snapped it shut. "Chris, you're still in a bad way. You haven't improved as quickly as we had expected you to. I'm sorry but, in hindsight, perhaps I shouldn't have signed your release."

"You're clearly not impressed", said Hubert. "Don't moan at me, right now."

Farmer was in no mood to be anything other than business-like. "Never mind that. I'm not speaking to your as your friend. I'm speaking now as your doctor. Chris, you're not fit for military service."

Hubert saw which way the wind was blowing. "Now, look, Henry, think on this. What's the alternative for me? Back to Canada or Switzerland to stay with my old man and wait to die. And I'd die all the quicker for it. Here in the Army, I can do something – anything – that might make a difference. That's what keeps me going. It means *everything* to me, Henry, believe me! You make a recommendation like that to the medical board and I'm dead for sure. And, besides, there are about half a dozen chaps like me working in 'Five' right now."

Farmer had seen too many young men go through his hospital not to understand Hubert's feelings. He looked into the young man's sunken eyes, stark against the pale face. "I know, dear boy," he said, patting him on the shoulder. But I have to think of what's best for you in the long run. And I really do believe that the Swiss air will do the world of good for your lungs if we could get you out there. The linings were all but stripped away by the chlorine. They'll never really heal completely." He held up a forestalling hand, seeing Hubert about to reply. "Yes, I know you're aware of that but you *can* make the most of things and put a few more years on the score card if you just take care of yourself."

"And what about the boys at the Front?"

"In what respect?"

"Do they 'take care' of themselves?"

"That's completely different, Chris. We are at war. No-one would *choose* to live like that."

"That's just my point, Henry. This *is* war. And you need me. Invalid me out and it will make not one jot of difference to your impending acting career. But you'll have to face it without me."

"That matters not in the least. I must think of what's best for you, not my own peace of mind."

"But Henry – what if it should all go pear-shaped just

because I wasn't there to help you? Yes, they'll probably put someone in my place, perhaps someone more knowledgeable or more genned-up on things, but will he know you as I do? Will he be able to spot the brickbats before they land on you? I'm beginning to get a line on these Intelligence sorts and, believe me, they're slippery customers. Think of what will happen if the 'charade', as you call it, is discovered! My health *has* to be secondary to that."

Farmer saw the logic but Hippocrates could be a stubborn companion. "I don't know, Chris. I hear what you say but ..."

"Do you think Kell would allow it, anyway?"

Farmer's head snapped round as he gathered up his greatcoat. "If I say a person is unfit, he stays unfit, Kell or no Kell!"

Hubert nodded in contrition. "Sorry, Henry, You're right, of course. But you must see that I *have* to go through with this. It may be the single most important thing I have ever done in my life or ever likely to do. It may even turn out to be the critical, unsung action of this war. It may not. All we can say is that, if we don't succeed, it's all over."

Farmer smiled, torn between his duty as a doctor and that of a soldier. "Very well, I'll say nothing for the moment." He held up a finger in warning. "But, remember, if we get through this, I'll have to make that recommendation – for your own good."

"Understood, Henry," said Hubert. "Understood."

****

In the last hours of Monday evening, Hubert and 'Kitchener' arrived at Broome. Henry had been equipped with an Imperial moustache of impressive proportions but had retained ordinary civilian clothes of the type Kitchener normally wore, courtesy of Solly. He had agreed to the clothes without demur but had questioned the moustache. Hubert had carried the day with the argument that *someone* would have to open the door for them. It would be as well to start the ball rolling. Word would get around like wildfire – particularly in the village. He hadn't told Farmer yet but he intended walking him around the local village tomorrow. It was a low-risk opportunity that could give him the early confidence boost he needed.

In the event, MacLaughlin opened the door to them, nose still on one side from his interview with Thompson.

"Good evening, sir."

"'Evening, MacLaughlin. You haven't seen us, understand? Particularly *this* gentleman." Farmer moved into the light that was spilling out onto the driveway from the hall. MacLaughlin's eyes widened as the two visitors walked in.

Hubert confided into Farmer's ear, "Told you, Henry. You'll do nicely." He turned round to MacLaughlin, who was closing the door after depositing their luggage on the floor. "Colonel Fitzgerald still up?"

"No sir, he went to bed hours ago. I was told to arrange for the preparation of two rooms in the east wing and then to dismiss the staff. I was to wait for your arrival and direct you to your quarters."

"Great, I'm dying for a bath and bed. Lead on, MacDuff."

"MacLaughlin, sir."

****

MacNeill turned sideways in the back passenger seat of the car to look more easily at Gallagher. "OK, Sean, give us the full SP."

"What's there to tell? We got in. We shot him. We got out."

MacNeill closed his eyes for a moment. "Sean," he said, "let's be straight on this. Brigade is pissed off w'your prima donna act. You, my son, are becomin' a liability. You're good at what you do but you're a wee bit unpredictable and that bothers people, y'see? Questions are bein' asked and that's a Bad Thing. Now I've asked you for a debrief and I'm not goin' to ask again, you follow?"

"Right, Eoin, don't get worked up. Let's just say I'm still around because I'm not always where I'm supposed to be. That's good for me and it's good for you, 'cause if you don't know where the hell I am, how're the Brits to find me?"

"You have to follow orders, Sean. Anyway, let's have the story."

"Riordan and me made our way down to Broome and then hung around the place. It was obvious that the only way we were goin' to get in was as ground staff. The place was crawling with Special Branch. So, we swiped some working clothes at the back of a house in the village and got over the wall of his gardens. After we had grabbed a couple of hoes and started pokin' at the ground here and there, sure, you couldn't tell us from the English Murphies. Anyway, we moved down the grounds towards the house, like this, lookin' for him. And that's when Riordan walked right into him."

"Jesus! What did he say?"

"Riordan or Kitchener?"

"For Christ's sake, Sean, you'd try the patience of a saint!"

"Kitchener said nothin'. He just stared down his nose at him. *Riordan* nearly wet his pants. We got away with it 'cause Riordan tugged the peak of his cap and we moved on before any damage was done. But I saw the big fellah watching us and that got me worryin'. Meant that we couldn't wait until darkness in case he got the Specials on to us."

"Good."

"We got ourselves under a bush at the back of the garden ..."

"What kind?"

"Christ, how the hell should I know?"

"OK, OK, get on with it."

Gallagher looked sideways at the other man. "We could see him from the bush but it was bloody hot under it, let me tell you. The two of us were nearly boiled away. In the end it got that bad that we were just about to get out. I gave it five more minutes. Just as well I did, 'cause he came past the bush a few minutes later. Anyway, we got ourselves out of the place half an hour or so after."

"Anybody hear or see you?"

"No. They were all down at the house end of the garden."

"Then what?"

"We found the local church in the wee hours the following mornin' and got into the tunnel. Brought us up in the kitchen. It was easy then to find the bedroom. No coppers in the house by royal command. I put four bullets into him and left the same way. Got to London and caught the train. The rest, as they say, is history."

"And Riordan, Sean, what about young Riordan?" asked MacNeill.

Gallagher stopped for a moment to think. "What about him, Eoin?"

"Well, y'see, Sean it's like this – the General Staff are a bit upset that he's not put in an appearance, so to speak."

"So? The operation comes first, Eoin, you should know that. Nothin' gets in the way."

"I'll come to the point, Sean."

"I wish you would."

MacNeill looked at him sharply. "You're to be court martialled, Sean. The boys want to know why you dropped him. Can't have our own soldiers goin' around killin' their partners. Sure, an' it would play the very devil wi' recruitment."

"And the General Staff have nothin' better to do than waste time on the likes of Riordan?"

"So it would seem, Sean. They're fair horn-mad about it. All down to them, my son." He looked hard at Gallagher. "Absolutely nothin' to do with him bein' my wife's wee brother."

****

For most of the time, the U75 had sailed on the surface on her way over from Heligoland, only submerging when enemy shipping appeared. The May weather being clement, Beitzen's passengers had enjoyed the experience. Casement, in particular, had been friendly and spoke excellent German. When Beitzen had picked them up, all three men wore large, bushy beards. Now that they were approaching the drop-off point, they had gone below to shave them off.

Casement climbed up into the conning tower to speak to Beitzen. Both men nodded to each other in greeting in the dim red light of the instrument panel and stood in silence for a few minutes. "You know, Captain," he said, "if your people had only listened to me and had attacked from the Pas de Calais, Britain would be in German hands by now."

"Such is military strategy, Sir Roger. The science of missed opportunities."

Casement smiled at the riposte. "How long before the drop-off point?"

"No more than half an hour. We've made good speed since most of the voyage has been on the surface."

"Very well. I should go back down below and start our preparations to leave you."

Within the hour, the *Bruder Walther* was rocking on the dark surface of the Bay of Tralee. All hands were on deck to say farewell to their Irish passengers and Sir Roger Casement went from man to man shaking hands and saying a few words to each. He ended up with Beitzen.

"So, Captain, this is goodbye," said Casement, shaking his hand.

"Indeed it is, sir. May I wish you all the very best of good luck?"

"You may, indeed, but that, as we say, is in the hands of the fairies." In the dim half-glow of that false dawn, he looked Beitzen in the eye. "And you, Captain, stay safe and come home to your loved ones, wherever they are."

"Amen to that."

"Gentlemen," said Casement, nodding to the crew in general. He climbed down into the dinghy where his two companions were already waiting among a number of bulky parcels and they pushed off from the hull. Shortly after, the dark outline of the inflatable rowed away into the gloom.

Beitzen turned to the Navigation Officer. "Right, Willi, take us back to the Channel. Quick as you like."

****

"Very well, Colonel Farmer. We have a single day to turn you into a Field Marshal." Fitzgerald hated the whole idea of impersonating Kitchener and clearly did not intend to go out of his way to help matters along. That said, he had to admit that as a temporary substitute Farmer had the looks sorted without the shadow of a doubt. And the clothes worked to perfection.

"Look, Oswald – may I call you Oswald?" asked Farmer, tentatively.

"If you must but …"

"Please call *me* Henry."

"Very well!"

"Oswald, I am petrified at the prospect of walking into the War Office on Tuesday. I know there's no possibility that I can ever truly *be* Lord Kitchener but I'm not doing it for myself, you understand. We'll be in a devil of a pickle if we can't hold this together for a few weeks. Anyone can see that you were very attached to Kitchener – what PSO doesn't eventually become firm friends with his Commanding Officer?"

Fitzgerald nodded.

"The problem is, old fellow, that I need you watching my back. The whole thing pivots around *you*. The only person who can make me into a facsimile Kitchener in the time we have available to us is Colonel Oswald Fitzgerald. So, please, help me."

"If you put it like that, it would be churlish indeed to refuse." He gave a frosty smile. "Well, then, let's start with the basics. Kitchener was born on ..."

"Excuse me, Colonel," said Hubert. "I think we should get into the habit right away of referring to Colonel Farmer as if he really *were* Lord Kitchener. He has to live the part right from the word 'go'. He needs to leave his past life behind him from this moment on, if he is to have any chance of looking the part tomorrow."

Fitzgerald, although annoyed by the interruption, surprised them both by agreeing. "You are right, of course, Hubert." He turned to Farmer. "*You*, then, were born on ..."

****

At about half past three that afternoon, Kell received a telephone call in his Strand office from Miss Joan Thorpe, Kitchener's secretary, to request an immediate interview. Fifteen minutes later and she was sitting in front of him, looking slightly dishevelled. Kell spent some minutes settling her down and ordering tea. It was one of the few anomalies of his character that he was cold, logical and calculating when dealing in matters of duty but was considerate to a fault when interacting professionally with ladies – particularly so, in this instance. Her red eyes told volumes. It was an open secret at the War Office that she had been *very* fond of her employer. Like Fitzgerald, she had no love for the idea of making use of an impostor but understood the practical realities of the situation.

"Now, Miss Thorpe, you had something to discuss?"

"Indeed I have. I don't know if you have heard that the Russian court has been angling to have Lord Kitchener pay them a visit?"

"I have not. I am surprised, nevertheless, but I'm responsible only for *internal* security, as you know. What happens beyond our shores is handled by Cumming and MI6. But carry on."

"I know that Lord Kitchener received a personal invitation from Czar Nicholas to go to St Petersburg and that His Lordship had indicated that, although he was agreeable to the proposition, it was a matter that could not be contemplated in our current emergency. One could hardly expect the Minister for War to go off on a trip in the current crisis. But he could not make the decision on his own. It would depend on both Governments discussing matters. All that was set in motion before … before ..." She lowered her head by slow degrees and, from nowhere, a handkerchief appeared, unbidden, in her hand.

"Please don't distress yourself, Miss Thorpe."

"Thank you. I'm fine, Major Kell. Excuse me."

"Please don't apologise. Now then, you were saying."

"Yes. I was saying that initial approaches were made to secure the visit. The point is that we have just been informed that the Foreign Office has prepared a mission plan for higher authorities to approve. I'm afraid it might expose the realities of the situation."

"When is Lord Kitchener supposed to arrive in Russia?" asked Kell.

"Around the ninth of June."

"This could be just what we need," said Kell, half to himself.

"Excuse me?"

"Nothing, Miss Thorpe. I was talking to myself, I'm afraid." He tidied an already tidy pile of documents. "How advanced are the arrangements?"

"As far as I am aware, nothing firm has been done at this early stage. Of course, the Prime Minister will have to sanction the trip. Possibly even the King, himself."

"Absolutely." He paused in thought. "Well, Miss Thorpe, I am extremely grateful that you brought this to my attention. You know that 'Lord Kitchener' will be with you tomorrow?"

"I do," she said, without enthusiasm.

Kell felt the mercury dropping. "Do give him all the help you can, Miss Thorpe. He is, I believe, a decent man out of his depth – which he knows – but he is also a man in great danger."

"Danger?"

"Well, dear lady, you don't think that the IRB will just give up once they work out that we are using a double, do you?"

****

Farmer's head was buzzing with facts and figures. He had spent all morning trying to absorb details of Kitchener's life – a brief history, which foods he preferred, how he walked, how he talked. One day was not enough – nowhere *near* enough. Fitzgerald had disappeared on estate business and Farmer was left, therefore, in the company of Hubert.

"Chris, this won't do. I'm struggling to remember even half of the things Fitzgerald's been drumming into me!"

"Relax. We're not expecting you to start spouting off an autobiography as soon as you walk into the office. Remember, you're the taciturn one. You speak only when necessary and, even then, short and to the point. You give *orders* not explanations."

"Really?"

"Well, of course you do!"

"I can't even get *Shaw* to do what she's told!"

Hubert laughed out loud. "I remember it well! Look, facts and figures are important – of course they are. But what is more important is that you acquire the *character* of Kitchener. That's what will carry the whole thing off. Just believe yourself to be the man and you'll have nothing to worry about."

"Wish I had your confidence, old man."

"I know, Henry. It's easy for me to rabbit on about what you should do, when it's you that's in the firing line. But I'm here to advise. I can *see* you – I can put myself in the position of someone meeting you for the first time in your character of the Secretary of State for War. The question is – do I believe in you? Or, if not, what do you have to do to convince me? That's where I make my contribution, if anywhere. Does that bother you at all?"

"No, no, Chris. All contributions gratefully received, as they say. Am I finished for the day?"

Hubert laughed. "No! And nothing like it! There's a lot more in store for you."

"Oh, God! What, for instance?"

"Well, you are just about to take a turn around the

grounds with me."

"But I thought that I was supposed to be hush-hush, and all that."

"*You* are but Kitchener isn't. You're going out as himself. And, if that goes well, we'll take a stroll around Barham later on. It's not far."

Despite Farmer's continued misgivings, they went out on to the terrace and stood there for a while, absorbing the sunshine. They went down the steps, past the ornate fountain and wandered off towards the rose bushes. A figure was down on his hands and knees, grubbing about in the soil. As they came closer, Hubert could see that it was Dudeney.

"Here's your first real test, Henry. If anyone, apart from the family, is going to see through you, it'll be Dudeney here," whispered Chris. Then, in a louder voice, he said, "'Afternoon, Dudeney. How're the roses coming along?"

The old man took some time to get to his feet, groaning and creaking. He turned round slowly. "They're comin' along right proper, sir. His Lordship would've been …"

At that point, he stopped and caught his breath. He staggered a little so that Hubert had to dash forward and catch him. Helped by Farmer, he sat him down on a garden bench a few yards away.

"Sorry, old man," said Hubert, "we were too sudden for you."

"I thought ... I thought …" whispered Dudeney, pointing at Farmer. Then, in a stronger voice, he nodded at Farmer and said, "I thought that you *were* His Lordship."

"*Thought*, Dudeney?" asked Hubert.

"Just for a moment, sir, I thought his ghost was back

with his flowers. You're very like him, sir. Maybe there's no-one else here that could spot you weren't him. But I could." he said proudly. "The Master and me were close. 'Cause of the roses."

"Well then, Dudeney," said Farmer, touched by the old man's affection, "be close to me, too. I'm going to need all the help I can get."

"That I will. You're a brave man, an' a good one, to do it. The likes o' them buggers won't win, then."

"So what gave me away?"

"Nothin' particular, sir. Just the way o' standing, maybe. It's nearly there – enough to gimme a turn, I can tell you – it just needs a little practice."

"What about his voice, Dudeney? That's not his own voice. He's trying to speak like Lord Kitchener."

"I can see that, sir, and it's good. Fool most people, I reckon. It's just the way he stands and looks at you. You know, his ... his *presence,* what you might call. But His Lordship's voice was a little higher than yours, sir. That's really the only thing."

"Thanks for that, Dudeney," said Hubert. "That's good advice. I'm sorry we startled you but I knew that if any man could spot him, it'd be you. And I was right, wasn't I?"

"Yes, sir. That you were."

"Now, look. I'm sure you can see that this is all to be kept quiet. As far as you and everyone else is concerned, the Master is still alive and well. That's why Special Branch has kept everyone on the grounds. No-one outside these walls knows what happened. And that's the way we want to keep it. 'His Lordship' here is going to walk around a little more, just to get the feel of things. Just keep an eye on us from time to time. If he does anything that you think would give him away, let me know."

"Right, sir. It'd be a real pleasure."

"Thanks. If everything goes well, I intend taking him for a walk around the church at Barham. That'll be the first *real* test. But I don't want to do it unless *you* are satisfied that he's up to it. Understand?"

The old man fairly swelled with pride. "Anything I can do to help, sir. Just *anything*. I'd be that proud to help."

"Right, then", said Hubert, "We'll see you later."

The two men walked off in silence. Henry nodded in what he considered a suitable 'Lord of the Manor' fashion to other members of the ground staff, receiving astonished stares in return before the automatic tug of the cap appeared. "You know, Chris, that was a fine thing you did for the old man."

"What do you mean?"

"You know very well. Letting him think he had an important part to play in all this. It'll take his mind off what happened here."

"OK, that was partly my intention. He's a good old stick and deserved to see off the few years remaining to him in his Master's service. But there was more to it than that."

"Oh, yes?" said Farmer, archly.

"Oh, yes!" mimicked Hubert. "He *has* known him for some time. That's valuable. He saw through you. *Why* he did so, is important. It's obvious from what he said that you have the essentials already. Not surprising, really, for you do look uncommonly like him, Henry. Much more so than I remember from Netley. You must be quite a thespian."

"No need to call me names."

Hubert chuckled and said, "Right, then. You're on your own. Wander around a bit. Talk to Dudeney again if you like but be seen by the staff in general. When you've finished, come back in and we'll have something to eat before going to the village."

****

Early evening not being the best time to find villagers in the streets, they had popped into the Barham pub – something that Kitchener never did, but which Hubert thought worth the risk in order to get Farmer seen. The customers were utterly awe-struck to find Kitchener walking in to their local and the landlord was beside himself. 'Kitchener' stood a round of drinks and his health was well and truly toasted before they managed to escape an hour later.

"Well, then, Henry my lad. You did well, there. Any remaining doubts about looking like the real thing?"

"No, you're right. I *must* look reasonably like Kitchener to get away with the sort of thing you chaps want me to do – the odd appearance and so on. Just don't ask me to direct a major offensive. The only niggling thing is the office, tomorrow …"

"Which the elderly and capable Miss Thorpe will manage for you."

Back at Broome House, Fitzgerald was waiting for them. "Where in God's name have you been?"

"Gallivanting," said Hubert and then hastily added a 'Sir' in response to Fitzgerald's frosty stare.

"You are meant to clear exits from the grounds with

MacLaughlin. We were about to notify Sir Basil just as you walked in."

"Oh, dear," said Farmer.

"I thought we needed to have Colonel Farmer test out his Kitchener impersonation under fire, so to speak."

"And how, exactly, did you do that?"

"We went off to the pub."

For a moment or two, Fitzgerald sat still, thunderstruck. "You went *where*?"

"To the pub. There was no sign of intelligent life anywhere else. I've no doubt that some estate workers were there among the villagers and certainly no-one questioned his identity. Or if they *did* have any doubts, they kept them to themselves. Which is precisely what would happen in London and Colonel Farmer needed to know that for himself."

Fitzgerald enunciated his words with care. "You will refrain from further ... *excursions* conducted on your own discretion. Do you understand? I have agreed to help maintain the illusion of his continuing existence but I must insist on being able to preserve his *reputation*, too!"

"Yes, sir."

Fitzgerald closed his eyes for a moment and calmed down, turning to Farmer. "Apart from that, were you satisfied with the results of your little ... test, Colonel?"

"Henry," prompted Farmer.

"Yes, 'Henry'."

"I was. Indeed, I was. I feel much better about the whole thing now."

"Good. Well, let's move the illusion up a notch. Your

uniforms have arrived. They have been laid out in your room. Be so good as to try one on and come downstairs, so that I can take you through the correct mode of dress for an officer of Engineers."

Ten minutes later, Farmer walked into the drawing room in working dress. Hubert stared in amazement and then settled back into an armchair with a quiet grin on his drawn face.

Fitzgerald stood up. "Yes, that will do very nicely, indeed. You know – *Henry* – I do believe, with a following wind, this might just work."

****

Bruce Lockhart sat back from the table at which he was decrypting the 'IMMEDIATE - EYES ONLY' signal he had just received. As MI6 Station controller in St Petersburg, he would expect to see anything from MI5 only under the most unusual circumstances. The two Services rabidly avoided encroaching on each other's respective patches since their separation a matter of only a few months before. And yet, here was a signal marked 'MOST SECRET' from Kell himself. Repeated, he noted, to Cumming.

"So Kitchener is to come to Russia!" he mused, spinning slowly from side to side in his over-stuffed swivel chair and chewing the end of his pencil. "But what the hell are Kell and Cumming up to?" He grinned to himself. 'Kell and Cumming'. Sounded like a dubious music hall act. He looked at the signal once more:

LORD KITCHENER TO ARRIVE ST PETERSBURG 9 JUNE - STOP - PASSAGE TO BE UNDERTAKEN BY ROYAL NAVY DEPARTING

CLYDE 5 JUNE - STOP - K WILL CONSULT WITH HRH THE CZAR AND REMAIN FOR 10 DAYS - STOP - YOU ARE TO LIAISE WITH OKHRANA CONCERNING SECURITY FOR VISIT - STOP - TAKE ALL ACTIONS NECESSARY TO BRING JOURNEY - BRACKET - WITHOUT PREJUDICE - BRACKET - TO ATTENTION OF PRINCE VORONTSOFF - STOP - SIGNAL TO BE DESTROYED WHEN READ - END

Vorontsoff was a noted sybarite of the Russian court who could not be trusted to keep his mouth shut were it to save the life of his grandmother. Why tell him? 'Without prejudice' was security service code for 'leak it to him by accident'. Perhaps this was a feint – leak the news and then let Kitchener disappear somewhere else while everyone's eye is off the ball – but that would mean that the Czar would have to be in on it. Unlikely, to say the least.

Of course, it was perfectly obvious why he *might* be coming. The Court was riddled with Russians playing for the other side. It was the only way they could afford to pay for the upkeep of their mistresses. Unless, of course, you were a member of the Government – then, it was a simple matter of pocketing your soldiers' pay, selling off their replacement equipment and issuing only enough food to keep them from starving. It was a good living and no-one ever got caught. Besides, who was looking? The Czarina was too busy with that flea-bitten mongrel Rasputin and the Czar did whatever the last person told him to do. Lockhart *had* heard rumours that an injection of gold was coming from Great Britain, so that was possibly the reason for his journey but then many other, less important people, could act as that sort of courier.

Being who he was – possibly the world's most famous soldier – Kitchener had a great deal of influence in military circles. Perhaps, Lockhart reflected, his visit was more to do with stabilising the rickety Duma and ensuring that the Russian Army stayed at the Front. All indications were that they were deserting *en masse.* Just about the only thing they were able to do with any sort of efficiency. True – a visit from someone like Kitchener might just do the job for a few months and stave off another revolution.

"He *must* be coming, then," he thought. "Bugger! That means I'll have to trawl for crockery through all those bloody flea-infested 'antique' shops in the city!"

Kitchener's love of fine porcelain and china was well-known, even in the Russias.

CHAPTER 4

Wednesday 24 May 1916 0800 hours – Thursday 1 June 1916 2300 hours

Beitzen relaxed against the conning tower as he powered the *Bruder Walther* slowly into Kiel on the diesels. "Coming home has to be the greatest feeling in the world," he said to himself as he nonchalantly acknowledged the 'welcome back' cheers of other U-boat crews, preparing for sea. One or two chuckles and Rabelaisian comments followed them in honour of the still-bent main periscope.

There was a slight breeze blowing as U-75 tied up, fluttering the tonnage pennants painted by the crew to advertise the success they had achieved in sinking the enemy. All hands were on deck for the arrival back in port and Beitzen felt a surge of pride as he looked down at them from his vantage point. They had done well and deserved a little relief from the unrelenting pressures of war. He inhaled a deep, calming breath – some well-earned shore leave for them but not for himself, right now. His successful mission had to be debriefed at Admiralty HQ then, maybe, he could go home to Magda for a little while.

While the boat tied up, he quickly arranged matters with Grassl – shore time for the crew, recall procedures, duty watches and so on. "I'll have to pop over to HQ, now, and tell them how the mission went. After that, I'll be off home. That's where you'll find me if anything turns up out of the blue." He made his way over to the Admiralty building near the quays, turning over in his mind half a dozen different ways to ask for two weeks' leave for his crew. It was hopeless, he supposed, but worth a try. Before he knew it, he was explaining his actions to the Commander, Fourth Flotilla, a very senior Captain.

"And so, you were able to pick up Sir Roger and his men?"

"We were, sir."

"Even with your reduced speed submerged?"

Beitzen said nothing but stared ahead at attention.

"Relax Beitzen," he said, "I'm really sorry to have to tell you this. It's a bitch of thing after all you and your men have gone through but the sad truth is that your efforts were in vain."

"I don't understand."

"I'm afraid Sir Roger was arrested by the Royal Irish Constabulary shortly after he landed. It would seem that MI5 had foreknowledge of the arrival location and were waiting for them. They shot his inflatable full of holes when it was a couple of hundred metres off shore and it capsized him and his people into Tralee Bay. The entire party ended up being washed on to Banna Strand and all their possessions were lost. I believe that Feld-Webel Leutnant Montieth escaped but Sir Roger has been taken to the Tower of London. The third man – Bailey – we don't yet know about."

Beitzen's shoulders drooped in defeat.

"You must be washed up. The pity is that I can only give you and your crew four days shore leave, I'm afraid. Something really big is about to blow and you'll all be involved. I'll tell you everything you need to know when you return. The main thing now is to go home and see your family. You've done an excellent job under very difficult circumstances, so try and recharge your own batteries."

"Thank you, sir." Beitzen saluted like an automaton, and left the office.

****

Near the end of his first morning, Farmer slipped into his ADC's office, now occupied by Hubert while the ecstatic owner was off on mandatory leave for the next month.

He looked up at his 'commanding officer'. "How are you doing, Field Marshal?"

Farmer grimaced. "You know, I think I have managed to undo all but the most stubborn of the knots in the pit of my stomach – largely due to Miss Thorpe."

"Henry! You've known her less than a day!"

"I don't … act your age, for goodness sake, boy!"

Hubert chuckled to himself, signed the document he was working on and sat back in his chair, observing his companion with a critical eye. "You *do* look a little more relaxed, Henry. Seriously."

"She really has been very helpful. When I arrived, I thought she was going to stick me with a hat pin right off but she's thawed in no time."

"I noticed she'd lined you up with two or three meetings. How did they go?"

"Well, they were rather junior individuals but working in areas of current interest to Kitchener. She chose them well. They had never met him in person and they were over the moon to be called in. And, of course, she ran me through what's on the board, so to speak. Everything she's done shows she's thought long and hard of what I *needed* to be told and what I didn't. Excellent woman."

Hubert said nothing but continued to observe Farmer with an innocent expression.

"Shut up!" exploded Farmer. "Anyway, now I remember why I came in to see you – why didn't you tell me Kell was coming round?"

"No! When?"

"This afternoon, according to Joan."

"Ooh, *Joan* is it?"

"You are a pathetic child, Chris."

"I am, indeed, Field Marshal."

"Wonder what he wants so soon?"

"He's probably just paying a social visit to see how things are going in general – no pun intended."

"I wonder."

"Don't," he said, pulling himself out of his chair, "Time for lunch."

****

Of all places, Gallagher found himself seated in a disused church hall just outside Dublin itself. Even in the musty light, he could make out the faces of those in judgement upon him. Butterflies flitted inside his stomach for an instant. He would take on any odds to complete a mission but this was different. There was no fighting or improvising his way out of this one and failure meant only one thing – a bullet in the back of his head. If he was lucky. There would be no extenuating circumstances, no court of appeal, no commutation of sentence – just death.

Iain MacDonald was presiding. That was the only good thing. He and Gallagher were no great friends but they shared a mutual, if guarded, respect for each other. MacNeill, to his left, was a different thing, as were his cronies, like Cathal Brugha on the right. This deck was stacked. Gallagher wondered if MacDonald knew.

"Sean Gallagher, you have been brought before this tribunal to answer the charge that you did murder a serving member of the Irish Republican Army, namely Patrick Riordan, in the pursuance of your operational objective, Field Marshal Kitchener, British Secretary of State for War. How do you plead to this charge?" MacDonald's voice was flat and devoid of any expression which would lead Gallagher to believe that he had a friend in the enemy's camp.

"I plead not guilty to this charge and I defy your right to try me. I'm entitled to a minimum of six members behind that table."

MacDonald held up a gnarled hand. "I'd advise you not to add contempt of court to the charges. You know very well that as Chief of Staff, I have every right to try you. But you're right about the six members. We lost most of those qualified to sit at this table in the wee upset on Easter Monday. You've been out of touch for a while, remember. And, since then, Kell and the RIC have been runnin' a bit of a purge on us – you'll have seen the check points and bloody uniforms everywhere – you can't scratch your arse but there's a Webley on your forehead five seconds later. Cathal and Eoin are the only ones that haven't been picked up yet. But I'll take all that into account. You know you'll get a fair hearing from me, Sean Gallagher, and most of the breaks."

Gallagher relaxed back into his seat.

"Anyway, where the hell do you come from, tellin' *us* that you didn't kill him, you bastard?" shouted MacNeill.

"And that's enough from you, Eoin, or this is a mis-trial and I let Gallagher walk out o' here!"

Gallagher looked at MacNeill and at MacDonald. "I didn't say that I didn't *kill* him. I'm just saying that it wasn't murder."

"Why did you have to kill him, Sean?" asked MacDonald.

"Self-defence. Y'see *someone* ..." Gallagher stared meaningfully at MacNeill and his cronies, "someone had persuaded young Riordan into holding on to the weapons we used."

MacDonald looked at MacNeill.

"I say 'weapons' but I really mean just 'weapon'. He kept *mine*. If he wasn't working for someone in this room, he was definitely working for the Brits."

"You bastard! He would never ..." MacNeill never completed his sentence but launched himself at Gallagher across the table. MacDonald and the others held him down while he continued to kick and scream abuse. Gallagher hadn't moved during the entire episode but sat calm and satisfied in his seat.

MacDonald shoved MacNeill back behind the table. "You and me'll have a two-handed crack later on, Eoin MacNeill. But right now, let me say to all of you that if this is true, this thing Gallagher tells us, there's goin' to be trouble. There'll be no personal vendettas in this Army. Every man bein' sent on a mission has to know that he can come back safe from his own kind, at least. There's no future for us else."

MacNeill sat back down, blowing like an exhausted horse. He had other ways to get Gallagher that didn't involve this old fart MacDonald. Patience.

"Right then, Sean Gallagher," said MacDonald, "I want to know every step that takes us from when you left Kitchener's place to Riordan ending up in a ferry toilet." He looked up from the charge sheet, "And it'd better be good, Sean."

Gallagher gathered his thoughts and made to speak but a movement in the far corner of the room caught his eye. The men at the table turned round to see what the disturbance was and saw one of MacNeill's bodyguards walk into the hall. Gallagher recognised him as Feeney.

Feeney came up close to MacDonald at the table and whispered urgent intelligence. MacDonald, in turn, started in surprise and peered at Gallagher.

"And you say, Sean, that you killed Kitchener outright?"

Gallagher looked at him as though he were mad. "Of course I bloody did! No question about it."

"Well, Feeney here – good lad yourself, Feeney, off you go – Feeney tells me that we've just received a report from one of our boys in London. Kitchener was seen goin' in to the War Office this morning, large as life and twice as ugly. Now, what do you think of that?"

Gallagher paused, momentarily left-footed by the news. "Look MacDonald, if I shoot you four times with a Mauser, you stay dead. It's an inevitable sort of affair. Somebody's got his wires crossed here."

"Aye, an' it's you!" crowed MacNeill. "Pity the boy's not here to stand up for you! You've no witnesses, now!"

Gallagher could see his point. Things looked very much like he had entered into some sort of agreement with the British Security Services to leave Kitchener alive and to return home, having bumped off the only witness to the contrary. He tried to put himself into MacDonald's position. Would *he* believe him, if their roles were reversed? But, if it were true and Gallagher was a traitor in league with the Brits, would they allow Kitchener to be seen so soon? Would they blow their own cover? It was this thought that brought Gallagher round to his senses. He knew damn well that he had killed the old bugger, so there was only one answer. He chortled, "The devious bastards!"

"What is it, Sean?" said MacDonald, watching his every expression.

"MacDonald, I'm tellin' you straight – I executed him and there's no question of that."

"So, how do you explain … ?"

"They're usin' a *double*! How the hell they managed to get a hold of one this quick, I don't know. Maybe they have one on tap. Maybe they've used one before an' we've never known! Maybe …"

"Maybe you just killed an actor, an' left the real thing alive and kickin'!" MacNeill said.

Gallagher stared at him, detached from the moment.

"You might be right there, Eoin – *maybe*."

"We'll need to think this one over – *bugger it!* – no we don't," said MacDonald. "There's only one answer to this. Sean, this is your business. I don't give a damn whether you killed a real one or not. Chances are, it doesn't even matter. It's what the workin' man thinks that's important. But if you *did* kill a double, the Brits'll be pissing themselves laughin' at us an' I'm not goin' to let that happen."

"And if I killed the real Kitchener?"

"Then we still haven't achieved the objective. The British Army don't know about it and neither do the British people. So you'll still have to do somethin' about it."

"You mean go back and kill him *twice*?"

MacDonald grinned a death's head smile. "Aye, Sean, somethin' like that. You get yourself over there and do the job. But this time do it somewhere less private. Don't give them another chance for a cover up. I want people in the street to see it."

Gallagher got up to leave.

"Sean, do this well and the slate'll be wiped clean." He held up a hand against MacNeill's wrath. "But if you don't manage it, don't come back. 'We clear?"

Gallagher held the other's stare, nodded, and left the hall.

****

Kell had been ushered into Farmer's office. Once the door had been closed behind him, he looked over at the other man and sipped the cup of tea provided by Miss Thorpe on his arrival.

"Almost finished your first day, *Field Marshal.* How do you feel now?" he asked.

"Like I said to Hubert this morning, the secretary has been a wonder. She kept all sorts of nauseous people away from me. The only thing I couldn't get out of was that trades' union visit. In the event, it went just fine, probably because none of them had actually *seen* Kitchener in the flesh, so to speak. After a while, I quite relaxed into the role. I seem to remember telling them that I wished the Government could keep secrets as effectively as the unions could!"

"That was naughty of you."

Farmer gave his self-satisfied grin, "I rather thought so!" He looked over at the other man and hesitated, as if unsure whether to reveal his thoughts or not.

"Did you wish to say something, sir?"

"Well, it's just that I can't understand this man Asquith. Before the war, I was all for him. Seemed to me that he did a reasonable job but, buffing up on what's been going on before I was volunteered for this nightmare, all I can see is that he has prevaricated and avoided taking any decisions where possible for the past two years. God knows how Kitchener ever got anything done."

"He doesn't come across as a great wartime Prime Minister, I have to agree."

"Indeed not."

Kell put down his tea cup. "But, putting that aside for the moment, Field Marshal, I have some news for you. The original plan required your services for about two to three months ..."

"Oh, God, don't tell me that I'll have to do it for longer!" Farmer was appalled and then struck dumb as a further more terrible possibility yawned before him. "For *ever*!"

Kell delivered a wintry grin that petered out before it reached his eyes. "No, no. Nothing of the sort. I have *good* news. We have a way of getting you out of the country on the fifth of next month."

"Where to?"

"Russia."

"Russia? Why Russia?"

"It seems that the Czar entertains a great admiration for Lord Kitchener. His Government are in the most grotesque pickle. His ministers, as you probably know, are licentious and unscrupulous to the ultimate degree. I'm informed by reliable sources that his generals are drunkards and the inevitable result of it all is that his troops are deserting in droves from the Front since they haven't been paid in months and are starving to death – no exaggeration, I assure you. Many, indeed, haven't even a pair of boots to their name."

"And Kitchener …?"

"The Czar felt that Lord Kitchener could talk some sense into his General Staff. Put some iron into their collective backbone so that they could all pull together – at least until the war is won." Kell sat back in his chair and steepled his fingers before continuing, "And there's another problem. Cumming is quite convinced that members of the Russian cabinet are German agents."

"Who is Cumming?"

Kell wheezed sibilantly. "Cumming is the head of MI6. One of his people, rejoicing in the name of Sidney Riley, has brought back irrefutable evidence that the Czar's Minister for War is working for the German High

Command."

"God save us." Farmer mulled it over for a moment and could think of nothing constructive to say about the Russians. "But I cannot believe you are suggesting that 'Kitchener' sail off to Russia in the middle of the greatest conflict this country has ever seen? You *know* I'm desperate to leave all this behind me and get back to what I do best, but won't this arouse suspicion among the dimmest of his enemies?"

"Good point, but yes and no. I have been with the Prime Minister this morning. He believes, as I do, that this could be the best thing for us. It gets you out of the reach of the IRB, keeps you out of the public gaze – although they will know exactly where you are – and it sets you among people most of whom have never laid eyes on Lord Kitchener."

"You intend to entrust a diplomatic mission of this magnitude to *me*?"

"Your pardon, but of course not! You are going to Russia but not on your own. You will have an entourage that will include members of the Foreign Office and military personnel. I am also given to understand that Lloyd George will accompany you in his capacity as Minister for Munitions. People of that sort are professional in their respective areas of expertise and will advise on every aspect of the mission, write your speeches and so forth. Your job will be to front the whole thing – that's all. We plan to depart from the Clyde – it's well protected from your point of view and there is an acceptable train service there from Euston, of course."

"I see. Well, that means that I can kick the War Office into touch in a couple of weeks' time!"

"Exactly so. And, while you are in Russia, you will

begin to show all the signs of incipient collapse. That's where your medical background will be a blessing – a very fortunate coincidence for us. When you return, you will go straight to Broome to 'recover' from the stress of the journey and, within a week or two of that, the Prime Minister will announce that you are retiring due to ill health, as we discussed." Kell smiled again, "You might even join the Choir Invisible, as it were, if you become *very* ill. So, it would appear that circumstances have conspired very much in our favour and that you will be relieved of your onerous duties, for which we are *so* grateful, far sooner than you anticipated."

"Hooray to that, say I!" said Farmer and pointed at Kell's cup. "More tea?"

****

Beitzen trudged made his way home to his hiring a mile or so from the docks. It was a very small apartment but this was war. It wasn't forever, anyway - he was an only child and would inherit a sizeable estate in Bavaria on his father's death – but at twenty-five, such things seemed a lifetime away. Then again, he and Magda loved each other dearly and when you're that lucky, he thought, one-bedroom flats just don't matter.

They lived near the top of a five-level tenement in a reasonable part of the town and Magda was overjoyed to see him return safe again. The minutes slid past in silent joy as he held her tightly in his arms, not daring to let her go. She was so tiny! He smelled the mass of glossy blonde hair and wished that he could stay forever and forget about returning to sea – pretty much the whole spectrum of thoughts countless sailors down the ages had felt on returning home. As though she understood his thoughts, she led him into the tiny living room with its frayed carpet and sparse furniture. He looked around. This isn't what he wanted for her! The British blockade made paupers of them all, but things would be different after the war. He would make it up with his father and they would all go back to Bavaria and live with him.

Magda was excited. "Karl, wait till you see this! Trudi, darling, look – Papa's home. She sat down on the sofa hand and stood the little girl between her knees in the age-old way. "Walk to Papa, darling. Go on."

The little girl tottered across the small space, tipping from one side to the other with arms outstretched, and ended up landed in a heap in Beitzen's lap as he sat on the floor. He gathered her up and hugged her.

****

The thought of ever becoming a permanent installation in the War Office horrified Thompson and, for that single reason, he was always happiest when walking out of its front door. But this time, in particular, there was something to celebrate. Young Fredericks had only been down at Broome to provide sufficient weekend cover for the protection – *protection!* – squad. Now he was back at the War Office, trying to track down this damn leak and, when they least expected it, he had found something to go on. A junior minister had coughed up the fact that he was passing information to the Ministry of Munitions – *funny old thing* – and that he agreed with others that Kitchener was a menace to the country and needed to be 'downed'. As he headed back to his own offices, Thompson reflected sourly on the information Fredericks had culled from the posturing fool. They were out to put Kitchener on the spot and that could mean exposure of Farmer and the assassination. There would be fun and games in the Commons – and damned soon – by means of a vote of no confidence against the Secretary of State for War. On the other hand, it was one more line closed down that might have exposed Farmer and, joy of joys, Kell had passed him the word that Bailey's hideous dossier was at the bottom of Tralee Bay. Pity Casement hadn't gone down with it but at least he and his kind wouldn't be exposing this Farmer chap.

****

Beitzen returned to Admiralty HQ as required. His shore leave, as always, had just evaporated before he realised it and now it was time to return to operations. Parting with Magda was always difficult but this time it seemed to be more so. She clung to him as though she'd never let him leave, despite his promises that he'd take no unnecessary risks and look after himself. For a while, they spoke about their plans for after the war but he knew she was just whistling in the dark to keep her spirits up – who could make plans in this madness?

Finally, with tearful reluctance, she let him go. Twenty minutes later, he was standing in front of his Commanding Officer once again, listening without much heart to his congratulations. Beitzen, it seemed, was to be decorated for winning his argument with the *Farewell*. Fortunately, he was able to drum up enough enthusiasm to smile and express his thanks. He got away with it at any rate, or perhaps his Captain had more perspicuity than he gave him credit for.

"Very well, enough of all that. Now, then Beitzen, listen up. This is classified 'Top Secret'. Next Wednesday, the High Seas Fleet will put to sea. The plan is to engage Jellicoe off Denmark. Our U-boats are moving at this moment to lie off targets close to the British mainland."

He stood up and moved over to his wall map. "U-44 is covering Scapa Flow; U-47, the Moray Firth; U-67, the Firth of Forth; UB-21 and -22 are looking after the Humber estuary and U-32, -51, -53 and -63 are being held in reserve near the Dogger Bank. The general idea is to drive or draw the British Grand Fleet over our submarines and sink every ship while, at the same time, bottling up reinforcements in their harbours."

"So, it's happening at last."

"I thought that might wake you up!" He turned back to the chart and gazed at it. "This is going to be the greatest naval battle in history – not a doubt of it. The British are fond of boasting that Jellicoe is 'the man who could win or lose the war in a single afternoon'. They're about to discover that the same might be said for Scheer." He turned back to Beitzen.

"I want you to act as catch-all to nail any stragglers who try to make their way northward from the battle area. Lie-to off the coast of Norway, around Trondheim."

"I'd prefer to be closer into the action, sir." If Beitzen's crew played second fiddle to the rest of the Flotilla, they'd never be allowed to live it down.

"I understand your feelings, Beitzen, but it's important that you follow these orders." He paused, as though about say something further, but then thought better of it. "We may have additional, more … more sensitive work for you to undertake so I'll need you to maintain daily contact with this HQ at 0100 hours on the dot."

"These additional duties - can you give me any hints?"

"Not right now, Beitzen, but I will say that they won't be *unconnected* with the work of your recent passenger. You did an outstanding job there and we want to put this into a safe pair of hands."

"I see."

"That's all, then. You are to put to sea by 0900 hours and sail directly for Norway. Let me be clear – under no circumstances are you to engage targets of opportunity. The prime objective is to maintain a screen against northern movements during the battle that is to come. Your secondary objective is to hold yourself in readiness for possible special operations."

"Very well, sir," he said, saluting.

"Good luck, Beitzen."

****

Farmer relaxed back into a deep garden-chair on the rear terrace at Broome. The few days he had spent at the War Office had exhausted him and then Fitzgerald, of all people, had suggested a recuperative trip down to Broome. Hubert and Farmer had arrived last night and had slept late.

Farmer threw down his newspaper and looked across at Fitzgerald, who was standing looking at the garden. The rose beds were just below them and also a little way off, beyond the double sweep of the stairs leading down onto the back lawn. "Thinking about *him*, Oswald?"

Fitzgerald turned round, a guilty smile on his face. "It's difficult not to. It happened a week ago now and I'm still trying believe it."

"I know, old boy. The main thing is that we have to move on from here." He levered himself slowly up from his chair. Now," he said, all business, "what tortures do you have in store for me today?"

"Actually, nothing. We have some more clothes that have been altered but that's just ..."

At that point in the conversation, a messenger appeared with a telegram from Whitehall. Fitzgerald opened it and found it was from Kell.

"I just cannot *believe* the double-dealing of politicians," he raved.

"What's the matter?" asked Farmer.

Fitzgerald slapped the message with the back of his hand. "The House is currently debating the issue of supplies to the Front – well, you already know that – but it seems that Markham and his cronies have been all fired up by Bonar Law, Carson and Lloyd George to call for some sort of vote of no confidence in Lord Kitchener's handling of the War effort. The effrontery of the fools! If it hadn't been for Kitchener, there would have been *no* war effort worth speaking about!"

"Will this affect us?"

"It certainly will. If they make a big enough noise, the upshot could be your complete exposure. Lloyd George and Northcliffe would just *love* that. We need to neutralise them somehow. So, Asquith has suggested to Kell that your under-secretary, Tennant, should drop a hint on Tuesday's debate that you'll meet any of them, either in private or as a group, at the War Office to discuss any matter which concerns them."

"What? How in God's name do they expect me to carry that off?"

"He seems to think that if we do not nip this problem in the bud, they will find other ways of embarrassing you. We'd run the risk of their discovering things we don't want them to know. I believe the offer is to be made *en passant* during a quiet period in the hope that no-one will notice. If they miss it, we can say we at least made the offer but if any of them are actually awake in the chamber, I'm afraid you're going to have to go through with it."

"Surely some of them know Kitchener, personally. I don't think I could perform well enough to fool them at close quarters."

Hubert joined the conversation. "Well, you know, Henry, I don't think things will turn out too badly, if we handle it with a little finesse."

Fitzgerald looked round at him. "How so, Lieutenant?"

"Well, once again, Kitchener is very uncommunicative – and notorious for it. He does things his own way and brooks no opposition. That's something you *must* bear in mind, Henry. If you don't like something, tell them you won't do it. Simple as that. Anyway, as I say, he is not well known as a garrulous man. That being the case, I think that the offer of this interview – being so out of character – is going to be seriously oversubscribed, to say the least. No one will want to miss the chance. Word of mouth alone will bring them flooding in from the Shires."

"How does that help me?" asked Farmer.

"Well, there's no way they could *all* be fitted into your office – that allows us to choose the venue."

"I see what you're getting at, Hubert. Go for one of the larger meeting rooms in the War Office or even the House of Commons where the audience is kept more at a distance," said Fitzgerald, interested now in the proposition.

"Absolutely. More to the point, with a larger audience like that, there would be fewer chances for individuals to button-hole Henry and get too close."

"Very well, that's the way we must do it. I'll get on to Kell."

"I wonder if our Prime Minister will actually put in an

appearance," said Farmer.

"Why do you say that?"

"Because, Oswald, in the short time I have been masquerading as Lord Kitchener, I have had no end of trouble getting Asquith to sign off on things – particularly this recruiting business that the War Office tells me is crucial if we're not just to throw open the gates of Buckingham Palace to Kaiser Bill. Yet, just before we drove down here, at the last hurdle, our Prime Minister declared himself too ill to pay attention to the needs of his country and the Bill remains unsigned. I thought he had exhausted every avenue of delay: I never thought of the diarrhoea."

****

U-75 was well out into the North Sea by now, on its way to a holding point just north of Trondheim, cruising on the surface at a relaxed pace which belied its deadly cargo of eighteen mines. Down below, in the Captain's cabin, Beitzen and Grassl were enjoying an illicit glass of schnapps.

"Go on, then, Kurt, How do you think Jellicoe and Scheer will measure up against each other?"

"Who knows? There's never been a battle of dreadnoughts before. Jellicoe is no great tactician, that's for sure, but he has some great ships. Beatty, on the other hand, is in a class of his own. If we have any problems, he'll be at the bottom of them." He lay back on his bunk and ruffled his dark brown hair. "You know, Willi, I can't wait for this battle to be fought."

"Me, too. I'm dying to have a go at sinking the 'Grand Fleet'."

"No, it's not just that. This could be *it.* A collision of the two greatest fleets in the world. It could spell the end, one way or the other. The war could slide to a standstill within a few weeks if there is a decisive outcome."

"'*One way or the other*?' Don't you expect us to win?"

"Don't know. I don't know if I care, really. I'm just ... tired of it all." He propped his head up on an elbow and looked at the other man. "It's been two years, Willi, *two years.* You only just joined up six months ago, but I've hardly seen my wife in all of that time and completely missed my little girl's first steps – I'll never get that back again. I suppose this is high treason or something but I just don't seem to have the same ... I don't know … *enthusiasm* for the whole thing."

"You're just tired, Kurt. I mean, you've done a hell of a lot of patrols. And that business of the *Farewell* – I don't think anyone else would've held his nerve."

"Thanks, Willi." He looked down into his glass. "And you may be right about the fatigue. Anyway, that's why I was annoyed at our being stuck out here while the main action's going to be taking place further south. We've got to make this a *decisive* defeat for the Grand Fleet or the whole thing will drag on for *another* two years. Both our countries will be beggared – and for what?"

"God preserve us from that! Yes, you're right, the destruction of the Grand Fleet is key to everything. If we can hammer it so hard that it never ventures out again, England and her sea lanes will just be lying open for the taking. There'll be no opposition *and* the blockade will be over."

Grassl got up, crouched in the confines of the tiny living space. "And so, with your permission, Kapitän, I'll get back to my compass-dynamo and stop us bumping into

Norway." He looked with affection at Beitzen. "Honestly, Kurt, you should just lie back and get some rest. I'll call you when we're on station."

****

Farmer wasn't too worried about the whole affair, now that he knew that he'd have so many experts to step in and help him if he was making a hash of things. Sitting in the main drawing room of Broome, he was listening to Fitzgerald's thoughts on how to deal with the military aspects of the Russian visit.

Dudeney continued to be a useful sounding board for his developing Kitchener impersonation and they were together often in the gardens and estate buildings. Farmer found it amusingly odd how he, too, had acquired a sort of proprietorial feeling for the roses, Kitchener's own pride and joy. Perhaps he was getting *too* good at this thing and he wondered just how he would manage when the time came to cast off his assumed persona. Would anything ever be the same again? He shivered in the warm breeze as Kitchener, figuratively speaking, walked over his grave.

****

"Mr Duquesne."

"Colonel Datchett."

The two, well-dressed men shook hands shook hands like old acquaintances meeting by chance. Datchett looked around with some disgust at the peeling paint of a rather seedy tea shop in the Cromwell Road. One could catch something nasty in here, he thought, and mentally made a note not to eat or drink anything just in case. He glanced across the greasy table at the other man while beckoning the waitress to take their order. "What can I tempt you to?"

In the end, just tea was ordered and, once the girl had scuffed away into the darkness of the kitchen, Datchett slipped a small package under the table. "Something *really* good for you this time, Mr Duquesne."

"Worth the journey I had to make from South America, I hope. My employers are becoming underwhelmed by the quality of information you're supplying. It doesn't always stand up to scrutiny. Personally, I'm not at all sure it's worth the money they're paying you."

"This one is for free," said Datchett.

Duquesne scowled. "Nothing's ever for free. Not if it's worth anything."

"This one is. And it is almost tailor-made for you, personally. That's the reason for your journey. Let's just say that our planets are in temporary alignment. Read the instructions carefully and make the preparations I've detailed." Datchett beamed a languorous smile, almost hugging himself. "Believe me, Duquesne, this is the culmination of everything you and I have been working for. All your Christmases are in that envelope."

****

Just off Birsay, the main island of the Orkney group, the destroyer *Unity* laboured to complete the last sweep of the channel to the west of Marwick Head. The deepening swell had made the entire operation difficult and her Captain was glad that he could head back for Scapa. In the radio room, the ship's operator transmitted his message, for the fourth time that hour, to Admiralty HQ in London.

`Channel to west of Marwick Head swept clear of mines - END`

He looked down at his written instructions as he had done before each transmission. They had just come in just before transmission began and were signed by old 'Badger' himself – Vice Admiral Sir Frederick Brockman, Commodore of Longhope Shore Establishment on Hoy. They were quite explicit – send the message, *en claire*, every fifteen minutes to Admiralty HQ in London. *Not to Longhope*. As he grabbed for his pen, which was in mortal danger of rolling off the table on to the floor, he puzzled over the order. Why *not* send the message to Longhope? That was the normal course of action. *And* four times, unencrypted, in one hour! Something important had to be going down soon for the Admiralty to give a damn about a place like Birsay. He stretched back over his chair, trying to get some feeling into his cramped muscles. Well, the whole thing was above his pay scale and, in any case, he was just about to go off watch.

****

When the news of Jutland broke early on the second of June, Hubert and Farmer were relaxing at the War Office after a conference of civil servants over which Farmer had presided. Monday, Tuesday and Wednesday had slipped past without incident, taken up with duties outside Whitehall and, so far, the rest of the week had proved to be equally inoffensive.

Hubert was reading over a brief on the situation Kell had couriered over. "It seems that Jellicoe did not give the High Seas Fleet the drubbing everyone expected. Looks like they fought to a sort of draw and the Germans made off under cover of smoke. Our lot are claiming victory, of course, but that's not the way it looks when you count numbers."

"Damn!"

"Succinctly put, Commander-in-Chief. Seems that we let ourselves down, partly by incompetence but also, apparently, by the quality of our *shells*." Hubert scratched his chin, scanning through the turgid prose. "At any rate, the High Seas Fleet has slunk back to Kiel, leaving us master of the field, so to speak."

"What about us? Any serious damage?"

"Well, yes. We lost some capital ships and a lot of pride. The fleet's back at Scapa, licking its wounds and feeling very sorry for itself." He tossed the report aside. "But there is a reason for telling you all this."

"Indeed?"

"Indeed. Kell has been on the phone. This Russian thing – it seems we could kill two birds with one stone. It's become apparent in the light of what happened at Jutland that we really should try to buck up the Navy's morale. You'll remember that we were supposed to be departing from the Clyde and, while that would doubtless have been the better idea – you know, short journey there and a well-checked channel to depart from – our sailors have been through such a God-awful scrap that the Admiralty think a visit from you to the Fleet at Scapa would do wonders. So, it's up to Thurso by train for you, across the sea to Orkney and from there to the frozen steppes."

"Fair enough. Makes no odds, really."

****

Infesting the basement of a building just off the Strand,

the Turkish Baths were dingy and depressing. Cracked green tiles abounded amid peeling paint to give the place something of a neglected look but appearances, as is so often the case, *were* deceptive – behind the scenes, the establishment was the most discreet vice parlour in London, attracting an endless supply of diplomats and the very wealthy.

A grim Anne Banfield folded yet another towel from the mountain of fresh laundry and stacked it on the neat pile just under the counter. She looked up at the clock. It was nearly time to go home, thank God, and her feet were killing her. Things were quiet – if it continued like this, perhaps she could just slope off ... but the outer door slammed, causing her to sigh at the thought of yet another customer.

Looking at her dispassionately, the average observer would see that she was not what classicists would call *pretty*. In fact, her face was perilously close to plain. Nose a little on the generous side, her hair was often mutinous despite her infuriated efforts to the contrary. Perhaps her bottom was even a touch too large. But her smile! When she smiled, her whole face seemed to glow from inside, as if someone had switched on an electric light. That, and a no-nonsense attitude to life, was all that was needed to encourage the proprietor to hire the impertinent twenty-five-year-old. Two or three abortive sorties and several painful jabs later, he gave up all attempts at scaling the north face of Anne Banfield. From there, her life had sagged into one of constant boredom, she thought, almost with regret.

Her new customer pushed open the inner swing doors and marched up to the counter. He scattered some coins down and demanded a towel. Anne noted that he kept his hat on and his eyes cast down, even after he'd stalked off into one of the cubicles a few doors away. She stuck her tongue out at his back disappearing round the door – rude people really made her mad! Exhausted, she turned to pick up another towel, fold it, put it on the pile, take another towel ... The way he just rushed in and ... Thinking again of what she could see of his face, Anne realised that she might have seen him before. But where?

Before she could bring him to mind, another man entered through the swing doors. She knew that she had never seen *him* in her life. But the other one? Her mind elsewhere, she provided the requested towel and he made his way to a cubicle next to the first customer's.

"*Casement*!" Although she said it to herself in a whisper, she stopped her hand over her mouth and looked around to see if either of the two men had heard. Nothing. She sat back in her chair. The first man was a known associate of Sir Roger Casement, who was taking a well-earned rest in the Tower for treason. What was his pal up to here? Within a few minutes, she heard the sound of a door open and one of them join the other.

Anne had arranged her own little cubby-hole so that the ventilators which serviced the cubicles opened out into her own. All she had to do was to stand on a chair and listen in. For a moment, she could hear only a low murmur and then a man, the second one she thought, whispered, "It seems that Mr Darlington's coming back. That worries quite a few people over here."

"Are you sure about that?"

"About Darlington coming back? Absolutely. And he knows far too much. So much, that he's likely to get off lightly in case he starts talking."

Anne's head was buzzing, trying to think of who 'Mr Darlington' might be. One possibility was Trebitsch Lincoln, the renegade Member of Parliament who had been resident in the USA for the past few months, employing his time publishing scurrilous material about Britain and the War through the German Embassy in Washington. Lincoln had been MP for the town of Darlington and it was a pseudonym he was known to use. The Government of Great Britain had been reduced to having to employ Pinkerton's to locate and return him to British soil. He richly deserved to join Casement in the Tower for treason but it was a crime not covered by the US extradition treaty. The upshot was that he'd be tried for fraud, instead, or the Yanks would not have agreed to hand him over. Her thoughts were dragged back to the present by the sound of the first man speaking again.

"Well, can we get in touch with him, then?"

"Not at the moment. We're all up to our armpits in crocodiles, right now. In fact, I just have time to grab a quick shower and then I have to be off. The important thing is to tell the boys not to be around when Darlington gets into Liverpool – he's got a 'very bad cold', understand? They might catch some of it.

"Understood."

"But even so, they mustn't lose sight of the Big Fellow. There's to be a party at the beginning of next month and he's to be the guest of honour."

"A champagne party, then?"

"No. Stronger stuff – vodka."

"Where's it to be held?"

"No idea, but we've just had word that they'll probably start off at Florrie's."

"Right. I suppose we can make it."

"You'd better."

Anne heard the door open and the man return to his own cubicle. Puzzled by the laconic conversation, she ran over everything in her mind. Who was to have met Lincoln and why was he being warned off? Were the Security Services watching? 'Florrie' or 'Florence' was a well-known enemy code-word for Scapa Flow. Whatever the party was, it was a naval one. 'Champagne' could be France and 'vodka', then, had to be Russia. But who was the 'Big Fellow'? The Prime Minister? Perhaps the King, himself? She dismissed the latter out of hand. No foreign power would wish to dispose of any member of the Royal Family. The inevitable popular backlash would undermine any political benefit sought.

Casement … Casement. She turned the name over in her head. The Irish traitor involved with separatism. It was the thought of Ireland that made the link in her mind – Kitchener was under threat from the IRB for nationalistic reasons and their recent activities at Easter placed them firmly in the forefront of her mind. Kitchener, himself, was born in Ireland and she was aware, through her work as one of the few female agents in Special Branch, that he was the subject of hostile surveillance. Was it possible that Kitchener was leaving for Russia, departing from the naval base at Scapa Flow some time within the next fortnight? If so, he might be in for trouble. The clock showing a little past five, she packed up her things and left for the Yard to see her commanding officer – Assistant Commissioner Sir Basil Thompson.

****

In the cold waters of the North Sea, Beitzen stood perched on the conning tower of U-75. In the rising swell, he wedged himself with his feet pushed against the safety rail, oblivious to the cold water running down his back from the superstructure. Grassl had just handed him a decoded signal and disappeared back down below. The paper fluttered like a trapped bird as he read the message – the battle had not gone as hoped. Not exactly a defeat but not the victory that was expected. Stalemate! And what of his new mission!

RECENTLY INTERCEPTED BRITISH SIGNALS COMBINED WITH CORROBORATIVE INTELLIGENCE INFORMATION FROM RUSSIA SUGGEST LORD KITCHENER WILL TRAVEL TO ST PETERSBURG PASSING CLOSE TO MARWICK HEAD OFF THE ISLAND OF BIRSAY ON FIFTH JUNE - STOP - MAKE FOR BIRSAY WITH ALL SPEED AND LAY FULL COMPLEMENT OF MINES THREE METRES BELOW WATER LEVEL IN SIX CHAINED GROUPS - END

My God! Kitchener! He leaned back against the bulkhead and looked up at the deepening blue of the evening sky, now flecked mistily with mare's tails.

Bad weather coming.

CHAPTER 5

Friday 2 June 1916 1930 hours – Sunday 4 June 1916 1300

Thompson sat still for a moment, his eyes screwed up, until Anne thought he was about to have a heart attack. No such luck, she thought, as he exploded into a large handkerchief. He looked at her with bleary eyes. "I'm sorry – dreadful, never-ending cold. Had it for weeks." He motioned towards a chair with his free hand. "Sit down and carry on."

Anne did as she was told, trembling inside. "You may be aware, sir, that I was detailed to observe callers to the Turkish Baths establishment in the Strand?"

"I do." He laid a hand on the thick file in front of him – her personal file.

Anne swallowed hard. "I overheard a conversation less than an hour ago. The long and the short of it is … I believe that there might be a significant new threat to Lord

Kitchener's life."

Thompson's eyes narrowed. He tucked his handkerchief into the breast pocket of his jacket with a single thrust. "Go on," he said, quietly.

"Well ... the conversation was somewhat coded but it was quite clear that the speakers were associates, or at least supporters, of both Casement and Lincoln. Scapa Flow was mentioned, together with oblique references to a Russian trip."

"What makes you sure that it's Lord Kitchener?"

"They referred to their target as 'The Big Fellow'. I agree that this could mean just about anyone but it does fit with Casement's background and the current Irish interest in Lord Kitchener. Putting two and two together, I thought it might be wise to get together with the War Office to check if he is to visit Ru ..."

Thompson held up a hand. "I'll decide what is *wise*, Miss Banfield, if you don't mind." He looked down at the cover of the file for a moment, gathering his thoughts. "Tell me everything that was said."

Anne paused for a moment to gather her thoughts and then recounted the conversation word for word, including her interpretations of the words "Florrie's" and "Vodka Party".

"This is something of a leap in the dark." The sardonic note in his voice was unmistakeable. "Am I to understand that you want me to alert the War Office on 'evidence' like this? Can you imagine what Kitchener's staff would say if I turned up and told them that we'd overheard a conversation in some Turkish Baths and that if he was planning to go to Russia in the future, he'd better call it off?"

He quickly held up a hand again to stifle Anne's retort.

"Look, I can see from your file you've been working long shifts with no back up. I know you to be a conscientious officer but with that sort of workload I'm not surprised this bee has become fixed in your bonnet. You're tired. It often happens. You've been doing too much work and you've let your imagination run away with you. That changes you from an asset to a damned liability! I'll see that you have a change of assignment in the near future – 'good as a rest', sort of thing."

"But, sir, I really think that this is important."

"You're probably so tensed up that anything seems important, right now. But I'm telling you that it isn't. Just forget it – and forget it immediately before your mind gets cluttered up even more."

Anne was fast becoming furious. She had been in this business for a few years now and had dealt with some difficult cases. She was not prepared to accept this sort of treatment without a fight and got to her feet, fists clenched. "Is there anything in my record that would give you the *smallest* basis for taking this line?"

"I'm not prepared to argue with you, Miss Banfield."

"I refuse to be silenced like this. I'm not some child you can rebuke without explanation."

Thompson's features slackened malevolently. "Now, you listen to me, woman. If you can't use the sense you were born with to keep silent about this, I'll find the means to *make* you silent. Do you understand me?"

Anne stood still, for a moment, her jaw trembling with indignation. In the end, all she could find to say was "Good day!" before spinning on her heel, furious at not being able to think of anything more cutting.

****

Fitz Duquesne sat back from his handiwork with a degree of care. Using this type of container for the device was a lovely touch, he chuckled malevolently, and it held a hell of a lot of gelignite. He *had* wanted to use dynamite but it sweated too easily and the weeping nitro-glycerine that resulted was a bitch to handle with any kind of safety – anyone might pick it up and cause it to explode just jiggling the damn thing. No – gelignite might be more expensive and harder to get in these trying times but it was completely inert unless a detonator was in the equation. Still, it still paid not to get too cocky with these things, he thought – thus, the exaggerated care.

He reached back in and shaped the charge a little more, feeling the slightly gritty texture of the putty-like explosive, until he was happy with the general arrangement. Screwing his eyes up against the incipient headache he always developed when handling gelignite without rubber gloves, Duquesne tried to think happy thoughts of a Kitchener converted in the blink of an eye into *aarbeikonfyt.* Some God-forsaken place was going to need a paint job. He laughed soundlessly.

All that was needed to bring it all to life was to slide a small, hidden metal contact on the outside of the container, just below its handle. The device would then explode when it was opened or when one of the two clocks inside reached its alarm setting. Reaching over to the side table in his tawdry but anonymous 'bijou' Paddington flat, he picked up his whisky glass and drew a long pull. He was finished.

****

Back home in her flat, Anne had changed out of her

work clothes and thrown something on the cooker – she had no idea what – with the vague intention of eating it in the immediate future. She was *incandescent*, so angry she could hardly think straight. Try as she might, she couldn't stop mentally replaying her meeting with Thompson. This was all *wrong*! Something was definitely going on that would do Kitchener no good – well, maybe not Kitchener, but she was sure it involved Scapa Flow, Russia and *some* highly placed political figure – the 'Big Fellow'. Then again, why *shouldn't* it be Kitchener? It all fitted. For God's sake, Special Branch and the Irish coppers had been up to their necks over the past few weeks, arresting every known member of the IRB they could lay their hands on. Kitchener's life was *known* to be in danger from extremists, so why discount even the faintest possibility that she had uncovered a plot to assassinate him at Scapa Flow, or on the way there? Could she be so far from the truth?

'Mr Darlington' was the key to it – she was sure of that. Trebitsch Lincoln had offered his services as a spy a while back but His Majesty's Government saw him as too much of a risk – and how right they were. He went straight off to the Netherlands to be recruited by the Germans as a double. Anne was part of the task force who went to arrest him when he returned, but he slipped the net and escaped to the United States where he made contact with Franz von Papen, the Military Attaché to the US. But it seemed that the Germans, had had enough of him. Now he was coming back to British soil and his 'friends' were planning to make some political capital out of it.

The smell of something burning brought her back to reality. The 'something' was carbonised – a black, smoking mess at the bottom of the pot. She stared at the ceiling, arms rigidly at her sides, and quietly growled.

****

Beitzen was on his way to the north of Scotland, having told no-one the purpose of the mission, except Grassl.

"Kitchener!" Grassl exclaimed, when they were alone in Beitzen's cabin. "My God, there's a target for you! How the hell did we get wind of that? Someone's been careless!" Grassl leaned back in the chair and gazed at the bulkhead, lost in thought. "This would change a lot of things, Kurt. The Tommies' morale would go to rock bottom if we were able to take Kitchener out of the equation. Everyone I talk to says that the Allies would make a complete hash of things in Flanders if it weren't for his control and – let's give the devil his due – the respect he commands."

"I know, Willi, but where's the *sense* in it? How in the name of God will this do Germany any good?"

Grassl looked at the other man through narrowed eyes and lowered his voice to little more than a hoarse whisper. Life in a submarine was like working inside a tin can – sound travelled. "I don't understand you, Kurt. It's not for you to question the whys and wherefores. You simply have to carry out your orders. If Kiel tells you to lay mines off Orkney, then that's exactly what you should do. Lay them and then get the hell out of there into open sea."

Beitzen was troubled and couldn't hide it. "Willi, I've looked at this from all sides and I believe there is only one conclusion to make – we *can't* win this war! Not just us, you understand – *no-one* can *really* win it! It's a question of who dies first."

"For Christ's sake, Kurt, lower your voice!"

Beitzen looked straight into the other man's eyes. "Willi, we can't win this war," he said quietly. "There are just too many forces ranged against us. And when it's all over, it'll be men like Kitchener who will make a decent peace – an honourable peace which might leave us some shreds of dignity. Something to build upon in peacetime."

"Kapitän, I don't want to hear any more of this." Grassl stood up to leave.

Reaching over, Beitzen grasped the other man's sleeve. "No, listen to me, Willi. Just for a minute. Sit back down and hear me out – I need your thoughts." Grassl lowered himself back onto the small wicker armchair. "Let's just suppose, then, that we send Kitchener to the bottom – congratulations all round. How do you think the British Army will react to that? How do you think Britain would take the news?" He looked steadily at Grassl. "I'll tell you – at first, they'd be devastated but then they'd come on us with a savagery the likes of which you and I have never seen!"

"Kurt!" said Grassl. "I never thought you *afraid*!"

"I'm not," he sighed, resting back against the ever-damp bulkhead. "What I'm trying to say is that the War would only be lengthened – doesn't matter who comes out top in the end. You, yourself, agreed when we were talking about Scheer versus Jellicoe. The British would *never* give up if we killed Kitchener. We'd just slug it out, year after year, like two old heavyweights who don't know when to throw in the towel. We'd put on a great show for the world to watch – and then, when it was all over, the world would go home and leave us both to bleed to death, drop by drop, on the canvas." He looked at Grassl. "We *need* men like Kitchener, not posturing politicians and warmongers. We need men of honour who know what it's like to fight for one's country."

"But Kurt, we *must* do as we are told! If you disobey, what will happen? You will be returned in disgrace, get yourself court-martialled and end up being shot, like as not. And even then, another boat will just be dispatched to do the job, anyway. It would all be for nothing. *Nothing*, Kurt!

You *have* to do it. Think of Magda, for God's sake, if nothing else."

"Willi, don't you understand what I'm trying to say? It's Magda and Trudi I'm thinking of. They're *starving*! The blockade is strangling our country." He turned, appalled, towards Grassl, "Do you know, Madga told me how she saw a group of people *butchering* a dead horse that had fallen in the very street – they were that hungry! It *has* to come to an end."

"You simply have no choice, Kurt." He tapped the flimsy in Beitzen's hand. "Your orders tell you clearly that you are to approach Orkney from the north-west just past Noup Head and mine the waters to the south – you *have* to lay those mines. The alternative is unthinkable."

Beitzen looked up at the dripping ceiling and sadly ran his finger along a weld line above his head. "I know, Willi. I'll do what I'm told. I'll lay the mines as ordered but remember what I've said. This will do Germany no favours – no favours at all."

****

Kell was less than pleased. Despite Special Branch's most strenuous efforts, backed up by the Royal Irish Constabulary, Gallagher and this phantom accomplice were still on the run. He was disappointed. And now this girl – he looked down at the open file lying untidily on the table – 'Banfield', was prowling around on the edges of the situation. Casement and his crew were out of the picture. Thompson had at least seen to that. There would be no further danger from them, especially now that they had Casement's appalling diaries to leak to his bleeding heart supporters within the British ranks. They made interesting reading, to say the least. Of course, they'd inevitably be labelled 'forgeries' by those with an axe to grind but Thompson was totally convinced of their authenticity and over the moon when he learned the glad tidings that they had not been lost at sea, as publicly leaked.

And now here was this 'Miss Banfield' and her slew of hysterical conclusions. Thompson had torn a strip off her, but perhaps that was just not enough. She was one loose end too many. Heaven knows what she might do if sufficiently frustrated. Her name had clicked something in his filing cabinet of a memory, causing him to call the Lady Superintendent for a check of the records, and there she was in a note written by his predecessor, Melville. Her undercover work in the Bank of England in the months leading up to the war had earned her a commendation – and Steinhauer himself had been batting for the other side – a *very* dangerous young lady, then.

He considered the matter for a moment and then, having come to a decision, pressed a lever on the intercom. A female voice answered and he delivered his order quietly into the microphone. "Send the Brothers Grimm to me, immediately."

****

In the darkness of that evening, U-75 laid its cargo of mines two miles off Marwick Head. Like obscene fruit, they slid out of the stern of the *Bruder Walther* and disappeared into the black, roiling sea. Beitzen watched them go, satisfied that he had done his duty. But 'duty' was a difficult concept to wrestle with after two years of incessant war. What *was* his duty, and to whom? Things were no longer as clear cut as they once had been. It wasn't that he had stopped believing in his country. That was still as strong as ever it had been – perhaps even more so, for he was thinking now of Germany in what would be her post-war years – but this had long stopped being a war of men or ideals. It was a war of industries, of men growing fat on the profits they made from the misery of human conflict. As far as *they* were concerned, things could go on as they were for as long as there were men to sacrifice. Kitchener's demise would suit them very nicely, indeed, but how would it help Germany?

Willi had been right, of course, it was not for him to decide which orders he would follow and which he would not, but he was still the Captain of the boat. *He* would decide *how* the orders would be followed. At 2304 hours on the second day of June 1916, he stonily watched the mines being laid. Set for a depth of *seven* metres. It would be a heavy ship indeed, and drawing a lot of water, whose hull would ride deep enough to strike them. Kitchener was safe – at least from him.

He saw the mine laying party safely back in, took a last look around at the headlands of Birsay, flickering silver-blue under a moon in its first quarter, and went below, closing the hatch firmly behind him.

****

Anne left the bus and walked the short distance to her flat in Blandford Street, hands behind her back, eyes down and scuffing an angry rhythm on the pavement with her heels. This Kitchener business was getting her well and truly down. Nothing of any consequence had happened at the Turkish Baths since that episode and she had been left with a great deal of time in which to mull the matter over. The end result was that she was convinced, more than ever, that she was right. She knew 'Mr Darlington' for the slimy bugger that he was and his supporters were cut from the same cloth.

Having struggled with her malevolent front door, she walked slowly up the stairs to her flat and let herself in. As she made to move into the little living room, she stopped instantly at the sight of a well-dressed man in his late forties, sitting in her favourite armchair at the far side of the room. He smiled genially. "*There* you are!" he cried, like an old friend who had been kept waiting. "Come in! Come in!"

"Thank you *so* much!" she said archly, and strode into the room, throwing her keys into a little Chinese pot she kept on the dresser for the purpose. The door closed firmly behind her, making her start and whirl round. A very different individual was leaning against it, arms folded and with a damn-your-eyes look in his face. This one was in his mid-twenties, a little below medium height, well-built and soberly dressed - even quite handsome, she thought. But all that stopped at the eyes. They were Billingsgate eyes – dead, without expression or life. She shuddered, as though she had found an earwig in her salad, and turned once more as the first spoke.

"I have no doubt she's wondering what on earth two unknown gentlemen are doing in her sitting room, Mr Pickup," he said in a soft, cultured voice. "And, indeed, she has every right to be indignant."

"What the hell *are* you doing in my room?" Anne said it forcibly enough but she was far from confident. The look in Pickup's face had unsettled her.

The older man's gentle face creased in mock horror. "Dear me, Mr Pickup, such *language*!"

"I could scream my head off right now, if I chose to. So just get on with whatever you're here for."

"I wouldn't recommend that, would you, Mr Pickup?

Her employer wouldn't welcome the attentions of Fleet Street just at the moment." He saw the confusion in her eyes as she tried to work out the relationship between the sleazy owner of the Baths and this man. He gave a light chuckle, "I really believe she thinks I'm referring to the proprietor of that ... *establishment.* No, no, I'm referring to Mr Thompson."

"I have absolutely no idea what you're talking about and if you don't ..." Anne looked at him closely, head on one side. "Have we *met*? Have I seen you somewhere before – a wanted poster or something like that?"

"Tell her to be quiet, Boissier," said a silky voice from behind.

"It talks!" she said.

Boissier smiled, as if at a private joke. "I wouldn't rub Mr Pickup the wrong way, Miss Banfield, really I wouldn't. Please sit down and let's talk shop, without any more fairy stories about who really pays your salary. You're Special Branch. Let's establish that and go on from there."

Anne said nothing but sat down anyway. She had been on her feet most of the day and was glad to flop down on the sofa, where she could watch both men. Pickup made no move and continued to stare at her in a very disconcerting way. Boissier, on the other hand, had made himself comfortable and looked every inch the much-loved uncle at ease in his niece's home.

"I *do* like your flat," he said, looking around. The smile faded and the avuncular eyes hardened, glittering in the soft light from the paraffin lamp on the table. "Now then, Miss Banfield, I am led to believe that you have been misbehaving yourself. I'm sorry to hear that of you. Apparently, your recent hysterics have upset certain parties and my colleague and I have been given the pleasant task of calling on you in the hope that we can straighten matters out."

"By which you mean ...?"

"Don't be coy," Pickup said through his teeth.

"Is all this a *threat* of some sort?"

Uncle was back and he was offended. "Miss Bancroft, *really*! Do you take us for thugs?"

"Do I *have* to answer that?"

Boissier looked long and hard at her. When he finally spoke, she was left in no doubt – of the two, Boissier was the deadlier. "Miss Banfield. This is just a social call." He looked up to the ceiling, as if searching for *just* the right words. "More ... more *permanent* action will come later – if required. At this moment, I am merely charged with asking you to let matters rest. You are a very small fish swimming in a dark, fathomless ocean, completely out of your depth. Believe me."

Anne bristled, in spite of the cold finger of fear running down the nape of her neck. "I am not to be threatened!"

"A *threat*? No, no – a request. Just a request," urged Boissier, as if it mattered to him.

"Boissier, leave her with me for ten minutes. She'll see sense by then." Pickup's tone had hardly changed in the few words he had spoken since Anne had returned. The menace was still there.

Anne looked at him up and down. "Just how old *were* you when you were potty trained?"

Pickup said nothing but smiled the small, secret smile of the cat waiting its chance.

"Miss Banfield, I *have* warned you. You'll upset my

friend. And then," he said, spreading his arms wide, "where will we be?"

Boissier stood up and adjusted the lie of his suit with exaggerated care. He took a deep breath and radiated affection. "Now, then, we have trespassed on your hospitality long enough and it's time for us to leave. No," he said, holding up a manicured hand, as Anne rose, "I won't hear of your asking us to stay a moment longer." He walked to the door, which Pickup had opened for him and turned round. "Remember what I have said, dear girl. *Let it lie!* If we have to come back, it will be under less pleasant circumstances." He smiled. "Well, anyway, nice to have met you. Try to relax after your hard day at work, now." He pointed an elegant finger down the hall. "We've drawn you a bath."

Anne was left alone in the room with Pickup who strolled over to her, where she stood frozen with fear. He reached out a hand and cupped it under her chin, squeezing it until it hurt. He smiled. "Everyone says you're a bad, bad girl. I *do* hope so." He released her slowly and, walking backwards towards the open door, he left, closing it quietly behind him.

In the silent room, Anne began shaking uncontrollably.

****

In the end, the dreaded Commons meeting took place on Friday in Committee Room 14 of the House of Commons. Lloyd George's vicarious attack on him in the House had fizzled out to nothing, partly due to the Government's confident handling of the situation but mostly because the vast majority of MPs were all for Kitchener.

Farmer, now *extensively* prepared by Fitzgerald and others, felt surprisingly confident. Perhaps it was the fact that this would be his last day 'in office', so to speak, before heading off for Scapa, Russia and then blessed oblivion back at Farnham House. 'End of term!' he smiled to himself, in memory of his schooldays at Shrewsbury.

Every man and his dog seemed to be there and, for a moment, Farmer was taken aback but – what the hell! – in for a penny ...

"Gentlemen, good morning. My time, as you can imagine, is somewhat limited, so let me start straight away. For some time now, I have felt that the circumstances attendant on the fact that I am an unelected Minister of State has imposed something of an artificial barrier between the workings of my Ministry and the House. No one regrets this more than I and, recently, it has been brought to my attention that it has even caused a degree of discomfiture among some members of this very audience."

More than one MP smiled to himself at the verbal paper cut targeted at people like Herbert, Markham and Lloyd George.

"Here is how I would like to proceed – I plan to take you through the current state of affairs as respects the conduct of the war and dwell particularly upon why I have felt that an increase in the number of divisions we field is absolutely necessary. I will then be happy to accept any questions from the floor and do my utmost to answer them fully and freely within the constraints of military security." Farmer smiled to disarm any remaining troublemakers. "How does that sound?"

Asquith, sitting in the front row, was taken aback both by the impersonation and also by the confidence radiating from the man. This doctor chap was positively enjoying himself!

Lloyd George was there, of course, but said little and nothing to the point. He made sure that his attacks were always made through third parties. As a result, Henry had to do a little fencing with people like Law and Herbert but the hardest thing was to justify Kitchener's decision to extend the call-up to married men. Questions on that particular point rained hard for a while until he held his hand up for silence.

"Gentlemen, it comes down to this in the end – Germany can field many more men than we and are already conscripting married men to the colours. If we are not to be swamped by sheer numbers, we have to do our best to match them."

He held his hands out as though cupping water. "We here hold the fate of this great nation in our very hands – we can only trust to God that this war, a conflict the scale of which we have never seen before, will end before we drain the last drop of that precious blood which runs in the veins of our country's manhood. Our losses each and every day seem to us all an intolerable burden. Yet, I tell you this – we *can* win and we *will* win – not simply because of the seeming legions of young men we expose to destruction but because we fight in a just cause. Yes, many have claimed such a cause in the past and many of them without justification but, to paraphrase my Right Honourable Friend over there, Mr Churchill, 'on the whole – and it is on the whole that such things must be judged – the British Empire has been a force for good.' We must *never* allow that moral force to be trampled upon by the expansionist dreams of an upstart Dictator."

The room erupted in applause and cheers and although, for an hour or more yet, questions rang out like shots from all quarters of the audience, no one was fooled by their attacks. All those who posed them were well-known to be in the pockets of either Northcliffe or the Welsh Wizard.

Farmer had been well-prepared and had delivered, as he would boast afterwards, a breezy, confident and well delivered performance. His audience was entranced, thrown off-balance by this unexpected apparition of an up-beat Secretary of State for War revealing his thoughts and intentions concerning the prosecution of the conflict. Farmer had all the facts and figures at his finger-ends: he *was* Kitchener.

Relaxing back into his chair, Asquith applauded with the majority of the audience.

And then, suddenly, it was over. Farmer sighed to himself in grateful relief and left the room with an elastic step to his walk, glad that it was done. The hardest aspect of it all, now, was to remain stern and unapproachable, instead of grinning from ear to ear like an idiot as he made his way back across to the War Office.

Hubert followed, three steps behind like a good ADC should, and smiled at the civil servant standing on the steps of the main entrance with another of those endless red dispatch boxes. Farmer, however, was temporarily immune even to those and waved airily in Hubert's direction who duly signed for it – noting that the signature chit declared the box's contents to be 'EYES ONLY' briefings for the Secretary of State concerning the trip to Russia, to be opened only when the ship was under way – and followed the Minister of State for War up to his 'borrowed' office.

****

On Saturday afternoon, Farmer, Hubert and Fitzgerald went back down to Broome for the last time before their departure for Russia. Farmer, accustomed now to wearing Kitchener's style of country clothes, was standing in front of the fireplace as though he belonged there.

"What're you up to, Henry?" asked Hubert, walking in after tea.

Farmer looked round and smiled, sheepishly. "Hello, Chris. It's this thing here. I thought I'd do a little bit more of it." He nodded at the chalk and charcoal drawing on the centrepiece of the heavy stone surround. "I suppose I really should be working on my dispatches but I just can't bear the thought of the bloody things." He jerked his chin in contempt at a red, ciphered box standing in one of the bay windows, forlorn and lonely. "That's the last one of this week's set and I *still* have the Russian one to do."

Hubert peered at it from across the room. "Very dilatory of you, Minister," he said, wagging a finger and turning to look back at the drawing. "Oh, right. I saw it the first day I came down – the day before I called on you at Farnham." He sipped the tea he had brought through with him and walked across to look more closely at the sketch. "Are you going to finish it?"

"Not, really. I thought I'd just put in the motto. I used to be pretty good at this sort of thing. No time for it in the past couple of years, of course."

"I know. I saw some of the water colours you did during your Boer campaigns."

"What? How?"

"The ever-flowering Shaw."

"The impudence of the girl!"

Hubert laughed. "They were very good, Henry. I was impressed, I have to say." He put his cup and saucer down on a side-table. "But enough of this, Your Lordship, spill the beans. You've been as quiet as a mouse since we left London this morning. I've given you, now, until – what is it – half past four and still you haven't opened up. So start talking – how did 'lunch with the King' go?"

"It went fine."

Hubert waited and then said, "And that's it?"

Farmer removed the gold pince-nez he sometimes used for close-up work and pulled out a handkerchief, spilling the contents of his pocket on to the hearth. Hubert bent down and retrieved the coins and oddments, returning them to his companion.

"Thanks, old chap."

Hubert looked at him closely. "Come on Henry," he said. "Let's have it. What happened?"

Farmer laid his chalk down on the mantelpiece and brushed his fingers together to clean away the dust. "Well, lunch went pretty well. I managed to spill very little, so I thought things were going swimmingly. We talked about a number of things – you know, the war, the visit and how I thought matters would turn out in Russia." He looked at Hubert. "You were right, Chris – you and Fitzgerald. No-one asks you for your family history. It's good to have a basic knowledge of his background, of course, but it's the way you walk and talk that's the important thing. Anyway, I was on the point of leaving. One of the servants had gone off to collect my cap and greatcoat, leaving the King and me alone for a moment or two. And then, he did a strange thing …"

"What?"

"He shook my hand and said that I was doing a great thing for my country. He was so sad, somehow. Just as I was leaving he said 'God go with you'."

"What's so strange about that?"

"That wasn't it. As I walked through the door, I heard

it. It was only a whisper but I heard him say '*whoever you are*'."

"He rumbled you!"

"I believe he did. I suppose it'd be too much to expect the King to be fooled. I mean, we know he was fairly friendly with Kitchener. He must have seen that I wasn't him at some point and I suppose he realised that if we needed a double to go to Russia, there was a good chance the real man was dead. Or perhaps he *has* been told about it all."

"My God." Hubert patted Farmer's shoulder. "We need to keep this from Old Ma Fitzgerald, Henry. It'd put the wind up him, no end."

Farmer nodded and turned back to the mantelpiece, inexpressibly sad. Looking at the drawing, he said, "He should have been allowed to retire here in peace, Chris. He'd done his bit. It's funny but somehow, in all of this business, I've come to understand him in a way I never did before, you know what I mean? Sometimes it's as if he's standing right beside me, helping me along, telling me what to do and how to say it."

"Complete bollocks, Henry, but I do know what you mean." Hubert retrieved his tea.

"Very odd feeling. His *murder* – I just can't see the sense in any of it. A peaceful end to a long and worthy life – that's what he'd earned. It just wasn't fair."

Hubert grunted. "'Fair' is for children, Henry."

Farmer turned round to gaze at the huge drawing room and leaned back against the mantelpiece. "Do you know, he never really *lived* here? Never had the time, I suppose."

"I didn't know that." Hubert shook Kitchener's shade from his mind and said, "Anyway, Henry, enough of all this or I'll start crying into my tea – and 'ration' tea is weak enough as it is. Are you happy with everything Fitzgerald told you about the mission?"

"Pretty much. I'm just to be shepherded around, looking poster-ish and wise but saying as little as possible."

"That's pretty much it. The plan is for us to board the train at King's Cross …"

"Just you and I?"

"No, no. The whole circus. You and your 'admiring crowd of sisters, cousins and aunts who attend you wherever you go'."

"I've never quite seen myself as Sir Joseph Porter ..."

"... KCB," chimed Chris laughing. "So, we all get on at King's Cross and travel up to Thurso. MacLaughlin, in fact, will be one of the team. He knows the real picture and that'll be good for you."

"And we get on the boat at Thurso?"

"Again, no, we'll travel by road along to a little place to the west, called Scrabster. It's only a few miles. And that's where we'll be met by a ship, probably a destroyer, that'll take us across to Scapa Flow. Two hours, they say, because of minefields and such like."

Farmer rolled his eyes.

"It's great scenery. Don't you like sailing, then?" asked Hubert.

Farmer pushed himself away from the mantelpiece. "Well, actually ... no. I haven't said it before. The whole idea of getting away from the War Office and all those people just waiting to point a finger at me and say '*this is the fake Lord Kitchener and I claim my five guineas*' rather outweighed the notion of being on a boat for that length of time."

"What's so bad about that? It'll be like a summer cruise. Are you sea-sick?"

"Dreadfully. But that's not the real problem."

"What is, then?"

Farmer looked at him half-ashamedly and blurted it out. "Well, if you *must* know, I can't swim!"

"You can't *what*?"

"Lots of people can't swim," cried Farmer, defensively. "I'm useless at that sort of thing. You know that. I can barely *walk* without destroying furniture that gets too close."

"I'm not worried about your not being able to swim *per se*, Henry. It's just that Kitchener was known to be a strong swimmer."

"So?"

"So you'd better make sure you don't let that particular cat out of the bag. Kitchener was so good, he was able to save a brother officer from drowning in the sea off Ascalon. That was years ago, of course, but if you let on you can't swim, even the thickest heads will start thinking. As it turns out, Kitchener *was* famously very prone to sea-sickness, so that bit's fine, but don't let anyone know about the other thing, for God's sake!"

"Very well. I can lie for my country when the trumpet sounds", said Farmer, sententiously.

"I call that noble, Henry, noble."

"What happens after the crossing, then?"

"You'll be taken to see Jellicoe on the *Iron Duke*. He *has* met you several times before but it was three or four years ago – any changes can be explained by the pressures of being War Minister under these circumstance – but if he rumbles you, too, I suppose we'll just have to brief him on the truth. He's Admiral of the Fleet, after all. The idea is that you have a nice cosy chat, talk about Jutland, tell him what a great job he did, how much you're looking forward to the trip and then clear off after lunch, with a couple of pink gins inside you, over to the *Hampshire.*"

"The *Hampshire?*"

"She's your transport to Russia. Kitchener was on her once before – in the Med, I think. It was Kell's idea, actually. He told the Admiralty that you had specially asked for her. It would be like 'coming home' for you, he told them. The Navy were beside themselves with joy. Anyway, remember – *you've been on her before.* We'll try to get you some pictures or drawings of her – that sort of thing."

"Right."

"And then we sail away with a couple of escorts to Archangel and then on to St Petersburg to arrive on the ninth or thereabouts."

"Sounds lovely."

"Absolutely. A summer cruise. Just what the doctor ordered!" he said, smiling at Farmer.

****

Anne looked up at the dull, overcast skies and realised that the early summer was over for the moment. A slight, but chill, wind was blowing thinly over the open countryside, causing her to pull her fox boa a little more tightly around her neck as she stepped off the local train. It chuffed and croaked off into the gloom, leaving her alone in the silence. Her encounter with MI5's pit-bulls had her starting at every sound. For a moment, she stood still, listening – nothing – and breathed tremulously. It didn't help that this little adventure might spell the end of her career with Special Branch and, for the twentieth time since leaving London that afternoon, she wondered if she was doing the right thing. A nauseous feeling in the pit of her stomach was the only reply.

Walking out through the little wicket gate, she spotted a pony and trap standing outside. Throwing her overnight bag into the back, she hired the driver to take her to Broome and headed off along the un-metalled road, turning around every few minutes to make sure she wasn't being followed. Fortunately, the driver was one of those morose, uncommunicative types so she could take stock of what she was up to. Thompson would kill her – possibly literally, if today's uninvited visitors were anything to go by – yet here she was, risking it all … on a hunch.

****

Fitzgerald had just finished dinner after a long day putting the affairs of Kitchener's estate into order prior to the next day's departure. He relaxed into one of the armchairs in the main drawing room and lit a cheroot, the single luxury he permitted himself in the day.

Mentally ticking off the personalities, he described the group who would accompany Farmer to Russia. "There will be myself and Hubert, of course. General Ellershaw from the War Office – you've met him, Henry – will be there to help you with the military side of things. Since Special Branch will have to have their finger in the pie, MacLaughlin will be with us, too – but, of course, you know that. Sir Harold Donaldson and a Mr Robertson will be representing Lloyd George and his Ministry."

Hubert turned round in his position at the window seat. "I thought the Welsh Wizard was coming with us."

"No. Cried off late last night. Apparently Asquith has given him the thankless task of looking into the Irish problem – particularly the reasons behind the Easter Uprising."

"I don't envy him."

"Absolutely not. Anyway, where was I? Oh, yes, O'Beirne will be doing his bit for the Foreign Office and there will be a few servants and a driver from the Royal Horse Artillery. That's it, I think."

Henry, dozing in his seat, sat a little more upright. "Just to show that I am not *quite* unconscious," he said, "what about the Russian side of things?"

"In what respect?" asked Fitzgerald, tapping some ash off his cigar.

"Well, we *are* all English, are we not? Well, all right – Hubert here is a colonial of some sort – but we are going to some God-forsaken country where ..."

"I see what you mean. Sorry, yes, we do need an interpreter, of course, and we're to have a young Scottish subaltern from the Cameronians – MacPherson. That definitely *is* it. As for the arrangements, themselves, it's off to the War Office tomorrow to tie up any loose ends, then down to Kings Cross and away to Thurso."

"Yes, Chris explained that side of things. But I was wondering about ..."

"Hullo," said Hubert, interrupting. "I wonder who this is."

Fitzgerald got up and joined Hubert, who had been standing at the French windows. Outside, in the dusk, a pony and trap was drawing up to the front door.

Anne stepped into the drawing room, having been announced by the butler. For a moment she stood rooted at the door until Hubert walked over to her.

"Come and sit down over here, Miss Banfield," he said. "It's turned cold outside. Can I get you anything?"

"No, thank you. I'm very well as I am," she said nervously.

Huber stood looking at her, a wide grin fixed inanely on his face. "Fine," he said, after an embarrassing pause. "Well, let me introduce everyone." He turned to Farmer and said, "My Lord, may I name Miss Anne Banfield of Scotland Yard? Miss Banfield, this is Field Marshal Lord Kitchener." Both shook hands and muttered the usual compliments and then Hubert repeated the process with Fitzgerald, leaving himself until the last. "And I am Lieutenant Chris Hubert, temporarily seconded to His Lordship's staff."

"I'm very pleased to meet you all."

The men sat down once she was seated. Farmer, knowing that he would be expected to take the lead, thought matters over for a moment. It was very unlikely that this girl would have been briefed on the real situation. He would have to be 'in character'. "Well now, Miss Banfield, what can we do for you? Is there a message from Commissioner Thompson?"

Anne looked tortured. "Well ... in a way."

"'In a way', Miss Banfield?" asked Fitzgerald. "I'm intrigued."

Anne took a deep breath and then related everything that had happened, including her interview with Thompson and the 'visitors'. When she had finished, there was a stunned silence. She looked at the three men in exasperation and turned to Farmer. "But don't you see, sir? I *really* believe that the IRB or someone from the Casement faction will try to murder you if you go to Scapa Flow. I'm here entirely on my own initiative. I'm not representing Special Branch in any way but I simply *cannot* understand why I am not being taken seriously. The men I overheard are committed and very dangerous. What's more, they have the organization and contacts to carry off something like this so, in my opinion, they should not be discounted quite so easily."

"I can see that, young lady, and I'm very grateful," said Farmer, emolliently.

Hubert had said nothing all the time she had been talking. He was conscious of a sense of wonder that this slip of a girl would thumb her nose at someone like Thompson – *just because she thought she was right.* As for the thugs, he could smell Boissier and Pickup and that meant Kell. He looked over at Fitzgerald only to find that the other was looking at him. Without a word being passed between them, both men knew that she had to be told. Not just because it was necessary to avoid any possibility of exposure if she took matters further but also because she had *earned* it.

Farmer cleared his throat and said "Are you sure that we can't tempt you to a brandy or something?"

Anne smiled at him. "No, really, sir but thanks."

"Well, then. In that case, I have a story for you. I'm sorry to tell you that, despite your courageous efforts, you are too late. Two weeks ago, Lord Kitchener was murdered by the IRB in this very house."

Anne turned pale. "But …" she stammered, staring at him.

"He's very good, isn't he?" said Chris, leaning mock-confidentially towards her. "Miss Banfield, let me do the introductions again. Colonel Fitzgerald and I are the real thing but this gentleman is, in fact, Colonel Henry Farmer of the RAMC."

"Oh my God."

"Well, not quite. It's a bit of a shock, isn't it?"

"May I change my mind about that brandy, please?"

"Certainly." Hubert poured out the drink while Fitzgerald carried on the explanation.

"You see, it was decided by Commissioner Thompson and Major Kell that it would be in the interests of the country if we could keep Lord Kitchener's assassination a secret for a little while longer to allow us to come up with some strategy to avoid the inevitable catastrophe which would ensue when the facts were made public."

"Lord Kitchener, dead? I can't believe it. Is that why you're going to Russia – to keep Colonel Farmer out of public view?"

"You have it exactly. He'll be 'retired' when we return."

Anne, elbows on knees, put her forehead in her hands. "And I nearly exposed *everything.* No wonder Thompson was so angry with me." She looked up frantically as another thought struck her. "I might have lost the war for us!"

Farmer smiled. "Don't be too hard on yourself, Miss Banfield. You weren't to know. I don't know about the other two gentlemen here but I think it reflects greatly to your credit that you were prepared to sacrifice everything to save Lord Kitchener. It's not your fault that it was in vain."

Anne looked up. "Thank you for that, sir." She sighed. "But it's not likely to do me much good *now.*"

"You mean, with Thompson?" asked Fitzgerald. "Oh no, I don't think we need to mention this to him at all. No, no, no. You have never been here."

"I know of no Miss Banfield," said Henry, expansively.

Hubert, for his part, said nothing but gazed contentedly at the young woman.

****

Sunday dawned breezy and cold. But even that couldn't dampen Hubert's new-found love of life. Anne had somehow added a little sparkle to things. She had stayed the night, of course. There was no way she could return to London. Instead, she had left early this morning but not before Hubert had been able to chat with her. Afterwards, he wandered into the garden, where Farmer was speaking to Dudeney.

"If you don't wipe that vacuous grin off your face, Chris, I may have to be violently ill," said Farmer, in an undertone.

Hubert chuckled to himself. "Sorry, Henry, but you must admit, she *was* rather nice."

"Yes, she was – much too nice for the likes of you. Do the decent thing and leave her alone."

"Henry, today you can say whatever you like. I forgive you, my child."

Farmer grinned and turned back to chat to Dudeney while Hubert's attention was occupied by the sight of a motorcycle being checked through the main gate at the top of the hill. Within minutes, the rider was walking along the path towards them and Hubert took the envelope from him, acknowledging the salute. It was from Kell. Hubert read the two sentences and handed it silently to Farmer. It read:

TAKE CARE - STOP - GALLAGHER ON THE LOOSE AGAIN - END

"Does this mean what I think it means, Chris?"

"Probably. They've worked it out. We're using a double and they'll want to do the job again."

Farmer turned pale at the thought. "I know I could face death if I could look at it. I saw it often enough in South Africa," he said. "But this ... a shot in the dark, never knowing when it would come …"

"Chin up, Henry. Remember, you have an identity to maintain." He pocketed the message and punched Farmer gently on the arm. "Come on! Things are moving in our favour. If Gallagher is out for you, he'll come here first. And where will we be? In Russia. Let him chase us there, if he wants. When we return, you'll disappear back to Farnham House and no-one will be the wiser. The odds are in our favour."

"I suppose you're right," said Farmer, not completely convinced.

"I am. Now, let's go. We have to get up to London and you have one or two things to do at the office before we get on the train."

"I'll join you in a minute, Chris."

Hubert walked off towards the house and Farmer turned round to the old gardener. "Well, Dudeney. This is it. I'm off. But I couldn't leave without telling you how grateful I am. I don't think I could have managed quite so well without your help."

"It weren't nothing, sir. I'm just that happy that I was able to do my bit for His Lordship. You take of yourself now, sir. It ain't over yet, or I'm much mistaken."

"You look after yourself too, Dudeney. And take care of the roses." He lowered his voice, "Make sure no-one tries to assassinate *them*."

CHAPTER 6

Sunday 4 June 1916 1700 hours – 2000 hours

It took almost until five o'clock in the afternoon before they reached Whitehall. Farmer immediately went in to his office, followed closely by Fitzgerald, while Hubert hung around in the anteroom for a few moments to speak to Kitchener's secretary.

"Do you know, Lieutenant", she said, "I will be rather sorry to see the 'Field Marshal' leave for Russia. I've become rather fond of him, these past few weeks."

"And no wonder, Miss Thorpe," he said with a smile. "You've been thrown together, as it were. I know he's valued your help very greatly, indeed. To be honest, I don't know how he could have done so well without your smoothing the path for him. We're *all* so grateful."

She blushed, ducking her head. Then, surprising him, she reached up to run his lapel between her finger and thumb, "You won't let anything happen to him?" she said in an undertone.

Hubert held her hand, "That's why I'm here." He smiled to comfort her and then said more briskly, "Anyway, I really must check how they're getting on. I'm sure he'll call for you in a moment."

Hubert knocked on the door and noticed the pause within the room beyond as Farmer and Fitzgerald 'arranged themselves' in case of visitors not in the know.

"Come", called Fitzgerald, casually.

Hubert opened the door and walked in, closing it behind him. Fitzgerald was standing beside Farmer who was signing documents at his massive wooden desk.

"Won't be long, Chris", said Farmer, "We're just finalising a few things from that last dispatch box before we leave. There'll be more of the damn things waiting for me on the train, apparently – plus the Russian one. Grab a seat and we'll be with you in a minute or two."

Hubert parked himself on a large, somewhat solidly sprung War Office sofa and looked around the room. Maps and military prints dominated – only the odd little porcelain cup or plate livened up what would have been real mausoleum of a room to work in. *Each to his own.*

"You just missed Sir Henry Oliver, Chris," boasted Farmer.

"What did *he* want?"

"It seems that he was responsible for setting up all the travel arrangements. Someone apparently told him that it was my idea to do this morale-boosting visit to the Fleet and it rather upset all his original plans for a Clyde departure. Of course, you and I both know it was really Kell. He came over to give me all the new details – rather decent of him, I thought – but it seems that Jellicoe is not happy at the thought of my travelling from the mainland to Scapa in the *Hampshire*. It's too dangerous, apparently, and telegraphed this morning to say that he wants me to make the trip in a destroyer, as you thought."

"HMS *Royal Oak*," said Fitzgerald. "But that's just the main party. The servants and luggage will follow in the Fleet pinnace."

"When do we get into Thurso?" prompted Hubert

Fitzgerald flicked through a thick operations order from a red box, "Around 1100 hours tomorrow – it's a 700 mile journey."

Fitzgerald took Farmer through some more paperwork until Hubert looked at his wristwatch. The 'few minutes' had now stretched to half an hour and he politely coughed to attract Fitzgerald's notice. "Sir, may I remind you that we must be at King's Cross by 1830 hours?" It was essential to maintain the pretence even within the confines of the office. There was no telling when an unguarded comment would be overheard in a rabbit warren like the War Office.

Fitzgerald nodded curtly. "Almost done," he said.

****

On the bridge of the *Hampshire*, Captain Savill watched the crew begin tying up operations following instructions from the C-in-C himself to manoeuvre closer to the *Iron Duke* in preparation for Lord Kitchener's embarkation. The weather, by now, had changed for the worse. The wind, already strong, had risen and veered round to the north, running a heavy sea. Scapa Flow was renowned for being well sheltered but it was fast disappearing behind a mass of white tops fading into a grey mist. Soaked by spray on the open bridge, Savill pulled the collar of his waterproof more closely round his neck and shouted down to his gunnery officer who was helping to supervise deck operations.

"Matthews!"

"Aye, sir?"

"Organise a party to rig safety lines for the Army – looks as though we'll need them soon."

"Very good, sir."

Savill returned to the tiny wheelhouse and sat back in his chair, wiping the sea water from his face. He was a sailor of the old brigade, having served during the Boer War. His exceptional skills at sea had enabled him to rise high enough to command the Royal Naval College at Greenwich before being brought back to active duty. Open bridges were no hardship to him, even in this sort of weather, but how His Lordship would take to being sea-sick was beginning to worry him. He reached underneath the seat for his charts.

On the deck, near the port capstan, Matthews watched the team starting the delicate, but strenuous, process of securing the cable from the buoy. Normally, this wouldn't pose too much of a problem but in these conditions, things could get nasty. It was all hands to the pump – even the ship's blacksmith and one of the few soldiers on board had been roped in.

The deck for'ard was completely awash with spray, periodically hiding it from Savill's view up on the bridge and, with the engines barely turning over, there was nothing to give the ship any sort of headway in the strong seas to provide stability. From time to time, he could see snapshots of action between successive explosions of seawater from the bows as the team wrestled with the enormous rope.

"Look lively, let's get that hawser over the capstan!" shouted Matthews over the shrieking of the gale.

"Aye, sir!" said Chief Petty Officer Wesson. "Come on lads! Oi, Greer! Blacksmiths are welcome too, y'know! Grab the end!"

The Herculean effort needed to press the cable over the end of the steel capstan had to be seen to be believed. Six straining men took all their efforts to complete the task in the dangerous conditions of the pitching, rolling deck. No-one noticed the small, wiry army private squeeze in amongst them. His mind was not on the hawser. With a sly sideways movement, totally masked by the gathering violence of the storm, he nudged the blacksmith just as the deck reached the top of a roll to port. Off balance, Greer's right leg slid underneath him as his rock hard blacksmith's boot skated across the holystoned decking. His cry was smothered by the gale as he slid towards the capstan, trapping his leg under the cable and virtually shearing it off above the knee.

The pounding of the seas smothered his screams.

****

"Well, Joan", said Farmer, "this is it, I suppose". He was standing awkwardly with Fitzgerald and Hubert in the outer office, trying to make his farewells to Kitchener's secretary. He jerked his hand out hesitantly towards her. She reached out to take it and then pulled him forward to clasp him in a warm hug.

"Do take care of yourself, Henry", she said in a whisper. It was the first time she had used his Christian name. He held her in his gaze and smiled shyly. He jerked his head.

“”Do my best”, he said.

A silence descended on the room as they looked at each other. Just as Fitzgerald was beginning to feel himself something of a gooseberry, Hubert suggested that it was time to make a move to the railway station. They picked up the last of their hand luggage and were on their way out of the door when the phone rang.

“Lieutenant Hubert”, she said, “It’s for you”. As he took the set from her and put the receiver to his ear she murmured, “It’s Major Kell”.

“I’m sorry, sir, could you wait just a moment while I take this call?” Fitzgerald and Farmer came back in to the office and sat down. Hubert listened while Kell spoke a few sentences and then hung up. “That was Major Kell, sir. We’re missing some classified travel documents. He’s requested that I pop over to his office and collect them. I’m also to receive a final mission briefing. In view of the time, I think the best thing would be for you and Colonel Fitzgerald to make your way over to King’s Cross and I’ll join you there with the papers”.

“It’s a bit last minute!” said Farmer looking significantly at him. “Don’t be late. Seven o’clock departure.”

“I won’t, sir.” Hubert winked at him, picked up his cap and left for Kell’s lair, as he liked to call it.

****

As the launch sheered away from the *Hampshire* in the pounding seas, Matthews climbed up to the bridge to report the blacksmith’s accident to Savill. “We’re transferring Greer across to the *Soudan*, sir”, he shouted over the noise of the wind.

“How bad does it look? Will he keep his leg, do you

think?"

"I doubt it very much. It looks pretty bad but at least he has a better chance in a hospital ship like the *Soudan*. The surgeons can get to work right away."

"Poor chap – it'll be the end of his time in the Navy. Well, best hope that we have no need of his services during the trip. Carry on, Guns."

"Aye, sir." Matthews, having completed his task, returned to Number One gun to supervise preparations for their forthcoming departure.

****

The instant Hubert stepped out of the lift in MI5 HQ, he sensed the two men standing on either side. Before he could do anything about it, he felt his arms seized. "Boissier and his pet poodle, I suppose. Frightened any more girls lately?" He gasped explosively, as Pickup punched him hard in the lower back.

"You'd better watch yourself, Hubert. Kell told us to grab hold of you and bring you to his office – but he didn't say to be gentle about it."

"Now, now, Pickup," said Boissier. "Don't let it get personal." He shook his head ruefully at Hubert. "He is *so* sensitive."

Expertly, they manhandled Hubert along the corridor, passing a white-faced Jane, and deposited him in a Chesterfield in Kell's office. "Chris!" she faltered. "Chris, what's happening?"

Kell glanced up and saw her peering round the door. "It's quite all right, Miss Sissmore. Lieutenant Hubert is just helping us with something. Please close the door, thank you."

Hubert rubbed his back, groaning. "What the hell is going on? Colonel Farmer is waiting for me at Kings Cross. If I don't arrive there in the next fifteen minutes, he'll have to leave without me."

Kell glared at Boissier and Pickup. "I asked you to bring this officer to me as soon as he entered the building. I gave no orders to assault him!"

Pickup actually shuffled his feet like a schoolboy. "He resisted arrest, sir."

"Arrest? Who do you think you are? Look, just stand there behind his seat, both of you. Keep an eye on him because this is not going to go well." He glanced down at a doubled-up Hubert. "Hubert. *Hubert!* Pay attention."

Hubert tried to sit up straight and look Kell in the eye.

"That's better. Now, let's get something straight – you will not be boarding that train. Colonel Farmer will depart as planned but those plans no longer include you."

****

Farmer never liked King's Cross, even at the best of times. Today, it was a bit chilly and miserably damp, he thought, as he stood on the platform beside his private train. Coupled with the usual mayhem of troops embarking and disembarking from transports, it was the least attractive place on earth he could think of.

He glanced around, almost forgetting to return the salute of a passing private soldier. The smell of coal smoke and hot oil was everywhere, stinging the eyes and smudging collars. On the furthest platform, he could see crowds of women, many carrying children, waving handkerchiefs tearfully at their departing husbands, unsure if they would ever see them again in this world.

Fearing the worst.

The shrieking of others, hidden from view behind a grimy cloud, he assumed was to welcome the return of those dearest to them. It all seemed to be a sort of dirty, mechanical staging post between the worlds of death and destruction and those of home and safety. A single platform change could take you from one to the other.

He snorted to himself. "Bloody business is turning me into a philosopher."

Fitzgerald touched his arm, causing him to start a little. "My apologies, sir."

Farmer smiled. "Not at all, Oswald. I was miles away. To tell the truth, I was concerned that we haven't seen Hubert yet."

"I'm afraid that's only one of our problems – the least of them, in fact."

"God!" said Farmer, "what next?"

Fitzgerald enumerated them on the fingers of one hand like a school-marm. "Firstly, I cannot persuade that fool of a Station Master to allocate a private waiting room for you. They are *all* under renovation at this very moment, which I find unbelievable, to say the least. You are very exposed out here – if I were to take a cynical view of the world, I might say 'almost deliberately so'. That being the case, I really think it would be best for you to board and wait for departure. It would at least keep you out of sight."

"I will but …" He pointed vaguely down the platform to the ticket barrier.

Fitzgerald flicked at a piece of coal cinder that had

drifted down on to the lapel of his greatcoat. "Yes, you are worried about the absence of Hubert. That's our second problem. I am too, frankly, but if he does not put in an appearance within the next twenty minutes, we will have to leave without him." He put up a hand to forestall Farmer's objections. "There is no possibility of waiting any further than that. We have to fit within the schedule allocated to us by GNER or we will miss point changes along our line of travel and probably be delayed by other rail traffic, into the bargain."

He paused, taking a brief look around. "And of course we have our third difficulty."

"Christ, there's more?"

"Mr O'Beirne has lost his manservant, a Mr Rix."

For a moment, Farmer stared at the other man, trying to work out why Rix's absence could, in any way, be significant. "Well, I'm sorry for O'Beirne but if we cannot wait for Hubert then I'm damned if I'll wait for this Rix chappie!"

"I agree completely, but for some reason which I am still trying to fathom, O'Beirne entrusted his Foreign Office cipher to Rix. Without it, he will not be able to send or receive coded signals."

"Why, in God's name, did he do that?"

"I feel sure it contravenes a large section of Foreign Ministry regulations but that is the situation we have on our hands. In any case …"

Fitzgerald stopped in mid-flow and stared into the distance behind Farmer, who turned to follow the other's eye-line, hoping it was Hubert. A rather hard-looking man in overcoat and bowler hat was hurrying up the platform towards them lugging a heavy suitcase.

"*Got to be Rix*," thought Farmer.

Another civilian appeared from inside the carriage and walked past them, confronting the newcomer halfway. Fitzgerald called out, "Mr O'Beirne, His Lordship would like an explanation." O'Beirne looked venomously at Rix, motioned him to carry on down the platform and join the other servants and then joined Fitzgerald and Farmer.

He peered up at Farmer through rather thick pince-nez. "Deepest apologies, my Lord. I have just heard the most extraordinary explanation for our delay." O'Beirne was clearly rattled and allowed his Irish accent to become more pronounced than he normally affected within diplomatic circles. "It would seem that Rix was just on the point of leaving my town house, when he received a telephone call from a Colonel Datchett."

He peered at the other two men, hoping to find that they knew Datchett, and receiving a curt shake of the head from Fitzgerald he continued. "It seems he told Rix that the departure was to take place from Paddington and excused the sudden alteration as a tactic to ensure your Lordship's safety. Rix tells me has just come from there, having being told by the Paddington staff that we were still, in fact, to leave from King's Cross."

Farmer and Fitzgerald glanced at each other. It had the feel of Kell all over it in a perverted sort of cloak-and-dagger sense. Fitzgerald motioned towards the train. "Very well, Mr O'Beirne but we really cannot delay any further. Would you and your servant please board and we can be off?"

O'Beirne gestured helplessly. "Unfortunately, Rix sent all our luggage to Paddington. It is on its way here but, with the traffic, could take up to an hour to arrive, he tells me. I really am most dreadfully sorry."

"Well, your luggage will have to follow later."

"Normally, I would agree but, as I explained to you earlier, I am afraid that I entrusted my Foreign Office cipher to Rix. You see, he is also my shorthand clerk. It is *with* the luggage. Without it, I cannot perform my duties as required."

Fitzgerald paused, fuming. "This is unacceptable," he said. "There's nothing for it. We can delay not a moment longer. I suggest you collect Rix from the carriage, arrange with the Station Master for a special train and follow us up to Thurso – at the Foreign Office's expense, mind you. Get your luggage and cipher and, with any luck, you'll be able to catch up."

O'Beirne made to object but a frosty look from Fitzgerald saw him scurry off to join Rix. "And now, sir, we had better board and be on our way."

"Very well, Oswald. See that everyone is on the train and I'll join you in a moment." He leaned closer to the other man. "I want to give Chris as long as I can." Fitzgerald looked at him, nodded and turned away to chivvy the rest of the party on board.

Farmer stood on the platform, momentarily quite alone, staring back through the oily smoke at the barrier in the middle distance. MacPherson, the interpreter, turned back from the train and approached Farmer. "Is anything wrong, sir?" Farmer swivelled round to face the young officer.

"It's Lieutenant ... MacPherson, isn't it – Cameronians, I believe?"

"That's correct, sir. I'm to serve as your Russian interpreter. But I was wondering if there was anything amiss."

Farmer looked sadly at him for a moment and then turned to gaze for the last time at the distant barrier. "No," said. "I was expecting someone but he hasn't turned up."

With that, both men boarded the train and a few moments later, emerging yard-by-yard from a dense, fulminating cloud, it plunged into one of the tunnels immediately outside King's Cross station to begin its long journey to the far north of Scotland.

****

"Sit where you are, Hubert!" snapped Kell.

Chris had tried to rise from his chair in sheer disbelief. "What the hell are you talking about?"

Kell looked over his desk at the younger man. "You are understandably disturbed but take caution in your tone, Lieutenant. I am fully aware that Colonel Farmer is a personal friend of yours and I'm making great allowances for that but there are limits. That aside, let's be clear about something. The fate of the '*Hampshire*', Hubert, is signed, sealed and delivered – to coin a cliché. Unwittingly, Colonel Farmer is about to do the greatest thing he could ever do for his country – *die* for it. This is going to be hard for you to accept because of your personal involvement – God knows, I don't believe I will ever sleep happy again, myself – and you'll probably feel somehow responsible for his fate, but I want you to think about this for a moment. Take all the emotion away and put the rest in the balance."

He pushed his chair away from the desk and sat back. "Yes, we can send 'Kitchener' off to Russia and I have no doubt he would even make a good enough job of it not to be unmasked. But when he returns …"

"We promised him that 'Kitchener' would retire. We

promised him!"

Kell threw him a sympathetic shake of the head, rose from behind his desk and walked over to look out of the window onto the unsuspecting London street. He exhaled long and quiet. "Must you be so naïve? Do you really think the British public would let the 'Hero of Omdurman' *retire* when the greatest conflict the world has ever known is in full swing? You know better than most the sort of casualty figures that come in each and every day, painting the same, hellish picture of our lads being massacred in countries that don't even *belong* to us. We have committees with people like Kipling tearing out their hair trying to devise ways to present the carnage in the best possible light."

He paused for a moment to gather his thoughts and then soberly, but strangely more angry than Hubert had ever seen him, hissed "*There is no best possible light!* It's the nearest thing to Armageddon we'll see *this* side of the Pearly Gates."

He paused to collect himself, conscious of having shown Hubert too much of the inner man, and continued in a calmer manner, "Don't misunderstand me – we will win the War, I have no doubt of that but, also without doubt, there are *years* of this still to come. You, of all people, should need no reminding of what trench warfare is really like – it is *interminable* – and you've seen the repercussions it has here in England."

Hubert leaned forward, ignoring Boissier and Pickup. "I also don't need to be reminded how to keep my word! This is a *doctor*, for Christ's sake! He has saved countless lives, put his *own* life at risk for Kitchener and now you expect me just to stand around while you throw him to the wolves because you have no further use for him! He's not a piece to move around your damn chess board. He's a decent man who put his trust in us."

Irritated, Kell wheezed asthmatically and rubbed his chest. He sat down and leaned back into the seat, weary of it all. "You still don't see to the bottom of this, do you? This *is* his 'further use'." Kell rapped the top of his desk with a knuckle. "This is his *ultimate* use! Think about it – what happens, God forbid, if we have another Ypres? Who will the public cry out for? Who will they expect to ride back on a charger to teach the General Staff 'How to Win a War in Five Easy Steps'?" He paused, waiting for Hubert to answer. "That wasn't a rhetorical question, Lieutenant – *who will they expect to take up the reins*?"

"Of course, they'll call for Kitchener …"

"Then you see our predicament. We cannot allow the Colonel, fine man that he is, to become the *de facto* leader of our war effort and nor do I believe that, in his worst nightmares, he would want to see himself in that position."

"We could still have allowed him to 'die' at home as Kitchener and then quietly return to his medical work as Henry Farmer."

"Certainly. But of what use would that be to the country? We would still have no 'Kitchener' to save the day for the public and we'd have the same public morale problem on our hands that we've been struggling to avoid. From this very office, your own work has shown you that domestic morale is already at rock bottom." Kell rose and paced around the room in precise steps. "For the first time since the Normans, war is being brought to the very doors of British homes by these damn Zeppelins. They've killed hardly anyone but now the 'Zep' has become the bogey-man that keeps our trembling citizens awake at night."

He paused and looked at Hubert's bleached face. "And now … now we have this pathetic show by the Royal Navy at Jutland. *Both* sides claiming victory! It should have been a new Trafalgar – but no – and so our families continue to get their telegrams from the King and somehow find the stomach to carry on the fight." He paused for a moment and looked out of the window once more. "The call will be for another 'Kitchener' – over and over – and when he fails to appear, what then? And should the truth get out that the IRB were at the bottom of it all, as it still might well do, there would be war in our own trenches – you said it yourself down at Broome. God knows what would happen to the Government but one thing is for sure – the War would be lost."

Kell sat back down with a bump. Picking up his pen, he intoned "I cannot let that happen."

Hubert stood and shook off his minders. Kell made a discreet sign that they should let him be. "What have you and Thompson done?"

For a moment, Hubert thought that Kell would keep his own counsel but it was clear, even at this late stage in the game, that he hoped to win Hubert round. "We need a disaster, Hubert", he wheezed.

****

Farmer looked out of the carriage window as Hitchin railway station flashed past. "What do you think happened to Chris, Oswald?"

"As I said before, Henry, I have no idea."

"Sorry ... *sorry*." Farmer held his hands up in mock-surrender. "I know I'm being an old woman. It's just that he was the only constant in this bloody nightmare. He was here before it all began and I was hoping he'd be in at the end. His not being here just has the feeling of doom written all over it."

Fitzgerald sat back into the corner of the seat opposite

Farmer and smiled. "I wouldn't be the least surprised if were to find him waiting for us in Thurso!"

"I do hope …" The clattering of the train across the points made the carriage sway violently, spilling the contents of his red box on to the floor. "Bloody hell!" He bent over to retrieve them and looked up at Fitzgerald. "How many more of these damn things do I have to go through?"

"Three."

"For God's sake!"

****

Kell gazed distractedly out of the window at the unappealing Sunday afternoon view of the park and the Thames beyond. A small puffer was butting its way downstream, leaving a short wake behind and a long memory in the sky. He looked back at Hubert. "Please, let's talk this thing through. I *know* that you will see the inevitability of it all if you just consider the matter without all the … passion."

He waited pointedly until Chris was back in the Chesterfield before continuing. "The idea of the visit to the Russian Court was a God-send. The Czar knows that the next revolution will finish him off so anything that can put some backbone into his General Staff and give him some breathing space has to be a good thing. Cumming, over at 'Six', was uncharacteristically helpful – I suspect something in his own nest of vipers is coming adrift over there. We were able to arrange for the story of the Field Marshal's trip to Russia to be leaked to a high-ranking individual at the Czar's Court we know to be hedging his bets with the Hun. However busy they might have been in the run-up to

Jutland, I had no doubt that Kiel would have made time to deal with someone like Kitchener and, of course, that miserable affair gave us the chance to arrange a departure point closer to open sea. The Clyde is so very heavily protected."

"What did you tell them?" Hubert could barely get the words out.

Kell was warming to his subject, keen to show just how he had engineered the 'perfect crime'. "Well, you must understand that we could not just tell our armed forces to give away information of this nature to the enemy. It had to be done with a degree of … finesse. We used the marine division of Sektion IIIb of the Nachrichten-Abteilung as unwitting accomplices. They have some very powerful signals intelligence capabilities and it's run by an officer who doesn't usually miss a trick – Colonel Walther Nikolai. We arranged for what appeared to be a harmless signal, announcing that a certain channel off Orkney had been swept clear of mines, to be sent from one of Scapa's vessels *en claire* – and not just once but four times in one hour – and not just four times to the local shore station at Longhope but all the way to Admiralty HQ, here in London."

He smiled self-consciously. "I confess was afraid that I might have over-egged the pudding, so to speak, with that last bit but it appears not. Things innocuous, when emphasised, really do acquire a spurious sort of importance to those already predisposed to suspect everything and everyone. People like us, in short. What you don't know is that we have a man actually inside Sektion IIIb – a Norwegian chap – who has informed us that the bait was duly taken. They're looking very hard at Birsay. If Nikolai misses the meaning of the signals, he's not worth his rations but I'm betting he'll match them up with the Russian leaks. Lloyd George's calling off the journey had nothing to do with the Easter Rising – we tipped him the wink, so to speak." Kell fell silent for a moment and had the grace to cough apologetically. "He is to be the new Secretary of State for War."

Hubert sneered. "It doesn't surprise me – the man is an opportunistic coward. And what do you plan to do if Nikolai doesn't fall for it?"

"As I say, our informer suggests that they already have but you're perfectly right: they could still mess it up. And so we come to Plan B. Clearly, we cannot rely on the Germans alone. Certainly, we want to heap the blame on them and we need some form of trail which shows that they got the original story from the Russian Court backed up, sadly, by the aforesaid lapses in our own naval protocols. But they *might* get a submarine to the correct spot, they *might* lay the mines in the correct position, the 'Hampshire' *might* run into them, the ship *might* sink, Kitchener *might* be killed in the explosion or drowned as a result." He smiled coldly at Boissier and Pickup. "Too many 'mights'. Thus, we come to our old friend and temporary colleague – Mr Duquesne."

"*Duquesne!*" Hubert leaned forward on Kell's desk, appalled. "Are you telling me we've climbed into bed with Fritz Duquesne?"

Kell wrinkled his nose at the metaphor. "Well, of, course, I wouldn't put it quite like that – the amusing thing is he doesn't *know* it's us. Cumming discovered that Nikolai had inserted Duquesne back into the country to report on shipping movements in the run-up to Jutland. He was supposed to contact 'Colonel Datchett' on arrival to get his exit instructions. The good Colonel, ably played by Mr Boissier here, changed his plans."

Hubert knew Duquesne to be a Boer working for German intelligence. "Duquesne'll stop at nothing to get a chance to kill Kitchener. He hates the British – and I'm beginning to see why." He looked Kell in the eye. "I'll see to it that the General Staff hear of this. Whatever the outcome, you're finished."

"I'm sorry, Hubert, but the Prime Minister himself has sanctioned this operation." He smiled benignly at Hubert's stupefied expression. "But where were we? You've made me lose my place. Duquesne … yes, we were speaking of Duquesne. Mr Duquesne had a further chat with our Colonel Datchett at Paddington Station. 'Colonel Datchett', by the way, is a suitably disaffected and entirely fictitious officer of the British Army who has been passing low-grade information, via Duquesne, to the German intelligence services for some time now. Boissier, or Colonel Datchett I should say, provided Duquesne with documents proving that he was Mr Rix – O'Beirne's manservant. Our Boer has developed, at Datchett's suggestion, a small but rather nasty explosive device to be planted in Kitchener's cabin. It will detonate when 'His Lordship' opens it and, should the ship hit a mine first, it will go off in what I am told is called 'sympathetic detonation'. It's in the form of a red dispatch box. You, yourself, signed for it the other day.

In addition, Cumming currently has two of his men on board the *Hampshire* who have been rather busy. A cleat which would normally secure one of the watertight doors to the boiler room has been cut almost through. You can't see the damage, unless you're looking for it, but it's there and, just in case, another of those enterprising lads from 'Six' has arranged for the ship's blacksmith to be removed. He will not be repairing it, even if it is discovered. Duquesne will ensure that the cleat is broken off by dint of a sharp blow with a lump hammer, meaning that the door will not be capable of a water-tight seal. The effect of cold seawater touching the boilers when they are under power is, I am assured, catastrophic. With U-Boat, bomb and boilers, we think we have all angles covered. The ship, I'm afraid, is destined for the bottom."

Kell sat back, steepling his fingers. "He really is a very talented individual, this Duquesne. Pity he won't work for us," he said, reflectively.

Hubert could not believe that even Asquith was in on the plot. *How far did it go?* "What about O'Beirne? Is he *aware* of the part he's playing in Farmer's death and that he might not even survive?"

Kell dismissed the question with an irritated wave of the hand. "Of course not! We have simply told O'Beirne that an MI5 agent will accompany him in the guise of his manservant. He has no idea that he is a very dangerous German agent. No-one else knows what Rix looks like and the real thing is currently enjoying an extended, if enforced, holiday at one of our nicer safe houses in the Lake District. Duquesne knows all of this but thinks Datchett has arranged it for the benefit of Kaiser Bill. It's quite neat, really."

This was enough for Hubert. Farmer's train would have left by now and the clock was ticking. He made a dash from his seat to the door but was tackled by Pickup before he had gone more than two or three steps. With his usual savagery, Pickup kneed him in the kidneys and pulled him to his feet. Pushing his left arm behind his back, he threw him back into the seat.

"Gently, Pickup. Remember that Lieutenant Hubert is still an invalid." Kell placed a hand on Hubert's shoulder. "You are an intelligent young man who sees his friend sleep-walking to an underserved death. It is natural that you want to warn him or to save him in some way but you must realise the arithmetic at stake here. I have proposed, and it has been sanctioned at the highest levels, that we sacrifice over 700 officers and men in order to avoid the immeasurably greater loss we would sustain should the true nature of Kitchener's death become public. I have done so in the belief that this strategy will give such a boost to public morale that we may *save* thousands at the Front – not just today but every day – and possibly shorten the War by God knows how many months. Years, perhaps. Instead of the somewhat tacky death Lord Kitchener suffered at the hands of an IRB thug, he will die an honourable one at those of the Hun and by that death help us avoid the inevitable defeat we would face in the trenches."

"You are going to kill hundreds of men on the off-chance that it will keep the lid on the assassination. Do the words 'irony' and 'stupidity' mean nothing to you?" Hubert spat.

Kell stood back from Hubert's seat. "Of course they do! I am no monster, whatever you may think." Kell paused for a moment, head drooping slightly, and muttered, "My part in arranging their deaths weighs heavily on my conscience and will continue to do so for the rest of my life, I suspect. I have no doubt of it. I'm not a murderer." He fiddled for a moment with his letter opener before setting it down sharply on the desk and glancing at Hubert. "But my duty is to make impossible decisions like this. In that respect, I hold the fate of the country in my hands. You *must* see that you cannot be allowed to interfere and, to make sure of that, I'm placing you under house arrest. It will all be over in a day or so and any allegations from you after that point concerning the 'truth' will seem laughable in the light of events."

He nodded to Boissier and Pickup, "Take the Lieutenant to his apartment and look after him until you are relieved."

****

Hubert moved to get up but groaned back into the sofa. With infinite care, he rolled over on to his stomach until he could slide on to his knees, facing the cushions, and lever himself up to an approximation of the standing position. Boissier and Pickup had decided to assume a broad, liberal interpretation of Kell's instructions. One of Hubert's eyes was closing and he suspected a cracked rib or two. The bathroom of his little flat was as least three yards away but, by taking the occasional rest to catch his breath, he made it in record time. Around ten minutes, he figured.

He teased his Sam Browne off and peered into the mirror which promptly advised him not to look again. He splashed his face with water, spitting bloodily into the wash basin. When he eventually stood up, the room was still spinning despite his gripping the ceramics. *Just go and lie down!* He pushed the thought away but another filled the vacuum ... *Henry!* That brought matters into more focus. *He had to get out and warn him!*

Boissier had said that he and Pickup were going to the 'Dolphin', across the road. Hubert stumbled back into his living room and looked down at the pub. Pickup, on the alert, saw him and raised a sardonic glass. From any window table on the Red Lion Street side, they were able to see the communal entrance to his group of flats, especially since the pub's original glass, frosted and patterned, was now ordinary glazing as a result of a Zeppelin attack last September. One of the regulars was killed outside when the front of the pub was blown in. The scorch marks were still visible on the pale brick of the buildings on the other side of the passage....

"Now *there's* an idea."

Suddenly, he was back in February standing outside the

pub with one of the Registry girls – Honoria – who had been given the task of finding him suitable accommodation after his release from Farnham. "I *do* hope you like it," she said, "I know you need somewhere quiet and this part of Holborn is still fairly peaceful." She paused and added, "In fact, I live just around the corner down there." Hubert leaned back against the wall of the "Dolphin", exhausted even by the exercise of getting here by cab from the Strand. He nodded his head upward at the scaffolding that marred the frontage of what was to be his new home.

"What's all this in aid of?" he said in a raspy whisper.

"Damage from the Zepplin bombs but I'm told that it'll all be gone in a month. Even then, isn't it a *lovely* little place?" She lisped the words through slightly prominent teeth.

Hubert concurred, although becoming aware of her pressing a little too close for comfort. Sure enough, by the beginning of April, the façade of the building had forgotten the attack had ever happened. The rear of it, however, out of sight of the world, was still covered with ladders, ropes and the assorted mysteries of the British workman. Hubert had complained time and again about it to the concierge but had received the stock answer in reply, "There's a War on, y'know!"

Now, sending up a silent prayer to little Napoleons the world over, he walked slowly through to the kitchen, holding on to almost everything vertical along the way and finishing off with an explosive coughing fit over the sink. There was blood again – not a lot but enough to make him feel sorry for himself. *Pickup was a real bastard.* He rinsed the sink, painfully pushed up the window and leaned out. A couple of feet away to the right and level with his kitchen was the top of a ladder leaning against the back wall of his flat.

****

Anne was back at the grindstone, still fuming about Thompson. It had been an easy day so far but the stifling monotony of it all was killing her by imperceptible degrees. So, when the creaky spring of the swing door announced a new arrival, she barely raised her eyes. And when no-one asked for a towel, she exhaled in exasperation.

"Would you like a …" She glanced around, searching for a customer, and was about to put it down to day-dreaming when she glimpsed a few locks of black hair just peeking over the far side of the counter. Cautiously, she jumped up to lean forward and get a better view. "Oh, my God!" She scampered around the desk and crouched down beside Hubert. "What happened to you, Lieutenant?" she asked.

"Chris! It's 'Chris' to you. I thought we settled all that down at Broome," he rasped in pain.

Anne rolled her eyes. "Shut up, stand up and let me get you round behind the counter. There's a pretty good first aid kit there."

For once, Hubert was in no mood to argue but time was pressing. "No," he said. "There's no time. Bring the kit with you and see if we can grab a cab. We need to get to King's Cross, pronto."

Anne looked at him for a second and knew that matters were serious. "Stay right there while I sort out transportation."

"My very thoughts."

Giving him an old-fashioned up-and-down look, she bustled off.

Five minutes later, on their way to the Station, Hubert

gave her the main headings of everything that had happened since they last met while she attended to the visible bruises and cuts he had sustained courtesy of Boissier and Pickup. His clumsy descent down the scaffolding had done nothing to help, either.

"I cannot believe it," she said when Hubert outlined Kell's plans for the *Hampshire*. "No, I know it *must* be true if you say it is but how can any man contemplate such a crime?"

Hubert grimaced for a moment while the cab swayed across a tram line junction. "To be honest, I think it has hit the old man fairly hard to come to this pass."

She looked at him aghast. "Are you seriously condoning this?"

"Of course not! Henry is my closest friend. All I'm trying to say is that, for Kell, he did the arithmetic and, while the answer appalled him, he believed the logic of it all to be unanswerable. He sees it as his *duty* to make the decision that will send Henry and 700-odd sailors to the bottom. It's that or the loss of the War – and, remember, he *could* have let me just go down with the ship." He sat still for a moment, looking at Anne. The real Kitchener was already dead but now, to create a more acceptable story, his friend would follow him. His eyes blazed. "Thank God it's not *my* job to take decisions like that but I'm damned if I'll let Henry die without a fight."

Anne sat back and smiled archly. "You believe you're – what was it – 'fit to fight'?"

"Fine, fine – mock the afflicted. Just patch me up, get me to the train and I'll wish you *adieu*."

She chuckled. "Not a chance. *One* blunt instrument in this enterprise is more than enough."

****

"You were told to remain with Hubert. Have I misunderstood my own orders?" Kell's voice dripped with sarcasm.

Boissier bristled. "We were only just across the road, sir."

"In a public house, was it not?"

"Yes, sir. But we could see the windows of his flat."

"But *not* the back." Kell sat back in his chair and looked over steepled fingers at the two men standing, shame-faced, in front of his desk. "We now have some serious damage limitation to handle because of you two. God knows what Hubert is going to do but we can be sure it will be connected, in some way or other, with pulling Colonel Farmer out of the soup. If he reaches the *Hampshire* and rescues him, the entire story will reach the ears of the Press. Certain as Christmas. It will make Repington's day."

Pickup made a snort of derision. "There's no chance he's ever going to reach the ship before it sails. And, even if he did, they would never let him on board. They'll just arrest him."

"You really are as foolish as you look." Kell was icy cold. "What do you think he'll be saying while they detain him? Do you think he'll sit there in silence while Farmer goes off to meet his Maker? He'll be shouting everything at the top of his voice to prevent the ship putting to sea. When it gets to Colonel Farmer's ears, he'll own up to the whole affair!"

Pickup looked at the carpet for a moment to allow Kell's anger to wash over him.

"And there's another complication – while you two were

heading back here, I had a word with Sir Basil. He tells me that Miss Banfield has also 'disappeared' herself. It takes no great leap of the imagination to assume that she is assisting Hubert. She already had concerns about Kitchener and, if they are in league with one another, our problems go up by an entire order of magnitude."

"She'll give us no problem," sneered Pickup. "We had a quiet word with her. She's probably taking a day or two off to recover." He giggled at Boissier, who remained stony-faced and silent.

"Be quiet," said Kell in a monotone. It was perfectly clear that, although Hubert was in a bad way physically, he had the sheer bloody-mindedness to reach Farmer somehow. Banfield's involvement would help to mitigate some of Hubert's physical weakness. They had to be stopped and, unfortunately, that meant bringing in Thompson.

"The Station Master at Kings Cross informs me that O'Beirne and Duquesne have reserved a special train to take them up to Thurso. Hubert will undoubtedly start at Kings Cross and he'll find out about the special. Once he learns that O'Beirne is on board, he'll do his best to expose Duquesne and we cannot allow that to happen under any circumstance. This is what the two of you are going to do – get over to Kings Cross before that train leaves and secure them both. Stay with them on the train and head for Orkney. Thompson will arrange for the Scottish police to take custody of your guests at Thurso and escort them back down to me. That should keep Hubert out of mischief for a couple of days at least. After the ship goes down, prevent anyone on the main island making successful rescue attempts. If Farmer were to be found alive we'd have serious questions to answer. The same goes for any sailor coming ashore with tales of an MI5 officer running loose around the ship, just in case you don't manage to lay hands on our Canadian. Thompson will also alert Police Forces up and down the line of travel with some story of a foreign agent, intent on sabotage at Scapa, heading their way."

He toyed with his paper knife again for a moment. "This is the last chance you have to redeem yourselves but …" He pointed the tip of the knife towards them, "... bear something in mind. Should you fail in this, I *promise* you shall find yourselves in uniform and heading for Flanders within twenty-four hours. Make no mistake about that."

Boissier blanched.

"Report to Major Haldane and sort out warrants, cover story and all the rest of it."

Boissier and Pickup looked at each other. Clearly, they had questions to ask but Kell was in no mood to prolong the interview. He had already picked up his pen.

"Get out of my office."

****

Anne scampered back into the space behind an abandoned gaggle of luggage bogies in the arches between Platforms 1 and 2. Hubert was sitting mournfully on the ground, clutching his ribs. She smiled sympathetically at him. "How're things with you, Lieutenant?"

Hubert knew – just *knew* – that this was 'the' girl. She just didn't know it yet, poor thing. "I thought we had sorted out the 'Lieutenant' business?"

"We've no time for all that nonsense, you idiot, so pay attention. I flashed my Special Branch warrant card and administered a one-way interview to the Station Master. Colonel Farmer left as planned but there was the problem with O'Beirne and this Rix man you told me about. They arranged a special to take them after the main party. It's leaving in forty minutes from Platform 9 and because it will make no stops apart from water and coal, it'll get into Thurso only an hour or so after them. I put the fear of God into the man and he's sworn to secrecy but he's in on something, I'm sure. If I'd had more time, I'd have dragged it out of him."

Catching sight of Hubert staring at her, she stopped. "What?"

"You're a bit frightening sometimes – did you know that?"

"As I say, shut up and listen. From what he said – and more from what he *didn't* say – there are dirty tricks afoot. I take it that's something to do with *your* brethren. He was *told* not to give 'Kitchener' cover in any of the waiting rooms so that the great unwashed could stare at him."

Hubert leaned back against the brick archway. "It's Kell and Thompson. They want him exposed and vulnerable." He coughed wretchedly and then added, "It also gives yet another lie to the IRB if they decide to announce his murder. Half the British Army and their families will have seen him today waiting for a train."

Anne leaned down to help Hubert, groaning, to his feet. "Well, we're getting on that train – baggage carriage sounds the best bet – and then we can start thinking about what we're going to do once we reach Scapa because I just don't see myself making any serious dent in the Royal Navy."

"You underestimate yourself," he gasped, as he tried to move into a more comfortable position. "It's all part of your charm."

CHAPTER 7

Sunday, 4 June 1916 2050 hours – Monday, 5 June 1916 1645 hours

Anne's warrant card worked its magic again – this time on the guard checking the luggage van. "Where can I get one of those?" whined Hubert dramatically. Commanding him – once again – to shut up, she helped him into the most comfortable spot she could find among the trunks and suitcases. That done, she disappeared for a moment back into the station to forage for things edible. He was getting worried the train would leave without her when she made a re-appearance, loaded with food and drink.

"Sorry. One of our friends up front kept sticking his head out of the window. I'm not sure why but I didn't like the idea of his seeing me get on board so I had to hide a couple of times."

The guard looked round the door, "Right, miss, we're off. Shall I let the party in First Class know you're here?"

Anne was about to agree when she felt the hidden pressure of Hubert's hand on her back. "No", she said, "Best not. Let's just leave it for the moment."

"Right-o. Oh, by the way, my name is …"

She held up her hand, "Really grateful for your help but it's better if we keep names out of it."

The guard tapped the side of his nose, as though he understood what was going on. "A nod's as good as a wink."

When the door had closed, she rounded on Hubert. "What was *that* in aid of?"

"I'm like you, only more so – I'm not sure it's a great idea letting *anyone* know we're on the train. God knows the people Kell's got in the palm of his hand. It seems clear as day that we should get ourselves into O'Beirne's compartment and give him the SP on his 'MI5' companion but I'm starting to think it might be best to let Duquesne relax – let his guard down a little. We can always get the Royal Navy to bounce up and down on him when we get to Thurso. Let's just lay low and figure out exactly what we're going to do once we get there. I had some time to think when you abandoned me and if you can come up with any other way to reach Henry except on board the *Hampshire*, then you're a better man than I am, Gunga Din. He'll have transferred over there from the flagship by the time we arrive. The good thing is that it won't set sail until that lot up front gets there – so it looks like *I'll* have to convince the Captain of the *Hampshire* that he and his men have been sold to the Hun by MI5." He smiled ruefully at Anne. "Won't be an easy sell."

She leaned back against a rather damp and peeling bulkhead. "Yes but when I'm able to back your story …"

He snorted inelegantly, "Use your head. When was the

last time a woman seen on a British warship at sea – apart from being stuck on the prow?"

"Ah ... hadn't thought of that ... you may conceivably have a point."

"Has Special Branch any resources we can use in the frozen north?"

She paused for a moment. "Well ... yes. There's a trawler we keep at Wick for all sorts of sneaky-beaky stuff, mostly to do with Irish Nationalists, recently."

He glanced up at her, hearing the evasion in her tone. "You're prevaricating, Special, what aren't you telling me?"

"Nothing – drop it." She looked down at him. "You still look pretty rubbish. How are you feeling?"

"I'll be fine in a little while. I just have to take a long run at breathing easily these days." He beamed at her, "But my curiosity is unimpaired."

"I *could* help you have a relapse."

****

"I'm very sorry, Mr O'Beirne, but I was inserted into this operation at very short notice. Colonel Datchett needed to brief me at the last possible moment at Paddington," Duquesne said soothingly.

O'Beirne remained ruffled. "I was made to look a fool in front of Lord Kitchener himself. Whoever is responsible for this nonsense will be hearing from the Foreign Office the moment we reach St Petersburg. I was only informed early this morning that you were to substitute for Rix and …" He peered myopically across at Duquesne. "Your accent – you're South African, are you not?"

Duquesne cursed inwardly. He *had* been trying to sound English. "I am," he said, curtly. "I was born there and lived in Durban until I was a young man. Does that bother you?"

The train, at that moment, entered the first of the series of tunnels leading the track away from King's Cross. The carriage had been hastily prepared for the unexpected group and the window had been left ajar by someone to air the long-unused carriage. Billows of sooty smoke flooded in. O'Beirne stood sharply up, snapped the window shut and looked down at his uninvited travelling companion. He appeared to be about forty years old, compactly-built and dark complexioned. A casual glance at that clean-shaven face would put him down as a terror with the ladies but anything closer would have to involve those sunken eyes; they shifted deceitfully in the shadows cast beneath prominent brow ridges – the eyes of a liar.

"Of course not. That particular disagreement is thousands of miles away and a long time ago, now." He sat down and adjusted his thick-lensed pince-nez. "But, since we are to work together, we need to straighten a few things out. For example, may I have the honour of your *real* name – or is that not permitted?"

"Certainly. It's Captain Claude Stoughton." He reached over to receive a reluctant handshake from O'Beirne. "Of the *British* Army," he added, just for spice.

"Really?"

"Actually, the Western Australian Light Horse."

"I see. Well, Captain, we will be in the company of the great and the good in a few hours and I have been given only the most elementary idea of the reasons for your appearance here. Before we make a complete shambles of the whole thing, is there any chance that you might enlighten me concerning the whys and the wherefores?"

Duquesne squirmed a little for effect and glanced across from under his eyebrows at the little bookworm. "As you might imagine, I am constrained by matters of security but I think I would be excused, given the circumstances, if I were to give you a general idea." He smiled at the other man, wondering how it would feel to throttle him. Right now. No – he had to be professional and concentrate on the big picture. Perhaps O'Beirne could be a sort of 'perk' of the job – something to be saved up and savoured at the right moment.

"Well?"

Duquesne trembled a little at the other man's irritation – one of your typical "milords" of the bastard English race. "Your time's coming *very* soon," he thought.

"Your pardon," he murmured, "I was miles away."

****

In a compartment of the second class carriage just in front of the guard's van, Pickup snickered as he collapsed onto the bench seat. "That was a lucky break, your spotting our boy Duquesne!"

Boissier finished stowing his luggage in the overhead rack and smiled frostily at the other man. "If he had, it would have messed up the whole Colonel Datchett story. Better that he plays his part and, hopefully, goes down with the ship."

"And if he escapes?"

"Colonel Datchett," he gestured, self-deprecatingly at himself, "is here to rescue him. Kell has plans to sort out the *real* Rix so that the story never gets out. *Our* Rix, as an individual, is due for a watery grave, I fear. We are supposed to extract Duquesne if we can and a grateful government will give the real Mr Rix, formerly resident of the Lake District, a new life – better than being a shorthand clerk and valet."

"And then we dispose of Duquesne." Pickup sighed contentedly.

Boissier looked at his reflection in the window to check that his tie was still immaculately centred. "That's the odd thing," he said. "Kell wants him released and I couldn't draw him on it. He has something up his sleeve with respect to our little Boer."

"What about Hubert and Farmer ... *and* Fitzgerald?" asked Pickup. "And there's MacLaughlin, too, of course."

Boissier patted his breast pocket. "I have a writ from Haldane authorising us to invoke martial law if we need to and we'll have the help of an officer of the Glasgow Police, no less – an Inspector Vance. We're supposed to meet up with him at Stromness. Kell has told him just enough of the story to make him useful. Then, straight onto the mainland of Orkney while that lot are enjoying their canapés with Jellicoe. If Duquesne can tell the time and doesn't blow himself up priming the ghastly thing, the *Hampshire* should have an irritating hole in its side while it's passing Skaill Bay or the Brough of Birsay. God, but I hate saying these bloody Scotch names. They leave a ghastly taste behind in one's mouth. Anyway, it's difficult to tell exactly when they'll get to the 'drop-off' point," he chuckled. "It depends on their departure time and weather, I suppose, but it should be sometime mid-evening tomorrow. We need to get ourselves a motorcar – perhaps Vance will have sorted that out – and patrol the shore road thereabouts to ensure that no-one connected with Kitchener gets rescued by the local 'heroes'. Our cover stories for the plebs are that I am *Lieutenant* Boissier of the RMA and you, believe it or not, are a Naval Surgeon. They really exist, apparently, both of them. We should look as though we're there to help but if any of the Broome lot come our way …

Now, as for Hubert and that Banfield girl, we'll wait until we're well away from London and pay them a visit. They must be *so* uncomfortable in the guard's van." He closed his eyes and lay back to take a nap but blinked awake again, "One final thing – we're to remember that Cumming has a couple of his boys on the Hampshire doing sneaky stuff. One of them is making sure the radios are disabled and the other is dealing with that water-tight door – supposedly a Navy rating and an Army private. We're to look after them if they survive."

Pickup gazed vacantly out of the window as the train left the tunnel. "And if any of those in the know get ashore?"

"We drown them like puppies."

****

Hubert was showing signs of recovering and was able to stand up without too much discomfort, even with the movement of the train. Anne gave him a professional look up and down. "I'm not trying to pry but someone told me that you were gassed at Ypres, Lieutenant. Is that right?"

"'Chris', woman!"

"For goodness' sake, all right – *Chris!*"

Hubert beamed affectionately.

Anne ignored it and persisted. "So why are you still in uniform? You're clearly very ill."

Hubert sat quickly down on one of the trunks as the

carriage swayed on a bend and grimaced at her. "The alternative is just too dreadful to contemplate – working for my father."

Anne's 'ah' said it all. "But you *are* going to get better, aren't you?"

"Sure," he lied.

"Do you mind telling me what happened?" asked Anne, when further details seemed to be unforthcoming. Hubert made to offer another flippant remark but she held up a hand. "No, no – don't. Don't deflect the question. No-one really knows what it's like over there. I have relatives who come home on leave and can't talk about any of it. All they want to do is to get back to the Front again – back among their friends. Everyone I meet says the same. If you can bear to, I'd like to know."

It dawned on Hubert that this tiny girl somehow *needed* to know, to make all her own efforts matter and – *somehow* – to put the miserable existence enforced, even on her, by the War into some sort of context. Yet again, he found himself admiring her "Head Girl" attitude.

"Actually", he began, "it was all rather fun …"

Anne was finishing off a sandwich. "What!" she choked, appalled.

"... except for the last bit, of course." He chuckled for a moment and then become sombre. "All that death around me yet, somehow, I never felt so alive. I suppose it was the excitement of the thing – you know, placing your life in the hands of others and knowing you were responsible for theirs. It was as if life just sort of ... made sense, you know? It was all so very ... well, *simple*." He came back to the moment and laughed self-consciously. "Sorry, I'm sounding a bit mystical."

Anne wasn't laughing. "Not a bit of it – go on," she said.

"Well, I was with Princess Pat's Light Infantry in a trench line on the Ypres Salient that had just been vacated by the French." He grunted. "Didn't clean up after themselves, either, the filthy swine. Anyway, my platoon was renowned as the best snatch squad on the Front."

"*Snatch* squad?"

"Yep, snatch squad. We'd snatch Germans. Same old route every night – along the trench, turn right at the barbed wire, past the Frog legs and …"

"Frog legs! What do you mean – 'Frog legs'?"

"Just what I say – the French had held this trench before us. They'd had to bury some of their guys in its eastern wall and the rain and shelling had caused it to subside a bit. The legs of one of the dead Frenchies ended up sticking out of the wall."

Anne looked slightly sick at the thought and placed the remains of her sandwich carefully down on its wrapper, perched on top of a nearby trunk. "Don't tell me any more about that, please."

"He was a very helpful chap," said Hubert, stoutly. "*Great* marker in the dark; we became quite fond of him."

"That image is going to stay with me for a long time, so *enough* of it, please! What did you do when you reached the wire?"

"We'd go over the top into the next trench, which was occupied by the Hun. The idea was to dispose of any guards who were ill-advised enough to have remained awake, grab the nearest non-commissioned officer and then drag him home for tea and questions. We did that many a time."

"And then?"

Hubert laid his head back against a brass-banded steamer trunk. "And then the Hun went and spoiled it all." He took a gulp of the tea Anne had brought and continued. "In April of last year, my unit was near St Julien – April 22nd it was – taking charge of a sector about 5000 yards long. We were ordered forward, sandwiched in between the French on our left and the Brits on the right, when suddenly we had to duck a bit because of a German bombardment. I jumped into one of the Hun trenches with my lads, ready for a bit of mayhem when everything seemed to go quiet. There was no more shouting and screaming – only this ... deafening silence." He shook his head, still amazed. "It was so *sudden*."

Absent-mindedly, Anne rubbed away the goose pimples on her arms. "Was that the gas?"

Hubert nodded. "It was in the shells they had just dropped on us. At first, we thought the Hun were advancing behind a cover of smoke but then the trench began filling up with this greenish fog. It sort of sinks to the bottom of things like a cold mist and *insinuates* itself everywhere." He closed his eyes against the memory. "And then my lads started coughing and retching. Most of them managed to jump back out but the Hun attacked in real force. They had their tails up, I can tell you. They knew we couldn't argue with chlorine."

"Why didn't you get away with your men?"

Hubert ran his fingers through his hair and exhaled, the memory jabbing at his conscious thought. "You don't know what Ypres is like. The water table is pretty high there – not far below the surface – and with all the rain, the shelling and heavy transport, the whole country is one big glutinous bog. It's like thick, sticky glue. So, with that, and then probably the previous impact of the shells, the walls of the trench suddenly slid in on me. I was turned over and over and eventually trapped."

"You poor thing," she whispered.

"It was not," he smiled sadly, "my favourite day. But here's a thing – being sucked in to that trench probably saved my life. It's right what they say about clouds and silver linings. My lads who got out were mown down to a man by the Germans. They machine-gunned all those boys who were staggering about, gasping for air." He turned to look steadily at her. "And you ask me why I'm still in uniform."

"I didn't know. Of course, I didn't know."

Hubert was immediately contrite and reached out to brush her arm. "How could you? How can anyone who wasn't there? But that's why I'd give *my* last, gasping breath to shoot the swine or bring us even one step closer to winning this thing."

"How did they find you?"

"It took a while. The Germans mounted quite a push and all our lot had to move back. It left a wide open door at the Salient but, of course, the Hun couldn't take advantage of it immediately because they would have had to breathe in the gas, too – the big problem with that sort of weapon. We recovered much of the ground later and that's when a lad from the Queen Victoria Rifles found me. I was half submerged upside-down in pretty solid mud but, luckily, my head had found the opening to one of the living areas below ground or I would have suffocated. The mud probably helped me not to breathe in any more gas, too. It's got an odd smell like pineapple and pepper mixed together. Did you know that?"

Anne shook her head.

"So I ended up in the CCS at Poperinghe – 'Pops' to you and me – it's only a few miles from Ypres. I remember that day so clearly – coughing and gasping for air. My lungs were burning yet they felt as though they had been filled with water – you know, like when you take a drink but breathe it down the wrong way?"

She nodded mutely, mouth slightly open.

"There were quite a few like me in that room. Sure, many others had the usual wounds but all I can remember is the sound of those men gasping like landed fish. The docs hadn't a clue how to treat them – it was all so new. I was there for two days and, one by one, those poor lads just … just drowned."

"How ... how could they *drown*? I don't understand."

"That's what it's called – 'dry land drowning'. The lungs just fill up with fluid. There's nothing that can be done. There was a man next to me, a trooper from the Royal Canadian Dragoons, a big strong lad. My abiding memory of him was his lips – they had gone a sort of plum colour. There wasn't a mark on him but he'd been gassed badly. I remember him saying over and over again to the staff, '*I can't die, I can't die – is there nothing you can do for me?*' He was the first to go."

Anne was moved by the suffering he had gone through and desperately wanted to offer words of sympathy and comfort but … what to say? His world had been so far beyond anything she had ever experienced, thank God. To all intents and purposes, he was a different species of Man. He might look like all the other boys she had known before the War but somehow he and his kind had been set apart by the horrors of the Trenches. And yet – somehow – he still showed these flashes of childish humour and, yes, *impertinence*. How could anyone retain the slightest vestige of what he once was after all that? But he did.

She shook her head slowly. "What can I say?"

He smiled and shook his head in reply. "Anyway, they shipped me back to Blighty and I ended up at the hospital at Netley. Do you know it?"

"It's near Southampton, isn't it?"

"That's right – not far from the port of entry – and that's where I first cast eyes on our Henry."

She beamed a damp smile. "You think a lot of him, don't you?"

"The man's a saint – a clumsy one, I grant you – but saint he is. When he goes through the Pearly Gates, my bet is that he rips his tunic on it but he's the man who put me back together."

****

"You mean that Casement's supporters are trying to brand His Lordship ... *homosexual*?" O'Beirne was disgusted. As an Irishman himself, the very idea of an Irish Knight of the Realm rebelling against the Crown was unthinkable. Casement was beyond the pale as far as he was concerned. Killing Kitchener was one thing but this ... "How do you know this?"

Duquesne had his part to play, as dictated by 'Colonel Datchett' at their Paddington meeting, and he dealt the hand deftly. He glanced around the room like a spy from a novel before leaning close to O'Beirne. "You understand that this must go no further," he murmured. O'Beirne nodded a shocked assent. "There is a Turkish Baths establishment in London where people of that persuasion go. Known associates of Trebitsch Lincoln were seen to enter it and part of their conversation was overheard. From then on, they were followed and they led us to others.

Their general idea, apparently, was to put together a dossier that described places and dates Lord Kitchener had visited. Later, a fictitious thread of 'activities' would be woven, making it particularly hard to disprove – especially after his death."

"His *death*! What on earth do you mean?"

"Once the dossier was complete, His Lordship's death would have been engineered. It's very hard to deny the facts when you are no longer living and, of course, one cannot libel the dead."

"This is despicable! And what is your role to be in preventing all of this?"

Duquesne began reeling him in gently – people *so* liked to feel that they were 'in the know'. "I need to be as close to His Lordship's group as possible during the voyage. I particularly need to see his cabin to ensure there is nothing in there he wouldn't like. The Navy will do their best to keep him from harm but, frankly, they have no idea of this sort of work."

"I do so despise this sort of 'Le Queux' stuff. It is so underhand."

"But necessary, sir. The enemy have their people everywhere."

"I pray to God that unnatural traitor, Roger Casement, gets his just deserts."

****

Farmer had asked, yet again, his opinion of Hubert's non-appearance at the station and Fitzgerald, remarkably composed, could only restate his earlier thoughts but it was becoming increasingly clear that something had detained

Hubert against his will. It had the worrisome smell of MI5 all over it.

He bent his head to resume the letter he had been composing to his family:

'If I do not return with my friend, you may be sure that foul play has probably been the means of our not doing so, but I hope for the best.'

He'd post it in Thurso. Looking over at Farmer, the vulnerability of the other man was clear to see – frightened, not of physical danger, but of letting Kitchener down. "Let's go over tomorrow's programme of events, Henry. Have you read the Admiralty's preliminary report of the Jutland business? I have a copy here, if you need it."

"No, I *have* seen it – turgid stuff and a very unsatisfactory ending."

"I have to agree but Jellicoe will want to discuss it all and probably Beatty's views on the shells we were using, into the bargain."

"Ah, yes. Chris mentioned something about that the other day. So what was the problem, exactly?"

"We were apparently hitting targets but doing no real damage."

"The shells weren't exploding?"

"No, in fact they made very loud bangs. The problem is that they are meant to be armour-piercing. The explosive is not meant to detonate until the fuse sets it off *after* the shell has penetrated the armour – *inside* the ship, in other words."

"And …"

"And it seems that the explosive the Royal Navy uses …" He flipped a page in the report, "... 'Liddite' is being set off by the shock of impact itself – the shell is detonating on the *outside* of the target. Apparently some very poorly armoured ships got away after direct hits from our fifteen inch guns. On the other hand, the German High Seas Fleet is using TNT that has no such problem. Beatty estimates that we could have sent another six enemy ships to the bottom of the North Sea if we had been using it. But what is worse is that the Admiralty have known about this problem for some time. In fact, Jellicoe himself tried to do something about it fairly recently but when he was made Admiral of the Fleet, the matter was quietly dropped by those who succeeded him."

"Well that's something useful I might do. I can get that back onto Jellicoe's agenda. Failing to reach a decisive victory simply because of poor quality materials is unforgiveable."

"Absolutely, but we *were* hampered by other issues, too."

"Such as?"

"The Germans made use of a great deal of smoke during the battle and, half the time, neither Jellicoe nor Beatty had any idea where the enemy was, despite many of our ships maintaining contact with the enemy. Jellicoe's battle plan clearly called upon all Captains to keep the Admiral abreast of the enemy's movements using *radio* but it appears that too many of our senior officers felt more comfortable using 'tried and tested' methods like semaphore. To be honest, it seems to me that it's a bit pointless flapping a few flags if you're enveloped in black, oily smoke. Quite simply, they are failing to move with the times." He looked up from the paper and smiled, "But, of course, I am no sailor."

"So Liddite and Luddite?"

For the very first time in their acquaintance, Fitzgerald gave a crack of laughter. "Very good! Put it like that to

Jellicoe. He'll enjoy it."

"After a quick meal on the *Iron Duke*, what then?"

"They'll have brought the *Hampshire* close to the flagship, so a quick trip across will see us on board and we can get you settled in after the usual handshakes all round." He shifted uncomfortably, "There *is* one thing, though, and I hesitate to bring it up …"

Farmer groaned. "Let me know the worst, Oswald."

"Well, I feel that they could have used any number of ships other than the *Hampshire* – more modern, faster and *definitely* better armoured. I'm puzzled as to why the life of the Secretary of State for War should be entrusted to a ship nearing the end of her useful life."

****

"And now they're going to kill Henry and blame it on the Hun," whispered Anne. "Kitchener is already dead but everyone will think he died on the *Hampshire.* Blackest of lies, indeed!"

"Sorry?"

Anne brushed away the beginnings of a tear and sniffed. "Tennyson, I think. '*A lie which is half a truth is ever the blackest of lies'*.

"Damn right," he said

Anne looked over at Hubert. "We still haven't considered how you are going to get on board the *Hampshire*."

"Well, I'm not going to be stealing any sailor's uniform, so it will have to be by hiding somewhere but I'll be damned if I can think of a way to get off this train without begin seen, get *on* the road transport without being seen and travel to Scrabster. Ditto as regards getting off there and on to the boat that takes me to the *Hampshire*. And as for getting on board …"

"What if we were to get a boat at Thurso and go over to Scapa from there?"

"And then bang on the side of the *Iron Duke* and say 'please can we speak to the Admiral?' – no, I don't think so. For a start, there are mines and booms and, bearing in mind that they've just had a God-awful scrap with the German Fleet, I'd say they'd be in no mind to offer hospitality to passing strangers. Even *with* warrant cards."

Anne stuck her tongue out at him and thoughtfully drummed a quiet tattoo with her heels on the trunk then stood sharply up as the door of the luggage van opened. It was only the Guard.

"I thought you might like some tea," he said, depositing a tray loaded with the necessities of life on to the top of a flat tin trunk.

"You life-saver," said Hubert in heart-felt gratitude.

"There's something else," he continued. "I don't know if it's important or anything but did you know that two other men got on the train just before we left?"

Chris and Anne looked at each other. "Can you describe them," she said, faintly.

"One was a middle-aged gentleman, very well-dressed but not someone you'd want to cross, I think, and the other was a younger chap. He was quite tall and looked a bit of a bruiser."

"Thanks for that," she said. "Don't let them know we're here, would you? And keep the door locked so that they don't accidentally wander in. My job is a highly sensitive one looking out for anyone tracking Lord Kitchener. If they get a whiff of the fact that I'm on the train, it could spell the end of the game and put him in danger."

The guard, like guards the world over, puffed himself up. This was important stuff – he might even get his name in the papers if he did well. "Just leave it to me, Miss. You won't be bothered."

He made to leave but Anne held him back. "The loading door – this sliding one here on the side of the carriage – is it unlocked?"

"No, Miss. That's locked from the outside for security's sake. We have to stop a few times on the way up to Thurso for coal and water and to change drivers. We don't want no-one on the platform just helping themselves to the luggage."

"Look," she said, "I need that door open. Not right now but near the end of the journey because this officer and I will not be here when the train pulls into Thurso. We'll be off chasing some bad people but I don't want anyone up front knowing that we're getting off. What's the last station we stop at before Thurso?"

"We'll be stopping at Edinburgh, Inverness and then Georgemas – we get a new driver and take on water. The old one gets off there and takes the branch line the long way down the east coast back to Inverness."

"Does that east coast train call at Wick?"

The guard ostentatiously consulted a timetable before intoning, "It does, Miss."

"Perfect! Right, then," she said, "when we stop at Inverness, unlock the padlock from its hasp and close it again on the other side of the bolt so that it still looks as though it's secure. Anyone seeing a missing padlock will come and take a look." Anne held up a warning finger, "But make *absolutely* sure no-one sees you. Are we clear?"

"Yes, Miss." The guard gulped and left to make his way forward to his den.

Anne leaned over Hubert's seated body to pour a cup of tea just as the train swayed violently from side to side over the points at a junction, depositing her firmly in his lap. "Well," he said, "this is turning out to be a real nice journey."

****

At 1035 the following morning, 5 June 1916, Farmer's train pulled slowly in to Thurso station at the end of its long journey. Fitzgerald had already been busy getting everything in order, just as he would have done if it had been the real Kitchener. Farmer looked up at him, "Oswald, just stick your head out and see if Chris is there."

"He isn't. I have already checked."

"Dammit!" he muttered.

The compartment being clear as the rest of the party disembarked, Fitzgerald sat back down beside him and patted the other man's arm. "You know, Henry, I behaved like an old woman, back at Broome." He held up a hand at Farmer's protestation. "No, let's be clear about things – to begin with, I didn't make it easy for you and I humbly apologise." He plucked a thread from Farmer's uniform and brushed the shoulder with his gloved hand. "You have carried out a very difficult task which was not of your making and you've done it in a way that I know 'he' would have been proud of. I don't suppose you know too much about my work with Lord Kitchener but he was more than just my commanding officer – he was a ... a dear friend – and I suppose that's what was at the bottom of my antagonism."

"My dear chap, there's no need to explain yourself to me."

"But there is, Henry, there is. It looks as though you and I are to be alone in all this crowd heading for Russia. It won't be an easy task but I want you to know that I am absolutely on your side. You have my greatest admiration for all your efforts and I promise to do my utmost to help you make a … a great success of it."

Farmer mumbled something inaudible while the other continued, "It *is* a great pity Hubert isn't here. As I say, he's a very resourceful young man and we could have done with him if things were to go a little off-piste – but we'll manage, you and I." Fitzgerald smiled encouragingly. "And, you never know, he might make it yet."

He patted Farmer's arm again and stood up. "At any rate, we'd better shift ourselves and get onto the platform to meet the welcoming committee."

Farmer sputtered and dropped the contents of a small valise all over the floor. "What welcoming committee?"

Fitzgerald was squinting out of the window again. "Well, for a start, there seem to be an inordinate number of police officers present and what could only be representatives of Special Branch. I do so wonder why they call it 'plain clothes' – there's nothing plain about it and you can spot them a mile off. There is also a gentleman wearing what appears to be the country's gold reserve around his neck so I'm going to make a leap in the dark and assume he's the Mayor of Thurso, if there be such an office."

Farmer stood up and joined Fitzgerald at the carriage door. Farmer sighed. "Once more unto the breach, dear friends."

****

Anne dozed off as the evening drew in, swaddling herself in her coat and a blanket provided by the guard. Hubert had been in too much pain to sleep and, when he heard the key turn in the door, he sat gingerly up in the first light of dawn, collecting the guard's tea things in the process.

"Thank you but I *have* breakfasted." Boissier was at his most amused but the gun in his right hand implied something quite different.

The crash of the tray hitting the floor of the van woke Anne with a start. "What's happening?" she mumbled, rubbing the sleep from her eyes.

"Yes, dear girl," grinned Boissier, as he the saw recognition dawn in her face. "It is I." He shook his head in sorrow, "Did I not say when we last met to *let it lie*? You didn't and now things have come to this unfortunate pass."

"Where's Mr Hyde?" she said.

"Please don't be truculent *and* ..." He waved the gun to his right as he saw her slide her hand towards her bag. "... keep your hands where I can see them. I don't doubt you have something nasty and effective in there for me. That's it - sit up straight. Now, you were asking about Mr Pickup. He's having a few words with the guard, explaining how both of you have gone rogue, so to speak."

Hubert quietly slid his legs underneath him. God knows if he had the strength left to launch himself at Boissier but it was now or never, before Pickup joined them. It was a pointless exercise anyway – Boissier spotted the movement and the gun was on him in an instant.

"Hubert – sit still, there's a good cripple. Kell has made it clear that you and this lovely lady are not to be harmed – *if at all possible* – but, whatever it takes, you're both to be stopped here. Don't make me do anything incurable."

Chris relaxed back against the packing case and turned to look at Pickup as he swaggered into the van.

"Well," sneered Pickup, "the gang's all here." Exultantly, he gave his Cheshire cat grin as his eyes lit on Anne, "I just *knew* you were going to be a bad girl."

"Play nice, Pickup," Boissier said warningly. He tilted his head to point just behind the other man. "There's some parcel string over there. Tie them up." He looked around the van disparagingly. "There's no way I want to be stuck in here for the rest of the journey – smells like a wet dog." He looked down at Chris and Anne. "Pickup and I have a date with destiny on Orkney but you two will be returning the way you came, accompanied this time by a couple of Scotch coppers we're to pick up in Thurso."

His mouth drooped in mock sadness. "I'm afraid the good healer's hours are numbered – about twelve, I believe."

****

On arrival at Thurso. Farmer was introduced to the Mayor – Fitzgerald was right, there, although the role was called something different – and conversation drifted around the usual subjects of the length of the journey and how the war was going from Kitchener's perspective up in London. All very banal stuff but the police presence was curious. Thurso was not internationally known as a hot bed of spies and assassins. Farmer made a mental note to ask Fitzgerald about it – were they expecting something to happen? As soon as they were able, the party made its way over on to the other train and settled themselves down.

The journey to Scrabster was only a matter of a few miles along the coast and the entourage was soon standing at the docks about to board the *Royal Oak*. Fitzgerald approached from behind and whispered in Farmer's ear, "It seems that O'Beirne and his people have made good speed and they're only a couple of hours behind us. They'll be making their way across to Scapa in the Fleet pinnace – dammit, what was it called ..." he consulted his notes, "*Alouette*. It'll take them about an hour and a half."

"Fair enough." Farmer looked up at the ship tying up in front of him. "So, this ship – do we know anything about her? I don't want to appear a *complete* Pongo."

Fitzgerald suppressed a laugh. "She's brand new – commissioned only a few weeks ago."

"Did she fight at Jutland?"

"Indeed, she did. And gave the *Derfflinger* a few thumps, not to mention the *Wiesbaden* – came out of the battle without a scratch." Hearing his name called, Fitzgerald turned to see a very young sub-lieutenant approaching him with an envelope in his left hand and his right in a perfect naval salute.

"Telegram for you, Sir", he said.

Fitzgerald thanked him, acknowledged the salute and broke open the envelope. It was from Kell and simply read,

GALLAGHER KNOWS DEPARTURE POINT - STOP - GET TO SEA WITHOUT DELAY - END

They both looked up at the sound of an officer being piped off the ship by the bo'sun. "This is the Captain – Crawford MacLachlan," said Fitzgerald in Farmer's ear.

Farmer acknowledged the salute of the officer stepping off the gangway and held out his hand. "Captain MacLachlan, how do you do? I understand I am to congratulate you on your ship's conduct at Jutland. I'd very much like to hear about it."

****

Edinburgh had come and gone without Anne having been able to free herself. Hubert was in no condition to do anything physical and, in fact, had taken half an hour to regain consciousness after a vicious kick from Pickup.

"I'm really sorry about Henry," said Anne.

"I know you are. But never say die – there's a lot that can still happen."

"Optimism runs in your family, then."

"No, just a blind inability to accept the facts. Anyway, now that we have some time on our hands, I think I ought to mention that I'm still waiting to hear about this 'Wick' business you're so modest about."

Anne growled quietly. "*Very well.* Before the War, I did some work for the Bank of England which involved my being attached to the Fisheries people in Arbroath."

"My God," he rasped in mock horror, "what had you *done*?"

Anne sighed in exasperation. "The point of what I'm *trying* to say … *damn it!*"

Hubert started in surprise. "What? What's wrong now?"

"*That's where I've seen Boissier before!*"

Hubert stared at her. "You've met him before? Where?

Why didn't you say?"

"That Bank of England job – I saw him there. It was two years ago and only for a few minutes but the swine left me in a real bad way – God, when I remember … I could kill him. What *was* the name he used? It wasn't Boissier, then." She paused in unhappy thought for a moment and then looked sharply at Hubert. "And what the hell were your lot doing there? And then *leaving* me!"

"Search me. It was before my time. What do you mean – 'bad way'?"

She shook her head in dismissal. "I'll tell you about it some other time. Let's get back to the trawler I mentioned yesterday – we used it to patrol the north-eastern coastline. It belongs to Special Branch and the skipper is one of our officers. I got to know him fairly well in my time there."

"Fairly well, eh?"

"Yes, *fairly* well! What of it?"

Hubert shook his head innocently. "Nothing, nothing."

"His name is Andrew MacDonald and he's from that part of the country. The trawler's been based out of Wick since the start of the War. Remember, the Guard told us that there's a train leaving Georgemas for Wick about fifteen minutes after this one continues on to Thurso. I had hoped that you and I could get to the trawler and persuade Mac to take us to Scapa. It might have been too late to stop Henry leaving on the *Hampshire* but we could perhaps have intercepted it or picked him up if it went down."

Anyway, even if we sail off into the sunset with Mac, how would we find the *Hampshire*?"

"*Howard!*" she shouted. "That was the name he was working under! Total swine."

"Boissier? OK, well, let's put that to one side for the moment and think about it later. What about the trawler?"

"Right, the trawler. One of the great things about *this* trawler is that it has some seriously powerful radio kit. We'd have been able to hear the *Hampshire's* transmissions had she been on the far side of the moon. If we had been too late, the trawler would have picked up the Captain's distress message."

"And if this 'Mac' chap isn't at Wick – if he's at sea."

"*Now* you're a glass half empty sort of person? Think happy thoughts." She looked away, tears in her eyes. "Anyway, it's all been for nothing now. We'll never get to him like this – we can't be far from Inverness and that's the last chance of our getting out of this van."

****

The train ground its way into the quaintly-styled station of Inverness. The gentle screech of the side door sliding cautiously open startled them both upright.

"Miss? Miss? It's me – the guard – we've just stopped at Inverness."

"Oh, God bless you, you darling man," said Anne. "Quickly, slide it behind you in case any of our 'friends' decide to take the air or get a newspaper."

The guard did as he was told and then trotted over to where they were lying trussed up like chickens for the pot. "I suppose this is the work of your 'friends', as you like to call them? Spun me a pack of lies about the two of you."

Anne, now free, helped him untie Hubert. "Why didn't you believe them?"

The guard looked pityingly at her. "Miss, really, I know

a fare-dodger when I see one – or two in this case."

"We're really grateful to you, sir. I wish I could tell you just how important your help is," said Hubert, grasping the other man's hand in sheer gratitude. "Now, the best thing is for you slink back out the way you came, leave the padlock on the other side of the hasp and keep your head down as you walk back up the platform. Don't let them see you, whatever you do."

"Best of luck, whatever it is you're up to."

****

His feet on the other bench seat of the compartment, Boissier reached over and prodded Pickup with a toe, who duly woke up with a grunt.

"We can't be far from Georgemas. That's supposed to be the last stop on this bloody camel train before we get into Thurso. Get back there to the guard's van and check our guests. Dump them out of sight at the back of the van. We don't want any virtuous railway workers – be there such a creature – 'discovering' them before the train heads back up to London and civilisation."

Pickup groaned upright and made to leave the compartment. "But make sure you leave Banfield alone." Seeing the other man's eyes light up, he hardened his voice. "I mean it, Pickup. She's Special Branch and we don't want any problems with them after this is over. Kell will have your balls – mine, too."

"You really know how to spoil a party, Boissier," he said, moving out into the corridor.

Bouncing from wall to wall as the carriages negotiated the rural, single-track line, Pickup reached the guard's van in a couple of minutes. As he opened the door, Anne hit him a hard as she could with a leather-bound cosh she had hidden in her bag. Pickup staggered to his knees, momentarily stunned, but with a roar of rage he got back up and charged at her, arms outstretched to throttle. Hubert managed to rugby tackle him, bringing him to the floor where Anne hit him repeatedly. Hubert stood up and, marshalling every ounce of strength he had left, kicked him on the side of the head. Pickup gasped and slumped into an untidy heap.

"Grab some more of that string," gasped Anne. "See how he likes it."

A few moments later, the unconscious Pickup had been dumped unceremoniously behind the trunks at the back of the van.

Hubert stood up, gripping his ribs. "Fine – now we have to be clear on what we're doing next. Georgemas can only be minutes away. If Boissier comes down to investigate, we'll have a harder time of it. He'll be suspicious, for a start."

"You know what we have to do," she said.

"Well, thank God for the guard. My faith in the human race has been restored. Even Boissier's lies weren't enough for him. I hope they won't take it out on the poor chap after we've left."

"If he keeps his head down like I told him, they shouldn't discover it was him. With any luck, they'll think the door was always open. They never tried it."

Both felt the jolt of the train slowing down for Georgemas Junction and Anne slid open the side door and they stood on the edge of the step. Anxiety made her voice tremble. "This is where we should wish each other luck, I suppose."

She pecked him lightly on the cheek.

****

"God *save* us!" Boissier threw his newspaper onto the facing seat in his compartment and stood up. Where the Hell was that idiot? "I'll lay odds he's enjoying himself with that Banfield chit." Irritably, he threw open the door, stalked down the corridor and stormed into the guard's van. Pickup was trying to vomit and groan at the same time, somewhere at the back but, apart from him, there was no-one else.

"Bugger!" he roared at the top of his voice.

Sliding trunks, suitcases and packing boxes aside, he dragged Pickup into the middle of the floor and cut him loose with a pen-knife. He grabbed him by the lapels and shouted at him in fury, "Where are they? Where the *hell* are they, you moron?"

Pickup could only slur a 'what?' Boissier examined a serious contusion on the side of Pickup's head and guessed there was probably a pretty severe concussion to match. There would be no getting any sense out of him – if that were possible in the first place. "Should improve your work immeasurably," growled Boissier, releasing him to fall heavily back onto the floor.

Plans would have to change now.

****

Anne was on the Wick train, having called ahead from Georgemas to the dockside offices to find out if MacDonald was ashore or at sea. Annoyingly, he was out with the trawler but he was due back in by about two in the afternoon. She left a message for him to refuel and not to go off for a pint after landing. Another couple of hours should see her in Wick and she'd run directly down to the quay.

The only worry at the back of her mind was Hubert – how in God's name was he going to survive her lunatic plan? The chances were that he'd die before even getting to Henry. For the first time, she wondered how she'd feel about that and surprised herself by realising that it would not feel good. Somehow, she and MacDonald would have to get Farmer and Hubert off the *Hampshire* before she got under way. "We'll have to tell the Navy *everything*!" she thought. "What other excuse could we have for stopping the journey to Russia?" Unless, of course, MacDonald could come up with something – but then thinking had never been his strong point.

She sat back and looked at the rain streaming diagonally down the carriage window and tried hard to remember precisely what *had* been his strong points.

****

The journey over to Scapa, on a battleship – even for Farmer – turned out to be a fairly undemanding business. MacLachlan had given them a balanced view of what had gone on at Jutland and bemoaned the fact that it had not been the decisive affair that it should have been. Fitzgerald politely declined the Captain's offer of a tour around the ship, suggesting that there was insufficient time to do her justice. Privately, he knew that a tour of the *Iron Duke* followed by another on the *Hampshire* were inevitable and unavoidable. Wandering round three ships in close succession in this weather would have been more than his patience could have borne.

When a suitable moment presented itself, Farmer leaned unobtrusively over to Fitzgerald and murmured, "Anything I should know about?"

"You mean the telegram I received at the dockside?"

"Just so."

Fitzgerald paused for a moment and looked sheepishly down. "I was debating with myself whether I should mention it or not – you have enough on your plate. It was from Kell. It seems, Heaven knows how, that Gallagher is back on our tracks. He has discovered that you're leaving from Scapa."

Henry turned pale. "God Almighty."

Fitzgerald gripped Farmer's upper arm. "I wouldn't worry too much about it. He'll never get on board any of the ships – but it's his ability to suborn others who *do* have access that worries me. The persuasive power of cash is a universal constant and I've absolutely no doubt that the IRB has supplied him well in that respect. Kell suggests that we get to sea as quickly as possible. I presume he's thinking along the same lines that the less time we give Gallagher to sort something out, the better."

Within a further hour, they found themselves in the impressive natural harbour provided by the rolling hills and islands of Orkney. The majority of the Home Fleet, some showing dismal signs of their engagement with the Imperial German Navy, lay spread around them as they slowly edged in to anchor at number four buoy, close by the *Iron Duke*. Fitzgerald pointed out the *Hampshire* lying a hundred yards away. MacLachlan, who had been on the bridge during the approach, slid expertly down the ladder. "My Lord, we are ready to transfer you over to the flagship by gangplank. Do take care – the decks are pitching a little, as you can see. I'll join you shortly, if I may, after operations are completed here."

Farmer smiled at the Captain and his assembled officers. "Thank you, Captain and you gentlemen, for your hospitality." He nodded to MacLachlan, "I look forward to seeing you soon." To the ear-piercing shriek of the bo'sun's pipe, Farmer and his party positioned themselves, ready to make their way across the rickety planking, protected only by some rather sulky-looking ropes.

"You know, Henry, your performance is getting a little ... *uncanny*. You've become *very* good. This Russian thing will be a cakewalk for you."

Farmer turned around, almost falling overboard in the process. "Bloody hell", he gasped, under his breath. He steadied himself and muttered at Fitzgerald, "Glad you think so but, to be frank, I don't even think about it now. It comes automatically – Chris said it would. *Chris!* I wish to God he were here. The little scamp."

Moments later, they were able to step onto the main deck of the *Iron Duke* to meet Jellicoe himself. "Welcome aboard, Sir," he said, genially. "Would you like to take a short tour of the ship before lunch?"

Farmer groaned internally – he was already feeling fairly green and the ship, at anchor, was rolling and plunging fairly vigorously by now. "Delighted," he replied.

Accompanied only by Fitzgerald, Farmer walked along with Jellicoe, mentally praying that the rain would hold off just a little longer. As it turned out, the tour was more interesting that he had expected.

Jellicoe held a hatch open for Farmer to step back out on to the main deck after seeing the engine room and said, quietly so that no-one else in the naval party could hear, "Your Lordship is not looking quite as I remember him, if I may say so."

Farmer suppressed a guilty start and glanced at Fitzgerald, who was occupied in conversation with another officer. "Well, the pressure of this office, let me tell you, has been almost intolerable over these last two years. I suppose it's inevitable that it would leave a mark. I haven't noticed myself, of course."

Jellicoe nodded sympathetically, "You *do* look somewhat worn down and exhausted, sir."

"It's the pressure of trying to work with a civilian government. You and I, Jellicoe, are used to making decisions and then simply having others carry our orders out. I cannot tell you how difficult it is first to have to convince a *committee* that your decisions are right and proper before those orders can be executed. I don't mean to imply that they're unintelligent people – they're not – but they are not military men. That's a lifelong study in itself."

"It sounds incredibly frustrating."

Farmer rolled his eyes upwards. "I have no words to express that frustration, truly. That's why I am so looking forward to this voyage." He smiled tiredly. "It'll be almost like a holiday to get away from the War Office for three weeks."

Jellicoe grinned at Farmer's comments as the two men approached the capstan at the prow of the ship. From there, the whole fleet at anchor could be seen, the furthest fading into the rain and low cloud. The Admiral pointed over to one ship, rather the worse for wear. "I have to confess that I've brought you out here in this rather damp weather for a purpose, sir."

Farmer grimaced. "Oh, yes?" he replied, simply.

"Do you see that cruiser? Not the nearest one – the one just beyond. That's the *Chester*. I intend to recommend one of its sailors for a VC – posthumously, sadly – and I would like to ask for your support back at the War Office to see that it goes through."

"Tell me about it."

"You might just be able to see the for'ard gun?"

"The damaged one?"

"That's it. Last Wednesday – in the early afternoon of the battle – the *Chester* went to investigate the sound of gunfire. She was attacked simultaneously by four enemy cruisers, each her own size, and came under a dreadful pounding. She fought as I would expect any ship under my command to fight – gallantly – but one of her crew, above all, stood out head and shoulders. Boy Seaman John Cornwell was a gun layer in that gun."

"You say a 'Boy Seaman'. Just how old was he?"

"Sixteen."

Farmer was appalled at the thought of a child being exposed to battle, never mind having to behave conspicuously. "Dear God!"

Jellicoe continued. "At least four hits were registered near the gun but you may be able to see that the armour in that particular type does not reach fully to the deck – nor is there shielding at the back. As a result, all of the gun crew were killed – not by direct hits – but from enemy shrapnel deflecting from the ship's own armour." He turned to face Farmer and looked straight into his eyes. "All except Cornwell, that is. When the *Chester* retired from the action with all her guns, bar one, disabled by enemy fire, the medics found young Cornwell still at his post, dreadfully injured about the legs, awaiting orders."

Farmer held on to a stanchion, unable to say anything.

"The ship was unfit for action and she was dispatched

to Immingham for emergency repairs and checks before she could sail on to Scapa. Cornwell was transferred to Grimsby General Hospital but, sadly, he died on Friday morning."

"Tell me what you wish me to do, Jellicoe."

"I tell you all this because the nay-sayers at the Admiralty are already declaring that since our recent engagement was not fought to the complete destruction of the German High Seas Fleet, it must be considered a defeat of some sort. As night follows day, that line of thought encourages the decision-makers in Government to believe that *no* conduct in the battle could therefore be worthy." Jellicoe thrust his hands into the pockets of his tunic and hardened his voice. "I beg you not to forget Jack Cornwell. There will be those, safe at home in the Admiralty while a child like Cornwell was facing injury and death, who will now courageously tie themselves in knots trying to prove that he was not a gallant sailor of the King, however well he behaved. Do not let them win. Let them stand in line and take their best shot at me, but men like Cornwell should not be forgotten in the cross-fire."

Farmer placed his hand unsteadily on Jellicoe's shoulder as the rain began to hammer down mercilessly. "Whatever I can do, I will. You have my word, Admiral."

****

Boissier watched O'Beirne, Duquesne and the rest of the party disembark from the train and crooked his finger at Pickup when the platform at Thurso was empty. Both men had only light valises to carry and they were soon out on Lovers' Lane which ran past the station entrance. "Quaint," he chuckled to a very pale Pickup. "Look, there's a pony and trap for hire."

Within half an hour, both men were standing at the quayside where they were able to commandeer a fishing boat to take them over to Stromness while O'Beirne and his lot were making their way to Scrabster. The wind was rising, making the journey tedious to say the least. Pickup spent most of the time leaning over the side – twice needing swift action by the deck hands to avoid being lost overboard. It wasn't that Boissier was the better sailor – it was just that he'd see himself damned first before showing any weakness in front of Pickup. He leaned back against the wheel housing, straddling his feet to gain balance. The first thing after docking was to get in touch with this man Vance. It was essential that no-one was rescued and that meant scaring the local yokels with threats of imprisonment. Vance would bring an air of officialdom to everything but they'd still have to keep him at arm's length.

He looked down at Pickup noisily bringing up everything he had ever eaten. 'Tough guy'.

****

At lunch in the Wardroom, Jellicoe tried hard to persuade Farmer to delay his departure enough to allow the storm to pass over. "A day or two, that's all, Sir."

Farmer, thinking of Gallagher on his tail would have none of it. "And what is the quickest time we can expect to Archangel?"

"Two to three days."

He shook his head, decisively. "No. I'm sorry, Jellicoe, I have a very tight schedule and cannot brook the delay of a single day."

The Admiral smiled, ruefully. "Yes, I was going to say just how appalled I am at the amount of work you intend to cover in *three weeks*. That being the case, I can completely understand your desire to be off but, nevertheless, let me caution you against it – the weather is looking rather bad. So much so, in fact, that I have been advised to send you by a different route."

Fitzgerald leaned forward, "Which route would that be, Sir?"

"Well, normally, we'd send the *Hampshire* up the *eastern* cost of Orkney but, since the storm is actually *from* the north east, the seas are running very high, indeed, in those waters. Not only will it be most uncomfortable for you all but it means our ability to detect submarines along your line of travel becomes substantially compromised by the weather. However, I have just been advised that we could use the western route, close inshore, to give you a lee effect. This should allow your escorting destroyers to maintain speed. On top of that, the route is known to be used mostly by our Auxiliaries."

"I'm sorry – the Auxiliaries – what difference does that make?"

"It is less likely to have been mined than one used by ships of the line."

Farmer shook his head again. "I thank you for your concern, Jellicoe, but – no – I'm afraid I cannot wait. The western route sounds ideal."

"I understand, Sir, but may I try another tack? I would like to have that course swept as far north as Birsay, just to be sure."

"And how long will that take?"

"About twenty-four hours."

"Since the weather is getting worse, rather than better, we'd still end up delaying by two or three days and I cannot countenance that. I'm sorry but I must impose upon you my original departure schedule."

****

O'Beirne threw his briefcase petulantly on to his bunk on the *Hampshire*. "What a God-awful crossing," he groaned at Duquesne. "I can't see my enjoying this voyage if the weather's going to be like this all the way."

"It's been pretty bad, certainly, but I've seen worse."

"Oh?" O'Beirne looked vaguely deflated. "You have? Where?"

"The Cape of Good Hope can be fairly unappetising, too."

"Yes … well … Oh, the cypher! Have one of the matelots bring my brass-banded trunk into my cabin – Rix would have put it in that one – then you can sort yourself out until Kitchener comes on board which should be in …" He pulled out a gold hunter. "… about thirty minutes if he keeps to schedule. By that time, I need to be on the ball just in case he needs anything sent ahead."

"I take it His Lordship will be travelling in the Captain's cabin?"

"Oh Lord, yes, you need to know about all that sort of thing, don't you? Well, as I said, I don't take to all this cloak-and-dagger stuff. I've done my bit by letting you pretend to be my servant. I really don't want to know any more about it, thank you," he sniffed.

While this suited Duquesne perfectly, he couldn't help but feel he was regarded as something even lower in the food chain than a manservant. Once again, he almost salivated at the thought of choking off this arrogant bastard.

"You could not do better, Mr O'Beirne. Leave it all to me."

****

Lt Cdr Macauly Leckie, Captain of the destroyer *HMS Unity,* was completing his final checks for sea, when his signals officer reported that he had received instructions from the *Iron Duke* to depart immediately with *HMS Victor*, to sweep the area around Hoy and then take station off Torness to escort the *Hampshire* to Archangel. "Very well, Signals, repeat to the *Victor* and let's get moving."

He moved across the bridge to stand beside his Executive Officer. "Filthy weather, Number One, but 'Ours not to reason why' sort of thing. I really was hoping for a couple of days' delay – they must be really keen to meet the Czar. Anyway, make ready for sea and get under way as soon as you can. Once we get to the rendezvous point I want as many eyes on deck as we can muster. Periscopes, mines – I don't care if they see a bloody mermaid – I want to know about it. We can *not* fluff this one up – not on my watch, anyway."

"Aye, Sir."

Within fifteen minutes both destroyers, chosen from many to escort their precious charge across dangerous wartime seas to Russia, were battling their way out of the western exit of Scapa Flow.

****

Hubert was moving in and out of consciousness. Anne had punched some air holes in the bottom of the trunk before she left but his damaged lungs meant that, after what seemed like days, suffocation was probably only minutes away - his chest felt as though it was filled with acid. He hacked feebly with Anne's knife at the inside of the trunk, not knowing whether he was on the train, on the journey over to Scapa or on board the *Hampshire*. The time was fast approaching when geography wouldn't matter a damn – survival was the priority now. Gradually, the stabbing motions became weak, powerless scratching until light and – thank God – *air* flooded back into his world. He looked up blearily at the man peering over the edge of the trunk, squeaking at him.

"Who the hell are you? Look what you have done to my trunk! *Look at it!* Have you any idea what it cost me? – it's a *Goyard*."

The voice paused, speechless, surveying the ruin Hubert had made of his prized possession until another thought struck. "And what the hell have you done with my clothes?"

****

Detective Inspector Vance moved out of the shadows of a public bar in Stromness and moved over to the two men. "Mister Boissier and Mr Pickup, Ah suppose?" he grunted in a thick Glaswegian accent, noting the purpling bruise now covering most of the right side of the younger man's face.

"Guilty, as charged, officer", Boissier oiled. Looking the policeman over, he got the overpowering impression of his simply being your average bobby, but Kell had given him a glowing reference before they left Whitehall. Vance, it seemed, was the Admiralty's right hand man in these parts and he had done all sorts of dodgy work for MI5 in the past. Boissier sat back in his seat and grimaced slightly at the uncomfortable springs pushing into his buttocks. So this was what passed for luxury in Orkney? Vance was in his early fifties, perhaps, with thinning prematurely-grey hair. He was wearing a rather soiled, ankle-length raincoat buttoned right up to his neck and kept his bowler hat on – even indoors. Boissier wondered if he wore it to bed. He looked carefully at the policeman – the face had all the qualities one might expect of a diabetic bloodhound but it told you, quite clearly, that if this man ever got on your trail, he'd never stop.

Boissier smiled. "What can we get for you Mr Vance?"

Vance simply shook his head imperceptibly and waggled his half-full pint glass of beer.

"I see you're sorted, so perhaps we should get straight down to business? Time is very short."

Vance nodded.

"Very well. I understand that you have already been briefed by my Director?" Seeing Vance nod again – he was clearly no conversationalist – he continued. "The key things here are that we must immediately have a vehicle to drive around the island and that you remain here and keep an eye open for an Irishman. On no account are you to interfere with his movements. Just watch him."

Vance took a draw at his beer and wiped his mouth with a handkerchief. "And while Ah'm daein' that, whit'll you two gentlemen be up tae?"

The voice sounded to Boissier like a couple of dogs fighting. He leaned forward to speak quietly but, with the racket going on in the pub, the precaution seemed, even to him, a little excessive. Still, appearances were everything and he didn't like the way this Scotch copper was looking at him. "We are on the track of highly classified materials stolen by German agents that may come ashore from a

Royal Navy ship currently at sea. We are to prevent them from reaching Germany or even falling into the hands of the civilian population. Apprehending the spy is a secondary consideration. The documents are everything. With that aim in mind, we'll be patrolling the western shoreline all this evening. We would appreciate your interceding with the local Police force on our behalf. We don't want them getting in the way."

"And that's it?"

Boissier relaxed into his seat and smiled, "That's it. Keep an eye out for our Mick around the docks and local cafés near Scapa. If he's anywhere, that's where he'll be. I understand that you have a full description of him?"

"Aye."

"Well, in that case, I suggest we meet back here at, say, nine o' clock this evening?"

Vance grunted, drained the last of his beer and stood up. "Yur car's parked ootside. It's the black Armstrong." Glancing around carefully to make sure he had left no traces behind, he turned and slid quietly out of the pub.

Pickup looked at his colleague through the one eye that remained open to him and growled, "What the hell are we meeting up with him again for? He's trouble. You can smell it."

Boissier turned sideways to look at him more clearly and enunciated his words with care. "You really are an idiot, aren't you? By nine we will be off this bloody island with Farmer, Fitzgerald and Hubert *dead* – that little snip of a girl, too, if we can find her."

He thrust his glass at the other man. "Here, get me another glass of this sheep dip and then we'll be on our way."

****

The lower deck crew of the Hampshire had been given permission to watch the C-in-C's pinnace come over from the *Iron Duke*. Speculation was rife as to the VIP they were to carry to Russia. One of the signallers had a pair of binoculars trained on the pinnace but the rolling seas made it difficult to keep it steady in the field of view. He had to fight off advice and questions from his mates until he caught a glimpse of "scrambled egg" on the caps of some of the officers. "A shower of bleedin' brasshats!" he moaned to his friends. "A real big nob, for sure."

"Hang on," said Leading Seaman Rogerson, "Don't you recognise 'im? It's the Chief Recruitin' Officer hisself! Just the spit of 'is bleedin' poster!" He ran an experienced eye over the situation. "They're goin' to have an 'ell of a time tying up in this sea."

Just then, a cry went up from the other end of the line of men. "What're they rollickin' about, Bill?" he said to Chief Shipwright William Phillips, standing a couple of men further down the line.

"One of the young killicks had an engagement ring for 'is girl. Just been jostled by one of the lads and it slipped clean out of 'is fingers into the sea. Had it for about a year and an 'alf but never 'ad a chance to ask her. Pore little bugger."

Rogerson's face fell. "Bad omen, that." Moodily, he watched 'Lord Kitchener' and his entourage disembark from the boat and make their way up the gangway to be piped on board.

After the usual introductory pleasantries, including a description of the ship's part in the battle, Captain Savill offered his cabin to Farmer and the ship was made ready for sea without delay. Farmer gratefully retired below to the cabin with Fitzgerald and MacPherson to look over some Russian papers. If anything could take Farmer's mind off the dreadful movement of the ship, it would be Cyrillic script.

Fitzgerald sent the junior officer out to arrange for some refreshments to be brought to the cabin. "Well, Henry," he said, looking over at Farmer who was gazing out at the hills of Hoy slipping in and out of the mists. "It looks as though we've been able to give Gallagher the slip. In a few days, we'll be in Archangel. He won't be following us there."

"Thank the Lord. I was beginning to imagine all sorts of things." He sat down and gazed at the deck.

Fitzgerald exhaled slowly. "Yes … Hubert. I've been wondering, too. What on earth could have happened to him? It has something to do with that man Kell – I'm certain of it – and, if that turns out to be true, I have to wonder what he has in store for us."

"I'm beginning to wish Gallagher had found us, instead!"

Fitzgerald smiled. "No you don't but I understand what you mean – the devil you *know*."

Within thirty minutes, at around 1645 hours, the *Hampshire* slipped her cable and began making slow headway towards the western exit to Scapa Flow, following the route taken by her escorts earlier, and out into the Pentland Firth.

CHAPTER 8

Monday, 5 June 1916 1645 hours – 1942 hours

Hubert reached an unsteady hand up at the trembling, high-pitched voice.

"Will you answer me? It was a bloody *Goyard*!"

"Means bugger-all to me, old man. Help me up – I'm done in," whispered Hubert, almost inaudibly.

"I will do nothing of the sort until I get some answers. Who the devil are you?" squeaked O'Beirne, indignantly.

"Christ! My name is Hubert and I'm on the staff of MI5. Are you O'Beirne?"

"Yes, indeed, and you can just explain …"

"Shut up", he groaned wearily. Anne was clearly rubbing off on him. "Are we on the *Hampshire*?

"Can't you *feel* the ship rolling all over the place?"

Hubert collapsed heavily on to the floor. "Look", he

gasped, "the way I feel right now, I'm not sure whether it's the ship or me."

O'Beirne help him up to sit on the edge of the bunk. "Mr Hubert, I think you'd better explain things. For a start, why would you want to stow away in one of my trunks?"

Chris felt like throwing up but willed himself to be calm. "It's as simple as this – there's a plan to kill Lord Kitchener."

"I know – but you already *have* a man looking out for him – this fellow Staughton who's acting as my manservant."

Hubert grunted in amusement but even that took more out of him than he could afford and O'Beirne had to support him against the movement of the ship. "He's actually a very dangerous man called Fritz Joubert Duquesne – a Boer working for the German Secret Service."

O'Beirne stared at him disbelievingly. "Are you sure of this? How do you know?"

"Never mind that – time's short. We have to alert the Captain of this tub that there may be mines ahead and that Kitchener's cabin has to be searched immediately for explosive devices. Your 'manservant' was provided with one before you left."

Things started to click in O'Beirne's head. "The Paddington delay!"

"That's the one." He stood unsteadily up. "Let's get moving."

O'Beirne moved over and opened the door of the cabin but backed away from it as Duquesne stepped in, holding a gun at waist level. "Move over to the bulkhead and sit on the floor," he hissed and turned to look at Hubert. "My

God, they're scraping the barrel at 'Five' if they think you're fit even for *light* duties."

"Fit enough for the likes of you, Duquesne."

"I seriously doubt it," he murmured and coshed him viciously with the gun barrel. As Hubert hit the decking, the Boer turned slowly towards O'Beirne, crouched in the corner of the cabin, and smiled. "*Now*, 'Milord' …"

****

On the bridge, things were going from bad to worse. As they rounded Tor Ness at 1745 hours, the ship hit the full force of the storm which, perversely, had now backed round to come from the northwest. Savill could just make out the two escorts waiting for them in the middle distance but the weather was incredibly bad. It seemed inconceivable that they could maintain the necessary speed to stay safe from submarine attack – not in these seas, possibly the worst he had ever experienced.

Speed was the key to it all – the *Hampshire* was poorly armoured and, even then, only amidships. He took the same line as the rest of the Navy that 'speed *is* armour' but without destroyer escort, they'd be dreadfully exposed. Mind you, with the ship yawing around like a fishing smack at anchor, it would be a very talented submariner who could get a decent shot off in these conditions.

"Signals?" shouted Savill as the *Hampshire* plunged in a torrent of spray between the two escorts, "Send to Unity and Victor, 'Take station and make revolutions for 18 knots'." He watched as the destroyers turned to follow the *Hampshire*. He gripped the rail out of sheer reflex as the *Victor* was nearly pooped in the heavy seas. The rain bounced off the superstructure, hiding the ships astern but, in a moment, they re-emerged through the mist.

"Jesus! Did you see that, Number One?" he shouted over the shrieking of the radio rigging.

"Damn close one, Sir. Someone on board said his prayers last night, that's for sure."

For quarter of an hour, Savill watched as the two smaller ships slipped ever further back into the grey vapour when he saw a faint yellow flickering between them, followed by a brighter signal to the *Hampshire*.

"The *Victor* informs *Unity* that she can only manage fifteen knots – relayed by *Unity*, Sir," called the Signals officer.

"Yes, I can see. They're taking a hell of a pounding." He turned to his First Officer. "What do you think, Charles? Fifteen is too slow."

"I agree, Sir. Sixteen is the slowest we can allow. We have to get Lord Kitchener out of these waters without delay." He ducked as a mountain of water roared over the weather shield of the open bridge.

"Right – let's bring her a little closer into land, too. We might get a bit more shelter there and stop the Army getting sick. Starboard five and make revolutions for sixteen knots. Relay that back to the escorts, Signals. Bring her back amidships on my command."

****

Hubert rolled slowly over and weakly rubbed the crusted blood gluing his left eye shut. As his field of vision came more into focus, he caught sight of O'Beirne's still body lying over in the corner. It had that 'pile of old clothes look' that meant Death was in the room – he'd seen enough of it to know – but nevertheless he crawled painfully over to check, his ribs hurting badly. O'Beirne's face was covered with a pillow taken presumably from the bunk above him. Chris removed it gently, uncovering glassy eyes staring sightlessly at the ceiling. Duquesne was an efficient killer – you had to give him that.

Using the furniture, he dragged himself up. His head was one mass of pain. "If anyone hits me again, I'm resigning," he thought and staggered towards the door. Wrenching it open, he tripped over the storm sill and tumbled into the passageway at the feet of a Royal Marine sergeant.

****

Savill scanned the horizon for the escorts and glimpsed them alternately appearing and then vanishing as they crested mountainous spume-covered waves far in the distance. He had already made yet another reduction in speed and had signalled the fact to the *Unity*, asking if Leckie could keep up. Suddenly the light of an Aldis lamp flickered through the storm.

"*Unity* says 'no', Sir," shouted the Signalman. "They're only able to maintain ten knots."

Savill swivelled on his stool and wiped the spray from his eyes. The two little destroyers were mere specks on the edge of visibility. Clearly, they'd soon lose contact all together. He thought for a moment and then made his decision. "Very well, Signals. Make to *Unity*, 'Destroyers return to base'. Ask them to repeat to *Victor*. Log the time."

Moments later, the reply glinted through the darkness of the storm. 'Message received and understood. Good luck.'

At 1820 hours, the *Hampshire* was on her own.

****

Duquesne, dressed in regulation navy oilskins, curled up in the lee of one of the superstructures topsides. He considered himself perfectly safe from detection – no-one in his right mind would be topsides in weather like this. The mines couldn't be far ahead by now and he had armed the bomb in Kitchener's cabin. It was timed to go off just before the mines – or perhaps a little later; it was difficult to finesse these things – and he'd made sure that the boiler room door wouldn't be closing properly when the ship went down.

Thinking of O'Beirne made him feel very good, indeed. Of course, he would *really* have liked to strangle him but, just in case the body was found, he didn't want it appearing in a post mortem. Smothering seemed a sensible alternative but, *honestly*, he would have liked more *time*.

He glanced round the corner, narrowing his eyes through the blast of rain and spray, to re-check the location of the nearest Carley raft. There was a pinnace but the officers would be in it and Datchett had warned him to stay out of sight as much as possible.

Besides, there would always be a better chance of survival with the lower deck types.

****

Captain Savill peered through binoculars at Marwick Head appearing through the low cloud. If anything, the weather had worsened, much to his complete disbelief. The *Hampshire's* bows were driving deep into the water, slowing her down. He turned at the commotion behind him as two Marines, accompanied by their Sergeant, brought what could only be described as a prisoner on to the bridge.

"What's the meaning of this, Sergeant?" he shouted.

"Beg pardon, Sir. Mr O'Beirne of Lord Kitchener's party has been found dead in his cabin. Looks like foul play and this man was found with the body. Claims to have information about a plot to kill His Lordship."

"For God's sake, Sir, listen to me. My name is Lieutenant Christophe Hubert of MI5. Until recently, I was attached to Lord Kitchener's staff. I can't go into details now but I was detained by force then managed to escape and get on board without being detected. Mr O'Beirne was murdered by a Boer working for the Germans. He has planted a bomb in your cabin with the intention of killing Lord Kitchener. Your route has also been compromised and is probably mined. We need to get His Lordship out of your cabin *now* and turn this ship around."

Savill looked disbelievingly at Hubert. "You were on his staff, you say?"

"Yes, Sir"

"Well, it's easy enough to check that out and, if it's as urgent as you say, we'd better do it quickly. Sergeant, take Lieutenant Hubert down to His Lordship's cabin – but guard him carefully. If he fails to recognise our stowaway, lock him in the brig for the duration." He turned to His Gunnery Officer. "Matthews, go down with them and speak to Lord Kitchener."

"Very good, Sir. Follow me, Sergeant."

The five minutes it took for Hubert to get from the bridge to Henry's cabin were probably the longest of his life. Matthews knocked on the cabin door and greeted

Fitzgerald who answered it.

"Apologies for disturbing you, Colonel, but this man here says he is known to you and Lord Kitchener." He swivelled aside to reveal a very battered Hubert.

"Hubert! Thank God you're here!"

Farmer, hearing Hubert's name came to the door. "Hubert, my dear boy … my goodness, you *have* been in the wars. Very glad, indeed, to see you."

Hubert knew Farmer was 'in character' and was really *overjoyed* to see him. "Thank you, Sir but no time to explain things. There may very well be a bomb in your cabin and we need to get you out of it – right now."

Without collecting any possessions, apart from grabbing their greatcoats, Farmer, Fitzgerald and MacPherson ran out into the companion-way as a violent explosion blew the door shut behind them, shredding the port bulkhead and killing the Marine on sentry duty outside the cabin. Farmer was thrown heavily against MacPherson and Hubert ended up underneath Fitzgerald and Matthews. For a moment, everything was stunned silence until he felt a hand helping him to his feet and found himself face to face with the Sergeant, who simply nodded and said, "Good call, Sir."

Fitzgerald, coughing in the acrid smoke, just looked ashen-faced at the wrecked cabin door and slicked back his hair into a semblance of neatness. "My God! That was on the money, Hubert. I thank you." He looked at the marines checking over the fallen man, his face hardening. "Is this the work of someone we both know?"

"Indirectly but, yes, Sir."

"Let's be clear, you're talking about Kell – the *bastard.* If we get out of this alive, Hubert, I swear …"

The companion-way was now filling with sailors

emerging from cabins but, in seconds, the Marines had Fitzgerald and Farmer stumbling quickly through the roiling fumes which filled the air. "Make way, there!" ordered Matthews, "Make *way* for Lord Kitchener!" Behind them, sea water began to flow over the cabin's storm sill.

****

Up on deck, Duquesne felt, rather than heard, the explosion and hugged himself at the thought of Kitchener in small pieces. This would make his name with German High Command – he'd be able to name his own price from now on – if he survived, of course. But the biggest satisfaction came surely from the knowledge that he had avenged his mother and sister on the man responsible for their deaths. Yes, he had tried and failed once before but that was now a distant and frustrating memory. At last, it was done. Even now, he could hardly bear the memory of the day he passed through his parents' farm in Nylstroom, serving with the British Army of all things, to find it razed to the ground on the orders of Kitchener's 'scorched earth' policy. The stink of burnt wood made him sick, still. That's when he found out that his sister had been killed and his mother was dying in a British concentration camp. And that's when he swore to devote his life to the destruction of Kitchener and the whole bloody British Empire. It would never really be over but Britain would not recover from this in time to win the war. Euphoria swept violently through him like a drug.

The noise of a metal hatch being blown open violently against its retaining cleats made him start – a naval officer was helping *Lord Kitchener* onto the deck, followed by that runt Hubert, supported by a couple of Marines! How many lives did the old bastard have?

They were making for the bridge. Stiffly, he rose to his feet, clutching at railings to avoid being flung overboard, and went to finish the job.

****

Savill snapped round to face the Signals officer, "Is Lord Kitchener safe? Was anyone injured?"

"One death, Sir – Marine Hughes. Took the brunt of the blast. His Lordship, Colonel Fitzgerald and that new bloke are coming up to the bridge."

"Thank God for that! Get a damage report sorted out immediately."

"Aye, Sir." Pressing his mouth tightly against the speaking tube, he shouted over the storm to organise damage control parties, almost losing his balance on the slippery deck as the ship's bows plunged to her deepest yet into the grey-green depths.

Luck was not with them that evening. Somehow, the downward movement of the bows seemed to stop abruptly, as if they had struck an underwater obstruction, like a reef. In any other weather, the ship would have passed over Beitzen's mines unharmed but the sliver of hope he had offered up was not to be realised. For a split second, the eyes of the bridge officers met as the immense explosion lifted the forepeak of the ship almost out of the sea, shattering the spine of one of the bridge officers and killing him instantly. The crew were thrown forwards as the ship decelerated from the huge drag forces exerted by the mangled bows. Savill pulled himself up from the deck, his head streaming blood from a wound rendered painless by shock, and peered down at the forward deck through the driving rain. One look was enough – she was going to the bottom. He had, perhaps, only minutes to bring the crippled warship closer into land. Pushing the dead officer to one side, he made his way over to the speaking tube and shouted down to the Quartermaster, two decks below the waterline. "Quartermaster, the ship is going down. Give me 30 degrees of starboard rudder and then get yourself and your men up on deck to abandon ship!" He turned to the other officers. "Gentlemen, I thank you for your faithful service but now it's time to leave. I ask one thing only of you – do your utmost to ensure the safety of our guests. Call 'Abandon Ship!'"

****

Once again, Farmer had been thrown heavily to the deck. Fitzgerald caught him by the collar of his greatcoat and held on grimly until he was helped by the returning MacPherson.

"We need to get abaft the bridge," shouted Fitzgerald into Hubert's ear as 'Abandon Ship' was announced. "The Captain's pinnace is secured there." He motioned to the Sergeant, who understood what was needed and they turned to make their way aft. The sudden deceleration could be felt almost immediately. Hubert knew exactly what had happened – it had to be one of Kell's mines rather than a torpedo. No submarine could usefully come up to periscope depth in these seas.

Moving towards the first funnel, grasping the lifelines that had been rigged earlier, the group moved out of the shelter of the superstructure. The force of the wind was unbelievable. Hubert felt that they'd never make it to the small wooden vessel rocking crazily on its stanchions. Every step aft, angling steeply up the sloping deck, blew them half a step backwards. The plunging of the bows constantly threatened to dash them against the bulkheads.

Matthews positioned them in the lee of the bridge while he moved further aft to manage the party already trying to make the pinnace ready to launch when a further eruption from below expelled dark clouds of soot from the four funnels of the ship as cold seawater flooded into the engine room, detonating the boilers. With no power, the *Hampshire* came to a halt in moments and corkscrewed in the pounding seas, making the lifeboats impossible to launch – the derricks were electrically powered with no mechanical back up. Matthews looked up one final time to see a towering wave come over the submerged port side before he and his deck crew were swept away.

Fitzgerald watched as the pinnace was shattered into kindling. "Hubert!" he roared. "The ship's dying. Fifteen minutes and she'll be down – I'm sure of it. We have to get the Colonel off the ship or we'll be sucked under as she sinks."

****

As yet another colossal sea hit the bows, Savill heard the ear-splitting screech of the mast aft of the bridge collapsing towards the funnels, covering the deck in a Gordian knot of tangled wire. None of the lifeboats would be capable of launching now. He grabbed the Signals officer by the lapels of his oilskins and shouted into his ear. "Lionel, get a radio message off to Longhope – damn pity we sent the escort home – but send off a distress call."

"No good, Sir, it was the first thing I tried when you ordered us to abandon. The set's been wrecked!"

Savill looked at him, appalled. "What the hell do you mean – 'wrecked'?"

"Just that, Sir. It's been sabotaged. Someone's been at it with a hammer. I checked the standby set, too. It's just the same – *and* the distress rockets. *They're* missing – probably overboard. All we have is the Aldis."

"But how …?"

"Must have been when we were all on deck to welcome Lord Kitchener. There's nothing to be done but get off the ship and make for shore."

Taking a final look around the bridge of his ship, Savill urged the other man towards the hatch. It was over for the *Hampshire.*

****

Farmer looked, terror-stricken, at Hubert. "Chris, this is going to upset me awfully." He started aside as a seaman officer, trying to run towards them with a pair of cork waistcoats, become tangled up in the wire covering the deck. Momentarily stuck on the open without shelter, he was thrown against the nearest stanchion by a wave and killed before their eyes. Fitzgerald grabbed the jackets before they were swept into the sea by the hissing torrent of water draining away through the scuppers. He glanced around to see of any other life jackets were about and, finding none, he snorted to himself. "Ah, well."

Sliding gingerly along with his back to the bulkhead, he gently pulled Farmer towards him and began to fit the floats over his head. "Did you know, Henry," he said, smiling sadly, as he carefully tied the braids of the life-preserver round him, "that Kitchener once had his fortune read – just once in his lifetime, as far as I know." Farmer dumbly shook his head. "Can you believe that she told him his death would come by water? Knowing what we know, how curious is that?" He pulled the bow tight and looked steadily into the other man's eyes. "Don't make it come true." He threw the other preserver to the Sergeant and pointed to Hubert, huddled on the deck.

"Oswald," stuttered Farmer through chattering teeth, "What are you doing?"

He patted him on the arm. "You're not to worry about me," he said briskly. "I'll be absolutely fine. I'll get on to one of the rafts and meet you on shore. Hubert's in a bad way, so there's no way you could both make it aft to the Carley rafts – not in this incline – and you'd never get through all this bloody rigging."

"But …"

Fitzgerald smiled fondly. "You did a *wonderful* job - simply wonderful and courageous and decent – and I *thank* you. I thank you for my sake as well as his but you *have to go*! We may only have minutes left!" He grabbed Farmer sharply towards him by the front of the lifejacket. "Go!"

Turning round, he pushed Farmer and Hubert ahead of him towards the rail facing away from Orkney, and hung on grimly to the remains of the mast as the ship angled a little deeper and rolled more to port. Farmer and Hubert, no longer sheltered from the gale, were struck by yet another powerful wave, thrown on to their backs and swept towards the rails.

Screaming in fury, Duquesne appeared on deck and charged towards them, trying at the last minute to reach Kitchener. He could *not* be allowed to escape his fate. He slithered quickly across space between them like a loathsome reptile – only a few feet more and he might be able to grab hold of Kitchener's lifejacket. He reached out and screamed in pain as Fitzgerald swung a wooden batten back again for another strike. But it never came. All of

Duquesne's fury became focussed on him alone and the two men wrestled on the pitching deck, inches away from the davits.

For a brief time, Fitzgerald seemed to have the upper hand. He punched the Boer again and again in the face and tried to throttle him but the ship angled suddenly downward when a hatch, deep below, gave way to air pressure. It was enough to distract Fitzgerald and for Duquesne to roll him off on to his face. Grabbing the nearest length of rigging wire strewn all around them, he wound it round and round Fitzgerald's neck, leaning back to pull it tight. As the ship lurched again in a roll to port, Duquesne jumped off the other man who slid down the slope towards the rails until the wire snapped tight. Within seconds, Fitzgerald was dead, sliding slowly from side to side at the end of the wire as the waves pounded the dying ship.

Duquesne grabbed on to a hatch coaming to stop him following his victim and looked down into the sea. Kitchener was gone. Stretching his neck as far as it would go, he scanned the waves but no sight of the two men could be seen. Kitchener was probably dead – no-one would survive in that sea – but he was meant to be *his*. To get so close and yet not be able to kill him personally!

Angrily, he wiped the blood from his eyes and looked up to see sailors struggling to launch a Carley raft over the starboard rail. By the time he reached the rail, the raft was in the sea.

****

Over on the starboard side, the sea was full of bobbing heads and all the detritus of a dying ship. Men were grasping frantically at anything that would float in the biting cold. Duquesne jumped and entered the water close to a group of men scalded when the boilers burst. The salt water lacerated their wounds. Even over the incredible noise of the gale, their screams pierced his ears. The *Hampshire* had minutes to go and, if he was not to be sucked down after it, he'd have to swim away from the ship and towards land. In those conditions, swimming fifty yards was more like half a mile but, exhausted by the waves and bitter cold, he made it towards the nearest raft where he was hauled in and unceremoniously dumped onto the submerged decking.

He looked back at the clouds of steam streaming out of the forward engine room. Just above, near the quarter deck, two officers jumped overboard holding wooden drawers under each arm. Someone in his raft sang out, "What do they think they're doing – committing hara-kiri?"

He turned around and took stock of where he was for the first time. The Carley raft was a large oval structure, about ten feet long and eight wide, with the edges encircled in a deep layer of cork. The deck was only a grating and the sea ran through unimpeded. About fifty other men shared the float with him – their weight pushed the deck deep into the sea, meaning that everyone was up to their waist in freezing water and the waves pounded over them constantly. Duquesne knew, knew for certain, he would not be able to suffer this for long. Clamping his jaw tightly shut to prevent his teeth chattering, he fought hesitatingly for breath.

Some men were furiously paddling. His brain beginning to cloud with encroaching hypothermia, he struggled to understand the reason until he looked back again. The forward funnel of the *Hampshire* was now going under the water, sucking their raft back towards the ship in her final agonies. Duquesne was hit by what felt like tons of water coming over the side, burning his wrists, twisted for safety around the Carley's ratlines.

"Look!" shouted a Petty Officer, "Look! She's going down!

The *Hampshire*, bow deep in the water, had suddenly lurched forward, her propellers high in the air. With a sickening noise of grinding steel, she began her descent. Perched high above, many of the crew were hanging to the rigging and derricks, hoping to float away when the ship went under. Others were now sliding down the exposed hull, trailing paths of blood as their skins were flayed by the exposed barnacles.

"She's going now," howled an older seaman, who retched over the side and slid, unseen, into the turbulent water.

The *Hampshire* tucked her bows even deeper and fifteen minutes after she struck the mine she disappeared from sight.

****

Over on Birsay, a gunner of the Orkney Territorial Force was watching the *Hampshire*, intrigued by her sailing so close to shore. Visibility was poor with driving mists of rain and black, lowering clouds. He grinned quietly to himself at memory of his Grannie's old saying – 'Orkney has three months of winter and nine months of bad weather'. He leaned on his gun post to watch the ship pound its way to wherever it was going, suddenly widening his eyes as he saw the blast of orange flame leap from abaft the bridge. The ship slowed and turned more into land. It was clear right away that she had been crippled – she began to settle by the head almost immediately. He raced over to his billet and reported in to his corporal. Within minutes, the NCO was in the Post Office, a couple of hundred yards away, drafting a telegram.

BATTLE CRUISER IN DISTRESS BETWEEN MARWICK HEAD AND THE BROUGH OF BIRSAY - END

"Jessie, get that off to Stromness and Kirkwall. I'm getting back to the lookout post to see what's happening"

As he raced back to the billet he called out to the gunner, "Joe, I'm back. What's happening?"

"I think she's going down, Corp!"

As the two men watched, holding on to their helmets in the gale, the *Hampshire* quickly sank.

"Jesus! God help those poor lads. I'll need to get back and let the Admirality know. Keep your eyes peeled."

Once again, he raced to two hundred yards to the Post Office and burst through the door, "Jessie, she's gone down. Can you add that to the telegram?"

"Oh here, now, that's terrible! " She sat still, hands over her mouth, trying to imagine the horrors of all those men in the sea on a night like this.

"Jessie! Can we add that to the telegram?"

"Right! Right! Honestly, I don't know. I'll need to ask Kirkwall. They'll know whit to do."

Moments later, she signalled to Kirkwall.

THE SHIP HAS SUNK. CAN THAT BE ADDED TO THE TELEGRAM - QUESTION - END

They waited for five minutes that seemed like five hours until the reply came through to say that it was 'all right'.

"'All right?' What does that mean? Are we sure it'll go into the telegram to the Admirality?"

"Oh, aye. If Morag say it's fine, you can be sure of it," she soothed.

Unconvinced, he thanked her and returned to his post.

****

Hubert vomited weakly into the water, aware that he could not keep Farmer's inert body afloat for much longer. Exhaustion and hypothermia were fast setting in. His broken ribs, the coshing and the salt water in his damaged lungs caused him desperate, dizzying pain while the incredible cold paralysed him, taking away all feeling from his arms and legs. Each wave carried them twenty or thirty feet into the air and then bore them down into a trough, submerging them in a tumbling mass of bubbles.

Gently, he tried to turn around, holding Farmer's head above the surface. Although it must have been well past eight in the evening, it was still day despite the bottle-green light of the storm and he could see the shoreline of one of the Orkney Islands about a mile or so away. That would have to be his target. He kicked round again, pulling Henry on to his chest and started to swim towards shore.

God knows how long they'd been in the water. It seemed like hours but couldn't have been more than twenty minutes or so, he thought. The older man had been drifting in and out of consciousness throughout but had been silent and unmoving for some time now. Hubert looked around for rafts or longboats each time they crested a wave but they were either all gone or deep in the troughs of other waves.

"Chris."

The sudden voice, close to his ear, caused Hubert to start. "Jesus, Henry!" he croaked, """You nearly scared me to death there!"

"Chris, let me go. Neither of us is going to survive if you try to keep me afloat."

"Not a chance, Henry," he choked as a wave hit him flat in the face. "Been through too much to do that."

"I'll be dead within the half hour. I know the symptoms." He grinned, ashen-faced. "I've had some medical training."

"Well, we'll just keep things going as they are until then."

"No, you …"

"Henry, you have to shut up and let me save my breath. With my lungs the way they are, I'm in desperate need of them."

Farmer did as he was told and within a few moments, Hubert could feel that he was unconscious once more. "Hang on for God's sake, Henry!" He looked around frantically. "Where the hell is the rest of the crew?"

****

Having second thoughts, the Post Mistress sent another telegram to Stromness instead of the signal she had made earlier to Kirkwall.

FOUR FUNNEL CRUISER SUNK TWENTY MINUTES AGO - STOP - NO ASSISTANCE ARRIVED YET - STOP - SEND SHIPS TO PICK UP BODIES - END

Up on the ridge, the Corporal had a clear view, but for the weather conditions, of the sea around. No ships had arrived yet to pick up survivors. Where were they? Men would be dying out there in these conditions. He ducked into his command post and cranked the handle of the field telephone. "Put me through to the Vice-Admiral at Longhope," he said with authority. While he waited for the connection, he imagined all the forms of torture he'd be subjected to for his temerity but what the hell did he care – it could be his brother out there. Thank God he was serving in warmer waters but, still …

The phone crackled into life. "Hello? Hello! I'm sorry but the Vice Admiral has left clear instructions that he is not to be disturbed." And, with that, the line went dead. Over in Longhope, Brock glanced at his ADC setting the earpiece of the telephone onto its hook. "Thank you, Jamie," he said quietly. "That'll be all for this evening but, before you leave, ask the Commander, Western Patrol to call me as soon as possible."

"Aye, Sir. Goodnight."

"Goodnight, Jamie."

When the door had closed behind the young officer, Brockman fished out the telegram from Kell, grabbed a lighter from the table and burned the message to fragments in the nearest ashtray, grinding them to a fine powder afterwards.

CHAPTER 9

Monday, 5 June 1916 1942 hours – 2300 hours

Twice the car had nearly been blown over as Boissier drove north. In fact, the savagery of the wind almost stopped them dead in their tracks as they turned right into its teeth, away from the lyrically-named Loch of Boardhouse. "Why the hell can't they have civilised names in this God-forsaken dump?" He wiped the rain from his goggles, muttering. "Arse-end of the world!" He turned to his sodden companion, "Where the hell are we?"

Pickup glanced at the small map he was pressing tightly against his knees to stop it being blown away. Vance had left it for them in the car with one or two important routes carefully marked on it together with some notes in a careful, copperplate script. With the rain and the fact that the gale had ripped the canvas clean off the car an hour ago, the map was now so sodden it was in great danger of simply falling apart at the fold lines. He pointed over to the half-right. "See that promontory over there? There's sort of peninsula at the end of it but in this bloody weather you can hardly see it from here – it all looks one spit of land."

"It's probably been blown away by this lunatic wind, too!" Boissier peered into the darkening sheets of rain and, little by little, he was gradually able to see huge waves smashing themselves at the base of the point's cliffs. "Right! Got it! I can't see the damn thing itself but there's a lot of spray over there."

"That's it!" Pickup had to shout in Boissier's ear to be heard. "That's the Brough of Birsay, so we're too far north if Vance's notes are as good as he thinks. Looks like the road we're on turns hard left in a mile and a bit and then it goes straight south," he shouted. "We'll get to Marwick Head about three miles after that and that's where he thinks there's the best chance of finding survivors." He prodded Boissier. "It'll be a hell of a job driving then – look, it's all small tracks from there on out westward towards the coast."

"Wonderful!"

"The thing is – there's almost no shoreline. It's all cliffs - the map calls them 'geos' – Nebbi Geo is the one to check out first, apparently. We'll have to watch that none of the yokels try to pull survivors up by rope or go down to help."

"So there's no beach they can come ashore on?"

Pickup looked again at the map, almost losing it again in the wind. "There's a golf course with a smallish beach. It's called the Bay of Skaill but that's a fair bit south of here. Can't see them lasting that long."

****

"Look, lads, we've too many people in here," shouted the Petty Officer in Duquesne's raft, "Some of you will have to get back into the water and hold on or we'll all go under."

Without discussion, a dozen men cheerfully jumped into the sea, some of them striking off for shore, "We'll get there afore you and grab all the skirt!" they shouted back.

Without the extra weight, the raft rose considerably but for the young boy seamen, it was still tough. They could still barely keep their heads above the water line. On the other side of the raft, Duquesne could see a private soldier, probably the one ordered to fix the blacksmith. He was talking to the Petty Officer but the wind and sea made it impossible for Duquesne to make out what he was saying. Using the violent movement of the raft as cover, he let himself be battered around the perimeter until he was within a man or two of the pair. God knows what he was saying to him – having the Grim Reaper in the raft with you would make most men garrulous and, to Duquesne, the private had a weasely, self-serving look about him. He might say anything.

"Shall we reach the shore?" chattered the 'solider', in agony from the cold.

The sailor looked carefully at him. "Sure we will. I think we'll do it," he said comfortingly.

"I don't think so, mate." Within a few minutes, his head had sagged backwards against the cork floats and he gently slid to the bottom of the raft.

Duquesne looked at the said shore – it was a bare mile away but the wind, being from the north-north-west was driving them *down* the coast rather than *towards* it. Despite clamping his jaw tightly shut to stop trembling, he was sure that he sweated at the thought of being blown *past* Orkney and out into open sea. He scanned the horizon. Was *no-one* going to come looking for them? His thoughts were shattered by a raucous noise – one of the sailors singing.

"It's a long way to Tipperary, it's a long way to go …" The old, grizzled gunner shouted out the song and called on his mates to join in the chorus. For a while, some of them tried, but, one by one, they fell silent, trying to conserve their energies.

"Tom!" called one, "Pipe down. You'll wear yourself out."

"No I bloody won't!" he shouted. "You buggers need to rouse yerselves or you'll nivir see land again." He staggered up and waved his arms stiffly like an arthritic conductor. "Right then. It's a long way to Tipperary, it's a …" He never saw the wave that came from behind him. When it had passed over the raft, he was gone.

"Christ," thought the Boer, "I'm not getting out of this."

****

"Hello, there. Who am I speaking to?"

Mr George Linklater Thomson was a man used to trouble at sea. The Honorary Secretary of the Royal National Lifeboat Institution in Stromness for many years, he had seen marine tragedy in all its uncompromising forms so when sailors were in danger, he was equally uncompromising. He knew the waters around Orkney and he knew the weather. This storm was probably the worst he had seen for a couple of decades at least and when the news of the *Hampshire* reached him, his first thought was to get the lifeboat to sea. He put a call through to the Naval HQ at Stromness.

"This is Lieutenant Rice. Who is this?"

"Hello there, it's George Thomson of the RNLI station. I've just heard that there's a ship down somewhere off

Marwick Head. Is that correct?"

"I'm sorry, Mr … Thomson … I really cannot discuss naval movements with unauthorised personnel!"

"Unauth…! Laddie, my job is to help save lives at sea. I'm as 'authorised' as I need to be. I'm not asking you to divulge the movements of the Grand Fleet. If there's a cruiser down in this weather, men who might be saved are going to die. Now stop wasting my time and give me the map reference. Minutes count!"

"I'm sorry, I know nothing about a cruiser. Good evening."

In utter disbelief, George turned slowly to look at the earpiece of his telephone. The man, barely more than a Snotty by his voice, had rung off: men possibly dying in freezing waters, *and he had rung off!* Well, damn him! He turned round to the lifeboat coxswain and nodded sharply, "Get her ready for sea, Alec."

****

"Boissier! Look! Over there."

Boissier saw the movement a few hundred yards away at the cliff edge. He'd be damned before he'd call it a 'geo' – it was a bloody cliff. "Looks like a group of concerned citizens with ropes and lanterns."

Pickup stood to look over the streaming windscreen. "The road ends here." He tried to chuckle at Boissier but the effort of getting up on his feet nearly made him throw up for the third time since leaving Stromness. He'd be seeing double for sure if his right eye wasn't completely closed, he thought. "You'll have to get those lovely hand-made shoes wet!"

Both men left the car, Boissier snarling at every flap of his cold, wet trousers clinging to his legs below the oilskin, and heaved forward into the violence of the wind coming straight off the sea. A hundred yards took them the best part of ten minutes to cover but they finally arrived at the cliff edge where they were welcomed by the group.

"Good evening, gentlemen! Have we found any survivors? No? Dear me, dear me. We're very grateful for all your help. I'm Lieutenant Boissier of the RMA and this is Surgeon-Commander Pickup of the Royal Navy." He patted Pickup solicitously on the arm. "We had a bit of an accident on the way over, as you can see."

Each of the locals introduced themselves but the names were snatched away by the wind and swallowed by the muffled clothes they wore. Boissier continued, "There will be other naval parties along shortly and they'll tell you what to do. Follow their instructions to the letter. You probably do not know that Lord Kitchener himself was aboard the sunken ship." The wide-eyed stares confirmed it. "That's why the Surgeon Commander is here – just in case His Lordship or any of his party makes it ashore."

One of the rescue party pointed down to the water line where the waves were bashing a Carley raft mercilessly. "Ten puir souls were clinging to that raft but they were washed away before we could get a line down to them." He shaded his eyes against the driving rain and scanned the sea. "We've been here about half an hour but there's no sign of anyone else and with the wind the way it is, I think if there *are* any other rafts they'll have been blown down the coast towards Skaill."

Boissier patted him on the shoulder. "Thank you so much for your efforts." He turned to the other men. "You, too, gentlemen. It would be a great help if you could stay here for a while longer, if you can stand it, just in case.

Meanwhile, since Commander Pickup and I have transport, we'll run down to Skaill as fast as we can in this weather and check for anyone coming ashore." Seeing them eagerly nod assent, Boissier and Pickup said their farewells and returned to the car.

As they reversed back to the main road, Pickup was deep in thought. "Surgeon-Commander," he announced, after a while. "That out-ranks you, doesn't it?"

Boissier smiled at him, pityingly. "Remember – it's all just fairy tales for the peasants. None of it's real." With an effort, he put the car into first gear and headed south once more. "Right. We should just make a bee-line straight for Skaill Bay in case they make it there like the yokel said. No-one's going to come up alive from those bloody cliffs but keep an eye out for any rescue parties, nevertheless, as we go along. I want that bastard Hubert."

"Banfield's mine – no arguments this time, Boissier."

****

A hoarse shout made George Thomson turn round from his thoughts. It was the coxswain. "We're ready, George! Everyone's standing by in their lifebelts. Do we launch?" Thomson looked down at the slipway. In the gathering dusk, he could just make out the crew in the backwash of light from the lanterns – all good lads, local fishermen who knew the seas around the islands as well as he did – but that damn Rice's attitude was puzzling him. Was it possible he'd make some naval manoeuvre *worse* by launching on his own recognizance? Was there something he didn't know?

"Wait a minute, Alec. Mr Gilchrist and I'll take a quick drive over there to see if we can straighten this out.

"Aye, but George – this weather …"

"I know, Alec, I know but perhaps the Navy knows more about this than they're letting on. Perhaps the area is mined to hell and back. We'd better be sure. I'll be back quick as I can."

Naval HQ at Stromness was only a short distance away and, within ten minutes, the two men were shaking the rain off their overcoats in the small office of a junior Naval officer who looked up at them petulantly.

"Yes? Can I help?"

Thomson saw the nameplate on the desk and leaned over it on his fists. "*Sub*-Lieutenant Rice, is it not? I have just had the dubious pleasure of speaking with you a little while ago. My name is Mr George Thomson of the RNLI and this is my friend and colleague Mr Gilchrist."

"How do you do, gentlemen?" stammered Rice. "I'm afraid that if this visit is anything to do with our conversation, then I'm very much afraid that …"

"I will *not* waste any further time with you, Lieutenant! There will be men dying out there! Now I want to talk to the most senior officer you can muster at this time of the evening. If Commander Walker is around, he's the man. He commands the Western Patrol – he, at least, should be able to give me the clearance I need."

"Well, I'm not sure I can just conjure him up at a moment's notice, Sir. I'm sorry to be blunt but we just do not need any civilian help. If there *is* a cruiser in trouble – and I make no admission of the fact – then it's a job for professionals." Rice looked at him defiantly. "Not *amateurs*."

Thomson drew himself up and looked down at Rice, trying to think of a way to eat him alive while still remaining civilised, when the door of the inner office opened suddenly and an officer with a lot more braid walked in. Thomson recognised him immediately and went across to shake hands.

"Commander Walker. I'm George Thomson, Secretary of the lifeboat station here and this is my friend Mr Gilchrist. I don't think you and I have met but I know you by sight. This is a terrible thing that's happened here…"

"Let me just stop you there, Mr Thomson. I believe Lieutenant Rice has made things quite clear to you. Thank you very much for your help but we do not require it."

"You do not *require* it? And what about the lads out there? Don't you think *they* require it?"

"Now look. I am trying to be polite. Lieutenant Rice has tried to be polite but you *bloody* people simply will not listen."

"It is my job to help save the lives of your men and we're standing here wasting time. How in God's name do you expect me …" Thomson cocked his head to one side to catch the muted sound of laughter coming from the inner office. The clinking of glasses was unmistakeable. He snarled at Walker. "While you drink your … your *pink gins*, mothers' sons are gasping their last."

"You will *not* interfere in Naval matters," bellowed Walker. "It is none of your bloody business!" He shook an infuriated index finger in Thomson's face. "And I'll go one step further – if you dare to put to sea, it'll be mutiny. Do you hear me, it'll be *munity!* If I hear another word on this subject, I'll have the whole lot of you locked up."

Walker turned sharply about and strode back to his office door, turning at the last minute to shout. "For the bloody duration!"

****

Duquesne's arms were rubbed raw by the abrasive ratlines of the raft but at least they had kept him from being flung out into the sea to die. Two men had already gone that way since the 'entertainer' and three or four more had simply succumbed to the cold – big men, too. Funny – the cold wasn't bothering him anymore. He felt warm and sleepy and ready to drift off. With any luck, he'd be picked up before he woke. And why shouldn't he have a quick nap? Hadn't he deserved it? Kitchener would never survive this weather – he was a dead man – and he, Fritz Joubert Duquesne, was the man responsible. Pride filled him with a comforting glow like strong liquor, swelling his chest. "I did it, Mama!" he whispered. Smiling quietly, he laid his head back against the cork lining of the raft, snuggling against it in an effort to make himself comfortable, and let the warmth engulf him like his mother's embrace.

"Oi! Wake up you stupid crab! Wake up!"

Duquesne found himself shattered out of his warm cocoon by the Petty Officer's boot in his side, snapping him awake. Christ! That had been close! That had been damn close! He had seen so many of his friends die that way in the Veldt when they were fighting the British. *He should have known better.* The constant, exhausting shivering had started again but at least it told him he was still alive. He glanced at the sailor who had saved him and nodded an exhausted 'Thank you', but he had to wonder how much longer he could take this. Time had ceased to matter to him now – how many times had he painfully vomited seawater, how many times had he almost been catapulted over the side, how many men in his raft had already died of exposure? "I'll *survive*," he croaked and, with that, the raft was driven abrasively onto the sands of Skaill Bay. Duquesne felt the constant movement of the raft cease and painfully – gingerly – he unwrapped his arms from the ratlines. He pulled himself wearily up and rolled over the top of the floats into the shallow water. A final wave hammered him up the slope ahead of the raft, leaving him beached there like a pin-striped whale just below the waterline of piled seaweed and other rubbish dumped by the storm. Blearily, he could see lights from a building not far away and he reached out a wavering arm towards it before he subsided face down into the harsh sand.

The last of his will power had gone just as he needed it.

****

Boissier was sure that he was close to Skaill Bay but this God-awful weather and the failing light were making things tiresome. He got Pickup to shine his torch on the map and checked the route so many times as he drove along that he almost collided with a crofter staggering down the road carrying a bundle. "Jesus!" exclaimed Pickup.

"That was a close one, sir!" shouted Boissier to the old man. "Where are you off to on a night like this?"

"A ship's just gone down. There's probably going to be some sailors from it coming ashore at Skaill Bay. It's where things wash up always. I brought some things to help them."

"That's all right, sir, you can go back home. No point in putting yourself at risk. My colleague here is a naval doctor and we have military forces meeting us at Skaill House. We have all the help we need without inconveniencing you. You get yourself back home before you catch your death." Boissier was at his most emollient.

"Well," hesitated the crofter, "if you're sure, now."

"Absolutely – but we'd better be off. Every second counts, you know." With a wave, Boissier drove off, leaving the old man to feel his way back home in the teeth of the gale.

"Every second counts!" sneered Pickup, gently massaging the bruise on the side of his head. "I don't know how you think them up."

Within five minutes, they were on the edge of the bay. Both men got out of the car and walked over the encircling grass to the edge of the sand. The bay was a mess – vast swathes of seaweed had been dumped almost up to the edge of the links below the house on the far side. A yellowish light in an upper window glinted but there was no movement from inside.

Pickup pointed to the grass below the house, covered in bodies cast there by the waves. One or two of them were moving feebly. "Don't look like army types," he said, mournfully.

"No, you're probably right. But this is about as far south as they'd get before being blown out into open water. Perhaps we should head back up …" A tiny flicker of movement at the north end of the bay caught his eye. A man, dressed in dark civilian clothing and almost submerged beneath a layer of kelp, was feebly gesturing towards the lights of the house. "Come on!" he shouted to Pickup. Both men ran down onto the sand towards the survivor. Who would it be? Perhaps O'Beirne or one of the other servants. Ten yards away, Boissier could see it was Duquesne. Pity – it might have been better for him to simply have disappeared in the sea but, then, Kell wanted him recovered if possible. A thought struck him and he nudged Pickup. "It's Duquesne. Now remember for God's sake, call me Colonel Datchett! That's how he knows me."

The Boer, however, was past caring and barely moving. Pickup carried him quickly to the car where they forced some whisky past his salt-caked lips and swaddled him in the rough navy blankets they had carried with them from Stromness. As Pickup cranked the car, Boissier dragged the unconscious body of a soldier past him and manhandled him into the rear seat with Duquesne.

"He was in the raft," panted Boissier. He gestured north and they set off again. A quick check of the cliffs on the way – just in case – then they'd head east to Evie to keep clear of any official rescue parties and turn back south again, this time towards Kirkwall. Vance had made arrangements for any survivors picked up by them to be given private wards in the Balfour Hospital under assumed names.

****

Like Duquesne, Hubert's last reserves of endurance were gradually slipping away from him. Twice in the past half hour, he found himself drifting off despite the bitter cold of the water, and only the sensation of Farmer slipping from his grasp woke him in time. Henry was a dead weight. *Dead – please, God, no!* The weather made it too dark to see if he was truly gone and his own fingers were so cold he couldn't feel for a pulse in the older man's neck. Once again, Hubert kicked vigorously to raise Henry's chin as far above water as he could.

Odd memories slipped in and out of his consciousness and he saw himself back in Ottawa, 'starting at the bottom', to use his father's hackneyed expression. Then there was that girl on the reception desk – the dark haired French one – hotel work clearly had its good points, he thought. But his father had noticed and, within the hour, she was gone from the building. He loathed him for that – not so much for spoiling his adolescent fun but for destroying her livelihood. He saw him standing there in those stupid tails of that stupid morning coat he normally wore … and then, smoothly, the black of the coat turned to khaki and his father had become his commanding officer, complete with Sam Browne belt and pistol holster. But with *tails*. Why was the CO in tails? Didn't make sense.

He coughed painfully and retched, bringing up a little more salt water. His cracked ribs moved a little, causing him to gasp in pain. Boissier and his side-kick – what *was* his name again? – flitted briefly through his thoughts but for no good reason that he could think of. He grasped Henry's life preserver tighter as a wave, steeper than normal, lifted them high up and submerged them into the following trough. For a terrifying moment, he thought he had lost Farmer in the dark, turbulent waters but a lucky sweep of the arm latched back on to his cork jacket. The relief brought him fleetingly back to lucidity. "Henry! Henry, old man, I don't know if you can hear me or if you've gone off to rip that tunic of yours but I think … I think we're probably finished. I've nothing left." The salt had left his voice a harsh whisper. "I'm sorry I got you into this hellish mess. Honest to …"

Guilty tears briefly flooded, unfelt and unseen, down his swollen face before he slipped finally into oblivion and drifted gradually away from his friend.

****

Pickup sat like a dark blot in the waiting room of the Balfour while Boissier did his smooth stuff with the Registrar. Bored, he picked up an elderly "War Illustrated" and flicked through some of the pictures of refugees from

"Plucky Belgium" being housed in Alexandra Palace – *bloody freeloaders* – and the usual jingoistic stuff about the beastly Hun. He snorted quietly to himself. Who could believe this manure?

The hospital had turned out to be a small, single-storied affair with quaint chimneys – more of a cottage hospital than anything else. Pickup thought he had seen better boarding houses but one of the nurses was a little stunner. If only he could hang around to 'look after our injured colleagues', he might get to know her better. That little Banfield piece had escaped justice, so to speak, and he was itching for some vicious fun.

Sensing someone walking past, he looked up from his magazine and *bloody hell* there she was – walking away from him, her shoes clack-clacking on the wooden floor … little tease! As she passed through the double swing doors at the end of the room furthest away from him, Boissier's voice floated through, talking to that doctor. Looked like the army bod had pegged it. No surprise, really – those 'Six' types were all chinless inbreds – but the doc was telling Boissier that the civilian was 'tougher than he looked'. Well, bully for you, Fritz of the Veldt. Now all we have to do is to spirit you away somewhere safe once you can walk.

****

In the end, it was a wooden toilet seat from the *Hampshire* that saved their lives. Sliding down the slope of a wave, it hit Hubert on the face *precisely* where he'd been coshed by Duquesne. The shock and pain brought him back to the real world, even if only for a moment or two. He could feel himself slipping back when the noise caught his attention. After being in the water for over three hours and hearing only the shrieking of the wind, his ears were sensitive to any man-made sounds. About fifty yards away, a fishing boat was looming through the darkness and sea spray. They'd never see them and *where was Henry!* Cursing his own weakness, he thrashed feebly around, frantically scanning the wave tops for any sight of him. "Henry!" he shouted noiselessly. *Nothing!* They'd have a better view from the deck of the trawler, though. He grabbed the toilet seat, almost out of reach within those few seconds, and ignoring the burning pain in his chest, waved it above his head. Shouting was out of the question and they'd never have heard him anyway.

The boat moved slowly to his left, maintaining its distance. It hadn't seen him and his last hope for his friend began to die when he saw the boat slow and stop dead in the water, pitching about in the swell. Through his swollen eyes, he could just make out something dark being dropped over the side – *a scramble net!* Perhaps they had found Henry. Each time he was lifted to the top of a wave, he could see the figure of a young boy climbing over the side and then grabbing hold of a heavy object in the water. Soon, a man joined him to drag a figure over the weatherboard. God! He hoped it was Henry and he was still alive! He relaxed back into the water, little caring if he were found or not, and looked blankly at the flag streaming back from the boat's main mast – *Dutch* – what the hell was a Dutch fishing boat doing up here?

Henry hopefully taken care of, Chris began to allow the warmth to insinuate itself back into his bones and seduce him to sleep when a further impact shattered him back to life. "Not another bloody toilet seat," he murmured as he felt a firm grip from above take hold of his life-preserver. The boy, clad in a sodden Arran jumper and tea-cosy hat helped drag him over and dump him in a pile on the deck. The smell of diesel and oil wafted around him like expensive perfume after his wretched time in the water.

Weakly, he tried to hold up his hand towards his saviours and thank them when he felt it grasped by the boy and held gently to his young cheek. For a moment, he found this puzzling, to say the least – they were clearly a friendly bunch in Holland – when recognition struck him.

“Took your time, Special.

CHAPTER 10

Tuesday, 6 June 1916 1100 hours – 1630 hours, Wick

Hubert strained until finally he could open his swollen eyes and peer groggily at his surroundings. He seemed to be in the living room of someone's house, lying on what felt like a sofa. Trying to move his head to take a look around turned out to be a big mistake – his head and neck exploded in pain like hot needles. Lying gently back to luxuriate in the gentle, domestic sounds coming from what was probably the kitchen seemed like a better idea. Outside, the rain was pattering against the window just above his head but from the sound of it the wind had abated from the madness of the night before. Well, he was *assuming* it was only the night before. God knows how long he'd been here – and where *was* 'here'? He tried to call out at whoever was working in the kitchen and was horrified at the hoarse croak that crawled out of his throat. But it brought results – Anne walked into the room and sat down on the floor near his head.

"You mustn't try to talk." Anne smiled archly at him.

"Although I *know* it'll drive you mad." She gently stroked a shock of his black hair away from his eyes, causing him to wince slightly at her touch. "Sorry. Your skin is a bit inflamed from being immersed in seawater for that length of time. We had one of 'our' doctors take a look at you both when we got here. I suppose you …"

His eyes widened at the sound of the 'both'. "Henry," he whispered, "Henry, is he alive?" Hubert felt the salt of her tears splash on his cheeks to join his. "Yes – he's alive. He's in a bad way but it seems he's going to make it." Anne looked beyond Hubert's head. "He's just behind you on another sofa at right angles to yours – no, you mustn't move yet. His head is only a couple of feet away from yours. When we picked him up, he was very nearly dead. It took us a while even to feel a pulse but his lifejacket had done the trick and kept his head clear of the water. It was the cold of Cape Wrath that nearly did for him. In that storm, and with his age, it was a miracle he survived at all. The doctor puts it down to your body warmth making that tiny difference between life and death. You saved him."

Played back in his mind, like a flickering biograph, Hubert saw again the tableau of Fitzgerald tying his own lifejacket around Farmer and calming him before their escape from the *Hampshire*. He shook his head weakly, squeezing his eyes shut against the misery of it all. "No, I didn't," he whispered. "It was someone else entirely."

Anne clasped his hand in hers and held it to her cheek, just like she had done when she pulled him from the sea. "Well, the main thing is that you're both safe."

"How ma…" Hubert retched a little and tried to swallow.

"Are you thirsty?" Seeing his nod, she poured him some from a jug placed between the two sofas and holding his head carefully up, helped him drink from the glass.

"Better?"

"Thank you. My throat … my throat is so swollen."

"The doctor says that your eyes and nose will be in a bad way from a few days and, because of all the salt water you probably swallowed, there will be other … more *unfortunate* effects, too. But with proper hydration, you should be fine soon enough. He also says that the orbit of your left eye is fractured. Nothing to be done about it, apparently – it'll heal itself. When you're a bit fitter, you can tell me about it all."

"How many?"

"How many survived?" She sighed and bowed her head. "It doesn't look like many. Probably only a dozen or so. Maybe fifteen"

"Out of seven hundred?"

"I know. MacDonald's been listening to the navy frequency. The recovery operations were criminally bad – apparently, the Thurso lifeboat boys are spitting blood over it and the worst of it is that many did make it to shore in rafts but they weren't rescued until it was too late."

"Kell – that'll be Kell. Pointless … destroy ship … let Henry survive in some hospital."

"Don't talk – you're exhausting yourself." She paused and closed her eyes against the news she had to break. "Chris, they recovered Colonel Fitzgerald's body. And that's not all – his neck shows signs of *ligature* marks." He didn't drown."

Hubert turned his face away.

"You *knew*?"

He looked back into her eyes and nodded slowly. "Duquesne … just as Henry and I went overboard."

For a moment or two, they sat silent. Anne took a deep breath and smiled tearfully. "Very well," she nodded, holding herself together. "I'll hear about that later, too. For now, I suppose I should do the talking. You'll want me to give you chapter and verse while Mac makes us a late breakfast." She shouted the last bit like a stage aside.

"I'm doing it – I'm *doing* it!" came the pained reply from the kitchen.

Smoothing the coverlet around Hubert's neck and shoulders, she chuckled at the thought of MacDonald as a kitchen slavey. She brought her face close to Chris's and stroked his cheek. "You've no idea how awful it made me feel to leave you locked up in that bloody trunk. Right up until we saw you in the water, I was imagining half the time that you had suffocated."

"Damn near did," he rasped.

"Glad you didn't."

Hubert grinned painfully. "Knew it was just a matter of time."

"Now don't start all that again!" She prodded gently with her index finger. "Anyway, where was I?"

"You were abandoning me in the trunk."

"Right. It took a couple of hours or so to get to Wick and then I had to find Mac. I went straight to the harbour area and, of course, he was at sea. By the time he came back in because of the worsening weather, refuelled and waited for the tide to change, I was pretty sure you'd have set sail but we headed off for Orkney."

Anne helped him to another sip of water, easing his throat a little. "Even although you thought I had snuffed it in a posh trunk?"

"There was always Henry – and anyone else we could find."

Hubert squeezed her hand. "Henry will be mortified you risked your life for him."

"Oh, for God's sake don't tell him. It's bad enough *your* knowing."

"All right, I won't, but I just don't see the point of being rescued if I can't embarrass you now and again."

Anne gave him her up-and-down look and went on with her story. "It has to have been the worst voyage I've ever taken in my life. I mean, the boat is designed for deep-sea, rough weather like you get in these parts – it isn't called Cape Wrath for nothing, you know – but I was so sick I can't tell you. When we got to the site, there was nothing to be seen but bodies and a bit of wreckage. And it was so dark. I was expecting it to be daylight until about eleven but the storm and spray made it hard to see anything. What *really* stood out was that there was *no-one* else around. We saw no other ships trying to find survivors. I'd have laid good odds that the place would have been crawling with the Navy trying to find Kitchener after they'd lost him. But – nothing."

A thought insinuated itself into Hubert's drowsy consciousness. "The flag."

"The flag? Oh you mean 'why were we flying the Dutch flag'?" She smiled sheepishly. "That's just a little conceit we use in our circles. Flying the neutral flag of Holland is a good way to move around and not be bothered too much by inquisitive types. The German Navy do it all the time. Anyway, we searched for two or three hours but all we found were bodies. We just had to leave them," she sighed. "But you and Henry had to be our priorities. We'd have stopped if we'd found anyone alive but we never saw a survivor in all that time. Right at the beginning we passed one of those big rafts with about forty men on board – all dead. I jumped into it to look at them in case …"

Hubert cradled her head on his chest as she sobbed for a moment and then shook herself upright.

"That wasted quite a bit of time," she continued in a firmer voice. "And I got damn wet. I was so scared of falling overboard. My sweater became so heavy and with that and the boots I'd have gone down like a stone."

"Why do your fishermen wear them, then?"

"Arrans? I think it's so that drowned sailors can be identified by the different family cable patterns."

"Comforting."

"Ye-e-e-s. Anyway, by the time we picked up Henry in the searchlight, I was exhausted by the cold and just hanging on for dear life." She looked sadly at Hubert. "I was sure he was dead – absolutely sure – but Mac found a pulse, got Henry into the cabin and I dried him off while Mac carried on looking for you. We searched for ages and that's when I began to believe you hadn't made it onto the *Hampshire.* I was sure that if we found Henry, we would have found you close by. Even worse, that … that you had never managed to make it out of that damn trunk and had gone down in the ship. And then – and then I saw a body in the water almost at the edge of the light. Trying to turn about in that weather was a nightmare. You just couldn't do it quickly but I kept the light on you all the time until we reached you. When I saw it was really you…" She hugged Chris, trying to hide her tears. "I'm getting the covers wet," she said after a moment. "Mac helped me to pull you in and I gave you the same treatment as Henry. We headed back for home, trying to follow the likely drift path of the rafts, but we passed only bodies or rafts with dead men aboard."

"So where *is* 'home'?"

"Oh, of course, you wouldn't know. You're in Mac's house in Wick. It's only a little thing with one bedroom. He made me take that since we could hardly fit you and Henry in a single bed and it would probably be better for the two of you to be together after all you've been through."

"I'm looking forward to meeting your 'Mac'. Henry and I owe him our worthless lives – you, too – and I'm looking forward to spending the rest of my life paying you back."

Kissing him for the first time, Anne cradled Hubert in her arms.

"You realise, of course, that I wasn't referring to Mac in that last part?" he wheezed.

The sound of crockery crashing disastrously to the floor made Anne jump from her laughter. "Mac! What the hell are you doing in there? Mac?" She stood up to go and see what MacDonald had done and instantly froze as the silhouette of a man appeared in the doorway of the kitchen.

"God bless all here!" he said, quietly.

"Who the hell are you?" said Hubert, feebly trying to rise.

"You lie where you are, son. You've been through some interestin' times by the look of it – you, too darlin'. Just sit back down there with your patient. I've no orders for anyone else other than the 'ould fellah' here, unless they get in my way." A silenced Mauser appeared from behind his back as he walked slowly into the middle of the room towards Henry's unconscious body.

"What have you done with Mac?" she trembled.

Gallagher cocked his head in the direction of the kitchen. "The pullover in the kitchen? Not to worry, love, he's just takin' a wee nap."

"So, you're Gallagher?" said Hubert

Gallagher looked up from gazing at Henry and smiled at Hubert. "That's it, son. D'you know, I spent every waking minute after Easter Monday planning that operation at Broome and then – when I kill him – you lot bugger it all up for me." He wagged the gun at Anne and Chris, "Have you any *idea* how much trouble I got into when I got home? They *court martialled* me! I'm sentenced to death if I don't bump your actor off." He turned to look at Henry again. "Doesn't look so much like Kitchener without the moustache."

Anne stood up, slowly, arms raised pleadingly. "Wait – just wait. Listen to me – he's not an actor. Not in that sense. He's a *doctor* who just happened to look a bit like him and was willing to help keep the secret a bit longer. It was never the plan for him to replace Kitchener. He's been through so much and all he wants to do is to go back to being a doctor. That's all – just to go back and save lives."

Gallagher shook his head firmly. "Sorry, darlin', my orders were to kill your double as publicly as possible so that there'd be no chance of anyone trying it again. Well, the public bit's out with him lying there like a log but what's to stop the British Government wheeling 'Kitchener' back out of convalescence when they cock something else up – 'oh, he's been on secret work in the Orient, don'cha know'?" he mocked. "No, he's got to die here and then you can find yourselves another double if you want. It won't be my problem."

Anne took a step forward as Gallagher pointed the gun at Henry's head. "Please!" she screamed.

He snarled at her, baring his teeth like a dog. "Sit down! Sit!"

Anne covered her face as Gallagher tightened his grip on the trigger and the sound of the double shot brought her, crying, to her knees. For a few moments Hubert pawed weakly at her back but nothing seemed to reach her senses. "Anne! Anne!"

Slowly, as though she was emerging from a winter of sleep, she raised her head from the floor and looked disbelievingly at Gallagher's body lying prone a few feet away from her. Blood was pooling from beneath his chest.

"Get the gun out of his hand," urged Hubert.

She moved the gun back towards Hubert and froze once more as a harsh voice from the living room said "Leave it! Move away from the gun!" A man stood behind the living room door, revealing only the rim of a bowler hat and a gun in his left hand.

"Christ in His Heaven! Who are *you*, now?" croaked Hubert.

"A'hm a police officer. Vance."

"Let me see your bloody warrant card!" screamed Anne.

"You jist settle down, Miss, till Ah find out what's what here."

"I'm Special Branch," she replied, more calmly in response to the sudden pressure of Hubert's hand on her shoulder. You'll find *my* warrant in the pocket of the overcoat that's hanging on the back of the door you're holding on to."

Vance retrieved it and, satisfied, threw his own across to Anne and walked into the room to check Gallagher. "Pity. He's still breathin' but Ah think he's done for."

"Mac!" screamed Anne, suddenly, and sprinted into the kitchen. Vance brushed past her to check the pulse of the man lying huddled up in the corner. It was clear he was dead, double-tapped in the head by Gallagher. The remains of a freshly-made breakfast lay scattered around the floor, mixed with fragments of the crockery that once held it. Vance stood up from checking MacDonald and looked at Anne. She was verging on the catatonic. Gently and kindly, he guided her back into the living room, past the body of Gallagher and sat her down at Hubert's feet. While Hubert spoke to her calmly, Vance went back into the hallway, dialled someone and murmured for a few moments. Hubert heard the sound of the earpiece being placed on the cradle and Vance re-appeared, closing the door behind him. He sat down in an armchair and looked over at Hubert.

"Maybe you and me should talk a wee bit. Take your time."

"But Gallagher …"

"He'll keep."

"Well, since you clearly know Gallagher, I suppose I can come clean on one or two things but I warn you – I can't tell you everything."

Vance grunted sardonically. "A'hm used tae that."

Slowly and hesitatingly, he began. "My name is Hubert and I was seconded to MI5 after I was made unfit for military service after Ypres."

"But you're American."

"Canadian!"

"Oh, right. Carry on." Clearly, to Vance, there was little difference.

"I was placed on board the *Hampshire* to prevent an act of espionage and to rescue the officer you see here."

"And who is he?"

Hubert grimaced. "That's the bit I can't tell you."

"Ah huh. Well, let's put that on wan side for now and move on."

Chris nodded towards Anne. "Perhaps you might get a whisky for her – she looks in a bad way."

"I take it she knew the deceased?" said Vance, pouring the drink.

"She did and he saved my life. The other officer and I would have drowned for sure if Mac and 'Special' here hadn't risked *their* lives to help us."

"He was ill-paid for it, then. Poor lad."

Hubert just shook his head and sat quietly for a moment. "Well, that's all I can say about my part – how did you end up appearing in the nick of time?"

"Because of two friends of yours – Mr Boissier and Mr Pickup."

"What?" Hubert snarled.

"So … not friends, after all."

"Far from it but – you're right – they're from my own particular sty. What were they up to?"

"Not sure. They told me that they were doing pretty much what you've told me *you* were doing and got me to arrange a car for them. My Superintendent back in Glasgow gave me orders that came from Moses himself. I was to give the two of them every bit of help I could. Well, I've been involved with Special Branch in the Port of Glasgow for more years than I'll tell ye, so the job came as nae great surprise to me. At any rate, I got them the car and one or two other bits and pieces and aff they went."

"But what about Gallagher?"

"Well, that's the thing. They sent me off to watch out for him."

Hubert chuckled painfully at the thought of Boissier and Pickup being too smart for their own good. Henry would have been dead but for them. "Go on."

Vance nodded across at the recumbent form, "At first, I thought this 'Gallagher' might have been a deserter from the Navy in Scapa but, I couldnae find any record of him at the Admiralty in Stromness. But any bad Irishman loose in these parts is a serious security risk so I kept a lookout for him. I found oot that a fisherman from Westray was supposed to be meeting Gallagher at a particular café doon by the dockside to sort out a trip back to Ireland for him, so I followed the fisherman." Vance sighed. "I must have drunk the best part of a gallon of tea waiting for that Irish bastard. And do you know what the best part of it was?" he asked, indignantly. "The waitress – a wee chit of a thing – was nearly in tears because he didnae show! He was supposed to be bringing her flowers. Talk aboot blarney."

A knock on the door caused Vance to get up with a grunt and go out into the hall to let the visitors come into the living room. "Ambulance," he explained laconically. The uniformed men loaded Gallagher gently on to a stretcher and returned to collect MacDonald's body, now covered respectfully by a sheet. Hubert hid Anne's eyes from the sight of her friend leaving his home for the last time.

When they had gone, Vance returned and knelt down by Anne, stroking her shoulder paternally. "Ah'll clean things up here for ye in a wee while. Jist you finish that whisky before it goes off." Carefully, he helped her sip a little more of the drink and then resumed his chair arthritically. "Anyway, we had our fisherman in custody but he was telling us all sorts of stories – 'maybe' the no-show was an Irishmen and, do you know, he wasn't so sure now that he was and, since he was a nice lad all round, there must have been a good reason for his not turning up so what was all the fuss about? I was that mad when we had to release him in the end – nothing to hold him on. But we learned a bit more from the lass – the waitress. Yes, he was definitely an Irishman – 'who could mistake that lovely brogue?' – and although he *had* said he was a seaman, he was such a gentleman, he might have been anything. He gave her flowers and a lucky horseshoe and told her to call him 'Sean'. I swear she must have been ordering her wedding clothes," Vance snorted. "The gullibility of some people. Only see what they *want* to see – but that's another story. I went over to ask around Kirkwall, too, and heard that he'd been there and was a very open, friendly sort so no-one was in the least suspicious about him. I spoke to quite a few people and heard a couple of his aliases used here and there. Then I got wind that he was planning to take a boat back to Thurso this morning and I managed to get on his tracks – we had to find oot if he was working alone or in collusion with somebody else – and that's how I got to know whit he looked like. From Thurso to Wick by train was easy enough but I lost him for about half an hour until I tracked down the driver of a pony and trap that had been hired by an Irishman to take him to this address. As ye say, it was in the nick of time."

True to his word, Vance cleaned up the stains on the living room and kitchen floors while Anne slowly recovered from the shock. In the late afternoon, he left to do the inevitable paperwork at the local police station and, eventually, to head off back to Glasgow. An hour or so later, Henry slowly regained consciousness and was able to talk a little and take some water. He was astonished to find himself still alive. Round about then, Hubert tried his first few steps and was dismayed at his own weakness but, with Anne's support, he managed to walk around the room, eventually settling beside Henry for a more extended chat before the telephone rang. Anne answered it while Hubert, unable to hear the words, caught tone of dismay. She came slowly back into the room.

"That was Detective Inspector Vance. Gallagher was operated on shortly after he reached the hospital and had the two bullets removed from his chest."

"I suppose the bastard is going to live a full and happy life?" grunted Hubert, sarcastically.

"I've no idea – all I know is that half an hour after he regained consciousness, he escaped. Vance doesn't think he'll get far in his state – and he's no longer armed, which is a mercy – but he's off now on his tracks again."

"Do you think he'll make another attempt on Henry?"

"What? What's this?" squeaked Farmer.

"Never mind, old man, you slept through it all. I'll tell you about it later if you behave."

"I doubt if he'll try again," replied Anne, shaking her head emphatically. "He'll be far too weak and, like I say, he's no longer armed. My bet is he'll try get back to Dublin and tell the rest of those animals that he planted a bomb in Kitchener's cabin on the *Hampshire* that killed him. Can't get more public than that."

"So it's over then?" whispered Henry, hoarsely.

"For you, yes," soothed Hubert. "Just don't expect any medals."

Over the course of the next hour, they brought one

another up to date on the parts they variously played to end up safe in that room. The ringing brought an end to it. "That bloody telephone!" groaned Hubert.

Anne stood slowly up. "It'll be Vance – I hope he's laid hands on Gallagher or he's found him dead in a ditch. However injured he might be, I'd be much happier hearing he's dangling decently at the end of some hemp." Within seconds she was back, worry etched on her face. "Chris, it's for you – it's Kell!"

"*Kell!* How in God's name did he track us here?" Hubert, with Anne's support, made it into the hallway and picked up the telephone set. The voice came through crackling and disturbingly remote as though the caller was not quite human. "Hubert, is that you?"

For a moment, Hubert seriously toyed with the idea of hanging up but realised the futility of it. Kell would always be able to find him. "Yes," he snapped.

"There's no need to take that tone of voice with me, Hubert. You knew the pressures we were under. If it hadn't been your friend, I suspect you'd have seen the logic of what I had to do. Appalling, yes, but it *was* necessary. But enough of this – we have to keep our conversation brief and careful. People can listen into these things as you very well know. Your doctor is quite safe now. The results are what we needed – provided he remains anonymous. Let him return to his previous profession with our thanks and wishes for his future health and happiness. I really mean that. But we now have to decide on *your* future."

"If you think I'm ever setting foot in …"

"You have no choice. It will be desertion otherwise. And I know you're thinking about your erstwhile colleagues who looked after you so well recently. I have decided that their talents would best be employed permanently at

Florrie's."

It took all of Hubert's self-control not to give a burst of laughter at the decadent Boissier being required to live and work on Orkney for the rest of the war.

"At least, you will have no trouble from them. They played their part, as instructed, and I have rewarded them by not putting them back in uniform," Kell said. "But I need you back here in the office as soon as possible. I will give you a week's recuperation but that's it. If you do not return and report for duty on, let us say, the twelfth instant, I will have you arrested and brought back in chains. That clear enough? Now put Miss Banfield on the line. Sir Basil wishes to have a quick word."

Wordlessly, Hubert handed the set over to Anne. "Hello," she said, tentatively. For a moment or two she listened, trying several times to interject, but ended up handing the telephone back to Hubert. She had gone a little paler.

Kell was back. "Right, then, Hubert. Listen carefully. Clearly, we have to be guarded in our conversation but I want you to think about this during your convalescence – Miss Banfield's 'Mr Darlington' was not idle during his enforced vacation in the United States. It seems Von Papen, in the Embassy over there, has some very bad people on his payroll who are intent on mischief and the American Government has asked us for some informal assistance in the matter. So get yourselves back in my office on the twelfth – you *and* Miss Banfield."

"Miss Banfield?"

"Yes. Miss Banfield. It seems Sir Basil has no further use for her services. She has been seconded to MI5." Kell paused so long, Chris thought he had hung up, when Kell's disembodied voice echoed through.

"I have plans for you two."

EPILOGUE

Tuesday, 6 June 1916 1701 hours, North Sea

Beitzen crumpled the signal Grassl had handed to him earlier in the evening and, alone, leaned back against the periscope high up on the conning tower of the Bruder Walther. So that was it – Kitchener was dead and his was the hand that killed him. God knows what would happen now. Would this hideous war never end? Would Magda and Trudi survive it? Would he?

He screwed his eyes shut against the sheer waste of it all and let the cold spray of the North Sea caress his skin, the wind rock him soothingly. Just over to port, the dark fjords of Norway slowly filed past his boat with whispers of trolls and fair Scandinavian heroes but the reality of the present butted their way into his consciousness, scattering all but the cold knowledge that he had probably killed the last honourable man in the British Army. Bleakness was all he could see ahead. Bleakness for his country and the crushing blight of poverty for its people.

Pushing himself off the superstructure, he moodily walked around to lean on the rail and watch the mist-shrouded mountains rise and fall in the sea's fading memory of the storm. They would all get leave, of course. The signal was almost ecstatic in its laconic text, hinting at honours and rewards for a job well done. The bile rose in his throat at the very thought.

Up there in the tower he was alone, not just physically, but separated from his men by the solitude that command imposed. He removed his cap and stretched back his neck to catch the rain, still pattering down from yesterday's downpours, while the words of Hesse's 'Lonesome Night' – one of Magda's favourites – filled his mind.

You brothers, who are mine,
Poor people, near and far,
Longing for every star,
Dream of relief from pain,
You, stumbling dumb
At night, as pale stars break,
Lift your thin hands for some
Hope, and suffer, and wake,
Poor muddling commonplace,
You sailors who must live
Unstarred by hopelessness,
We share a single face.
Give me my welcome back.

ABOUT THE AUTHOR

Bill Aitken is an IT specialist who served for 20 years as an officer in the Royal Air Force. It was during a tour with NATO in Norway that he first came across Donald McCormick's 1959 book "The Mystery of Lord Kitchener's Death" and he has maintained that interest ever since. This has expanded into a fascination with the First World War in general, particularly where it involved the Security Services. In his spare time, Bill writes too much computer code for his own good and has a soft spot for 19th Century fiction.

MAP OF ORKNEY

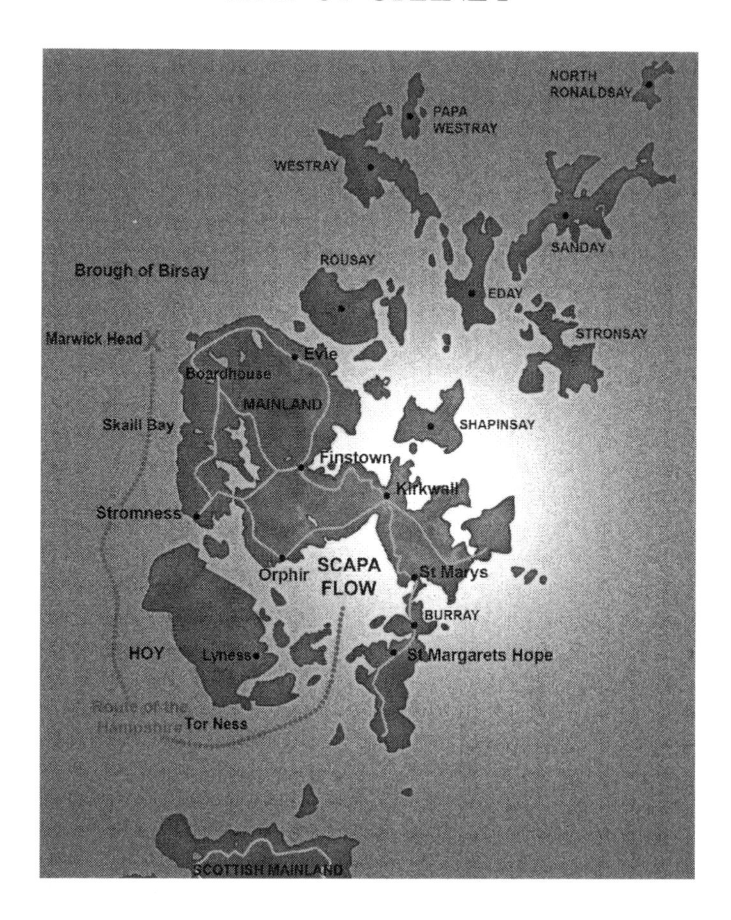

Sweet Sorrow

1916

Far north of the Arctic Circle, Baron von Rosen delivers arms and food to Finnish rebels, fighting against their Russian occupiers. This time – well – this time he's bringing something very special, indeed.

Chris Hubert and Anne Banfield have returned to MI5 after recovering from their ordeal in the waters of the Pentland Firth. German saboteurs are working in US harbours to destroy ammunition bound for the European Front. They're "old friends" of MI5 and the US authorities have asked the War Office to help them stop a planned "outrage".

Reluctantly, Hubert and Banfield join forces with the civilian authorities in New York to prevent the best efforts of von Papen and the German Embassy to cause mayhem in the still-neutral county. But the plot is too advanced and Black Tom pier is devastated by their destruction of ammunition barges and trains.

In the chaos surrounding them, Banfield takes hold of a new thread – a programme of bio-warfare devised and managed by Doctor Anton Dilger to spread anthrax and bubonic plague in Europe. Horses and mules, destined for the Front, are being infected with anthrax by German sympathisers. Baltimore harbour is where it starts.

But Dilger is not a man to be easily caught and he slips back to Germany, leaving Hubert and Banfield to mop up his operations while he continues to weaponise his cultures for the Kaiser. His newest creation will change the course of the war.

Von Rosen keeps his promises to the Finnish rebels. Dilger has presented him with boxes of sugar cubes, each containing its own tiny ampule of anthrax. The Russian mules will love them and, when they become infected, so will their masters. But Dilger, of course, wants something in return – a repeat performance on *English* soil.

Hubert, supported by MI6, head for Finland, following a tip-off by the Norwegian Secret Police, while Anne remains behind in London. Hubert breathes a sigh of relief when they recover the anthrax but, in each box, one cube is missing.

Captured members of the von Rosen group reveal that a human subject in England is to be victim number one – some woman from the Security Services.

Dilger bears grudges …

Printed in Poland
by Amazon Fulfillment
Poland Sp. z o.o., Wrocław

51048126R00179